PRAISE FOR *Portable Childhoods*

"Ellen Klages writes about childhood in brilliant, primary colors. Like Ray Bradbury, her nostalgic stories are like myths."
— MAUREEN MCHUGH

"Ellen Klages's work seems as transparent as spring water, but this is a woman who knows that clarity and simplicity can pierce the heart."
— PETER STRAUB

"This delightful collection showcases the best of Klages. Her protagonists are lovable, her prose natural, and her charm evident throughout. In time for the holiday season!"
— KAREN JOY FOWLER

"Welcome to Planet Klages! These stories are warm, witty, occasionally wise, and always wonderfully written. Ellen Klages is going to be big as big. Buy this book now, read it today, and become her fan forever."
— MICHAEL SWANWICK

"I haven't been writing prose very long, but I've been reading prose long enough to know this – Ellen Klages approaches greatness."
— JANIS IAN

"Ellen Klages writes like a dream – a dream from which you wake up laughing, and that fills the rest of the day with its strangeness and sweetness."
— MARGO LANAGAN

"Like childhood, these stories run deep with not-yet-happened nostalgia and fierce yearning for what never was. And, like children, they brim with joy, wonder, and wickedness."
— NICOLA GRIFFITH

"When you surface out of an Ellen Klages story, it's like arriving home after a long trip: your kitchen table, your car, your living room are all recognizably yours, but strange, and not half as real as the place you just came from. That place is the real world, and the people in it are as complex, unpredictable, and solid as you. It's a hard place to come back from."
— EMMA BULL

"Ellen Klages's stories combine the clear-eyed wonder of an intelligent child with the beautiful, controlled prose of a craftsman. And they have heart. What more could one ask of fiction?"

— DELIA SHERMAN

"Reading any fiction by Ellen Klages, whether it's set in the basement of a home in Detroit or on the green glass desert sands near Los Alamos or at the favorite fishing spot of a father and his very special son, you are always submerged deep in the rich and strange magic of life."

— CHARLES VESS

PRAISE FOR *The Green Glass Sea*

"Klages makes an impressive debut with an ambitious, meticulously researched novel set during WWII."

— PUBLISHERS WEEKLY, STARRED REVIEW

"...an intense but accessible page-turner, firmly belongs to the girls and their families; history and story are drawn together with confidence."

— HORN BOOK, STARRED REVIEW

"Many readers will know as little about the true nature of the project as the girls do, so the gradual revelation of facts is especially effective, while those who already know about Los Alamos's historical significance will experience the story in a different, but equally powerful, way."

— SCHOOL LIBRARY JOURNAL

"The story is [a memoir of the life of the small daughter of an atomic scientist, who recounts the events leading up to and following Trinity] in heartbreaking Klages style: simple, subtle, emotionally powerful writing that will knock you on your ass again and again as you read it.... If you haven't read Klages before, you're in for a treat."

— CORY DOCTOROW, BOING BOING

"Ellen Klages is a very careful writer – which is to say that she is full of care for her craft, and allows her readers the intelligence to take care of themselves. To take care, for instance, of the differences and resonances and contingencies between reality and fantasy, between real life and fairy tale; and to take care of what one can say to and about the other."
    — EDSF PROJECT

"Klages gives us sympathetic characters and slow-building suspense in an absorbing novel with a unique view of wartime."
    — NEWHOUSE NEWS SERVICE

"This beautifully told and historically accurate story makes you feel what it would be like to be a kid in this surreal, secretive world of scientists, mathematicians, and their families."
    — NOT YOUR MOTHER'S BOOK CLUB

PORTABLE CHILDHOODS

ELLEN KLAGES

PORTABLE
CHILDHOODS

TACHYON PUBLICATIONS | SAN FRANCISCO

Portable Childhoods
Copyright 2007 by Ellen Klages

Cover photo ©2007 Ellen Klages | Small cover images from the collection of the author
Design & composition by John D. Berry
The typefaces are Aldus nova and Palatino Sans
(Special thanks to Linotype GmbH for advance use of a pre-release version of Palatino Sans)

Tachyon Publications
1459 18th Street #139
San Francisco, CA 94107
(415) 285-5615
www.tachyonpublications.com

Editor: Jill Roberts

ISBN 10: 1-892391-45-7
ISBN 13: 978-1-892391-45-2

Printed in the United States of America
by Worzalla

First Edition: 2007

9 8 7 6 5 4 3 2 1

All stories copyright by Ellen Klages. "Basement Magic" © 2003. First appeared in *The Maga-
zine of Fantasy & Science Fiction*, May 2003. | "Intelligent Design" © 2005. First appeared
in *Strange Horizons*, December 2005. | "The Green Glass Sea" © 2004. First appeared in
Strange Horizons, September 2004. | "Clip Art" © 2007. Previously unpublished. | "Triangle"
© 2001. First appeared in *Bending the Landscape: Original Gay and Lesbian Writing: Horror*,
edited by Nicola Griffith and Stephen Pagel (Overlook Press: New York). | "The Feed Bag"
© 2003. First appeared in *Tales of the Unanticipated* #24, 2003. | "Flying Over Water" ©
2001. First appeared in *Lady Churchill's Rosebud Wristlet* No. 7, 2001. | "Möbius, Stripped
of a Muse" © 2007. Previously unpublished. | "Time Gypsy" © 1998, 2006. First appeared
in *Bending the Landscape: Original Gay and Lesbian Writing: Science Fiction*, edited by
Nicola Griffith and Stephen Pagel (Overlook Press: New York). | "Be Prepared" © 2002.
First appeared in *The Infinite Matrix*, September 2002. | "Travel Agency" © 2002. First
appeared in *Strange Horizons*, February 2002. | "A Taste of Summer" © 2002. First appeared
in *Black Gate*, Winter 2002. | "Ringing Up Baby" © 2006. First appeared in *Nature*, April
2006. | "Guys Day Out" © 2005. First appeared in *Sci Fiction* (*www.SciFi.com*), April 2005.
| "Portable Childhoods" © 2007. Previously unpublished. | "In the House of the Seven
Librarians" © 2006. First appeared in *Firebirds Rising: An Original Anthology of Science
Fiction and Fantasy*, edited by Sharyn November (Firebird: New York).

SC
KLAGES

Contents

Acknowledgments

I WAS MIDDLE-AGED when I finally found my tribe, and learned that Madison, Wisconsin is one of the centers of the world. Thanks to Jeanne Bowman, who took me to a party in Hayward against my will and changed my life. To Pat Murphy, who told me the secret to being a writer: *Write Something*. To Karen Fowler, Debbie Notkin, and Jeanne Gomoll for introducing me to WisCon and the Secret Feminist Cabal. To Delia Sherman, my writing sister, and her partner, Ellen Kushner, who are my role models for how to make words and singing and laughing all an integral part of life. To Walter Jon Williams, for founding Rio Hondo, and to Nina Hoffman, Leslie What, Maureen McHugh, Ted Chiang, Sean Stewart and others who critiqued my stories there. To Laurie Winter, my writing and poker buddy. To Michael Swanwick for kicking my butt in the right direction. To Margo Lanagan for the best conversation about punctuation I've ever had. To Emma Munro and my other Clarion South mates, for crits and companionship. To the Cajun Sushi Hamsters from Hell, my writing group in Cleveland, who saw some of these stories through their larval stage. To Neil Gaiman, for taking time out of the world's busiest schedule to write an introduction for this book. To Nicola Griffith, who bought my very first story, and to Kelly Link and Gavin Grant, John O'Neill, Gordon Van Gelder, Ellen Datlow, Jed Hartman, Eileen Gunn, and Sharyn November, extraordinary editors all. To Jill Roberts and Jacob Weisman of Tachyon Publications, for gathering all my fictional flotsam and putting it in one place. To Kurt Vonnegut, for *Welcome to the Monkey House*, Jack Finney for "The Third Level," and Rod Serling for *The Twilight Zone*. And to J.D. Salinger for "Uncle Wiggly in Connecticut," which made me want to be a writer.

To the Secret Feminist Cabal.

Introduction | *Neil Gaiman*

TO BEGIN WITH, a physical description: Ellen Klages is shorter than I am, and she grins more. Her hair is shorter than mine, too. I think she's around my age, more or less, but she bounces more than I do and sometimes she bustles, which I never do at all. There. Now you'll know her if you pass her in the street.

I met her in person first, which is dangerous for authors, because we don't fit preconceptions and the stories on the inside and the stories on the outside are very different. The Ellen I met in the flesh was funny and bustling and smart, a force of nature: the second time I met her I wound up shaving off my beard and giving it to her to auction, and she made this seem like a sensible thing to do. I'm not even sure I knew she was an author back then. And then I started to notice her name cropping up in story collections, and online.

The stories mapped slowly onto the person. I expected them to be funny and bustling, and they weren't. They were something else entirely.

It's not that there aren't jokes in the stories you are about to read. There are. But most of these tales are stories of wide-eyed childhood, fables of powerlessness and of taking what power and control one can from one's life. These are stories of families, the ones we are born into and the ones that we create. They are tender stories, most of them, betraying a love of and respect for people of all kinds and shapes and minds. They contain wisdom – you will learn here, if you had forgotten, that a book can be a safe place to hide, for example, and so can a library. They are about the bonds between people. They exist in a place on the borderland between genre and mimetic fiction, sometimes walking the line one way, sometimes the other, often leaving the reader unsure until the final paragraph what kind of story this has been, what kind of escape Ellen's characters have taken, what kind of mercy they have been given...

This is her first collection of stories.

I do not believe it will be her last. There are writers with their own voices and their own agendas, who have important things to say, and who say them in their own way. Ellen Klages is one of them.

Enjoy.

NEIL GAIMAN

In a hotel room somewhere in America, November 2006

PORTABLE CHILDHOODS

Basement Magic

MARY LOUISE WHITTAKER believes in magic. She knows that some-where, somewhere else, there must be dragons and princes, wands and wishes. Especially wishes. And happily ever after. Ever after is not now.

Her mother died in a car accident when Mary Louise was still a tod-dler. She misses her mother fiercely but abstractly. Her memories are less a coherent portrait than a mosaic of disconnected details: soft skin that smelled of lavender; a bright voice singing "Sweet and Low" in the night darkness; bubbles at bathtime; dark curls; zweiback.

Her childhood has been kneaded, but not shaped, by the series of well-meaning middle-aged women her father has hired to tend her. He is busy climbing the corporate ladder, and is absent even when he is at home. She does not miss him. He remarried when she was five, and they moved into a two-story Tudor in one of the better suburbs of Detroit. Kitty, the new Mrs. Ted Whittaker, is a former Miss Bloomfield Hills, a vain divorcée with a towering mass of blond curls in a shade not her own. In the wild, her kind is inclined to eat their young.

Kitty might have tolerated her new stepdaughter had she been sweet and cuddly, a slick-magazine cherub. But at six, Mary Louise is an odd, solitary child. She has unruly red hair the color of Fiestaware, the dishes that might have been radioactive, and small round pink glasses that make her blue eyes seem large and slightly distant. She did not walk until she was almost two, and propels herself with a quick shuffle-duckling gait that is both urgent and awkward.

One spring morning, Mary Louise is camped in one of her favorite spots, the window seat in the guest bedroom. It is a stage set of a room, one that no one else ever visits. She leans against the wall, a thick book with lush illustrations propped up on her bare knees. Bright sunlight, filtered through the leaves of the oak outside, is broken into geomet-ric patterns by the mullioned windows, dappling the floral cushion in front of her.

3

The book is almost bigger than her lap, and she holds it open with one elbow, the other anchoring her Bankie, a square of pale blue flannel with pale blue satin edging that once swaddled her infant self, carried home from the hospital. It is raveled and graying, both tattered and beloved. The thumb of her blanket arm rests in her mouth in a comforting manner.

Mary Louise is studying a picture of a witch with purple robes and hair as black as midnight, when she hears voices in the hall. The door to the guest room is open a crack, so she can hear clearly, but cannot see or be seen. One of the voices is Kitty's. She is explaining something about the linen closet, so it is probably a new cleaning lady. They have had six since they moved in.

Mary Louise sits very still and doesn't turn the page, because it is stiff paper and might make a noise. But the door opens anyway, and she hears Kitty say, "This is the guest room. Now unless we've got company – and I'll let you know – it just needs to be dusted and the linens aired once a week. It has an – oh, there you are," she says, coming in the doorway, as if she has been looking all over for Mary Louise, which she has not.

Kitty turns and says to the air behind her, "This is my husband's daughter, Mary Louise. She's not in school yet. She's small for her age, and her birthday is in December, so we decided to hold her back a year. She never does much, just sits and reads. I'm sure she won't be a bother. Will you?" She turns and looks at Mary Louise but does not wait for an answer. "And this is Ruby. She's going to take care of the house for us."

The woman who stands behind Kitty nods, but makes no move to enter the room. She is tall, taller than Kitty, with skin the color of gingerbread. Ruby wears a white uniform and a pair of white Keds. She is older, there are lines around her eyes and her mouth, but her hair is sleek and black, black as midnight.

Kitty looks at her small gold watch. "Oh, dear. I've got to get going or I'll be late for my hair appointment." She looks back at Mary Louise. "Your father and I are going out tonight, but Ruby will make you some dinner, and Mrs. Banks will be here about six." Mrs. Banks is one of the babysitters, an older woman in a dark dress who smells like dusty licorice and coos too much. "So be a good girl. And for god's sake get that thumb out of your mouth. Do you want your teeth to grow in crooked, too?"

Mary Louise says nothing, but withdraws her damp puckered thumb and folds both hands in her lap. She looks up at Kitty, her eyes expressionless, until her stepmother looks away. "Well, an-y-wa-y," Kitty says, drawing the word out to four syllables, "I've really got to be going." She turns and leaves the room, brushing by Ruby, who stands silently just outside the doorway.

Ruby watches Kitty go, and when the high heels have clattered onto the tiles at the bottom of the stairs, she turns and looks at Mary Louise. "You a quiet little mouse, ain't you?" she asks in a soft, low voice.

Mary Louise shrugs. She sits very still in the window seat and waits for Ruby to leave. She does not look down at her book, because it is rude to look away when a grown-up might still be talking to you. But none of the cleaning ladies talk to her, except to ask her to move out of the way, as if she were furniture.

"Yes siree, a quiet little mouse," Ruby says again. "Well, Miss Mouse, I'm fixin to go downstairs and make me a grilled cheese sandwich for lunch. If you like, I can cook you up one too. I make a mighty fine grilled cheese sandwich."

Mary Louise is startled by the offer. Grilled cheese is one of her very favorite foods. She thinks for a minute, then closes her book and tucks Bankie securely under one arm. She slowly follows Ruby down the wide front stairs, her small green-socked feet making no sound at all on the thick beige carpet.

It is the best grilled cheese sandwich Mary Louise has ever eaten. The outside is golden brown and so crisp it crackles under her teeth. The cheese is melted so that it soaks into the bread on the inside, just a little. There are no burnt spots at all. Mary Louise thanks Ruby and returns to her book.

The house is large, and Mary Louise knows all the best hiding places. She does not like being where Kitty can find her, where their paths might cross. Before Ruby came, Mary Louise didn't go down to the basement very much. Not by herself. It is an old house, and the basement is damp and musty, with heavy stone walls and banished, battered furniture. It is not a comfortable place, nor a safe one. There is the furnace, roaring fire, and the cans of paint and bleach and other frightful potions. Poisons. Years of soap flakes, lint, and furnace soot coat the walls like household lichen.

The basement is a place between the worlds, within Kitty's domain, but beneath her notice. Now, in the daytime, it is Ruby's, and Mary Louise is happy there. Ruby is not like other grown-ups. Ruby talks to her in a regular voice, not a scold, nor the sing-song Mrs. Banks uses, as if Mary Louise is a tiny baby. Ruby lets her sit and watch while she irons, or sorts the laundry, or runs the sheets through the mangle. She doesn't sigh when Mary Louise asks her questions.

On the rare occasions when Kitty and Ted are home in the evening, they have dinner in the dining room. Ruby cooks. She comes in late on those days, and then is very busy, and Mary Louise does not get to see her until dinnertime. But the two of them eat in the kitchen, in the breakfast nook. Ruby tells stories, but has to get up every few minutes when Kitty buzzes for her, to bring more water or another fork, or to clear away the salad plates. Ruby smiles when she is talking to Mary Louise, but when the buzzer sounds, her face changes. Not to a frown, but to a kind of blank Ruby mask.

One Tuesday night in early May, Kitty decrees that Mary Louise will eat dinner with them in the dining room, too. They sit at the wide mahogany table on stiff brocade chairs that pick at the backs of her legs. There are too many forks and even though she is very careful it is hard to cut her meat, and once the heavy silverware skitters across the china with a sound that sets her teeth on edge. Kitty frowns at her.

The grown-ups talk to each other and Mary Louise just sits. The worst part is that when Ruby comes in and sets a plate down in front of her, there is no smile, just the Ruby mask.

"I don't know how you do it, Ruby," says her father when Ruby comes in to give him a second glass of water. "These pork chops are the best I've ever eaten. You've certainly got the magic touch."

"She does, doesn't she?" says Kitty. "You must tell me your secret."

"Just shake 'em up in flour, salt and pepper, then fry 'em in Crisco," Ruby says.

"That's all?"

"Yes, ma'am."

"Well, isn't that marvelous. I must try that. Thank you Ruby. You may go now."

"Yes, ma'am." Ruby turns and lets the swinging door between the kitchen and the dining room close behind her. A minute later Mary Louise hears the sound of running water, and the soft clunk of plates being slotted into the racks of the dishwasher.

"Mary Louise, don't put your peas into your mashed potatoes that way. It's not polite to play with your food," Kitty says.

Mary Louise sighs. There are too many rules in the dining room.

"Mary Louise, answer me when I speak to you."

"Muhff-mum," Mary Louise says through a mouthful of mashed potatoes.

"Oh, for god's sake. Don't talk with your mouth full. Don't you have any manners at all?"

Caught between two conflicting rules, Mary Louise merely shrugs.

"Is there any more gravy?" her father asks.

Kitty leans forward a little and Mary Louise hears the slightly muffled sound of the buzzer in the kitchen. There is a little bump, about the size of an Oreo, under the carpet just beneath Kitty's chair that Kitty presses with her foot. Ruby appears a few seconds later and stands inside the doorway, holding a striped dishcloth in one hand.

"Mr. Whittaker would like some more gravy," says Kitty.

Ruby shakes her head. "Sorry, Miz Whittaker. I put all of it in the gravy boat. There's no more left."

"Oh." Kitty sounds disapproving. "We had plenty of gravy last time."

"Yes, ma'am. But that was a beef roast. Pork chops just don't make as much gravy," Ruby says.

"Oh. Of course. Well, thank you, Ruby."

"Yes ma'am." Ruby pulls the door shut behind her.

"I guess that's all the gravy, Ted," Kitty says, even though he is sitting at the other end of the table, and has heard Ruby himself.

"Tell her to make more next time," he says, frowning. "So what did you do today?" He turns his attention to Mary Louise for the first time since they sat down.

"Mostly I read my book," she says. "The fairy tales you gave me for Christmas."

"Well, that's fine," he says. "I need you to call the Taylors and cancel." Mary Louise realizes he is no longer talking to her, and eats the last of her mashed potatoes.

"Why?" Kitty raises an eyebrow. "I thought we were meeting them out at the club on Friday for cocktails."

"Can't. Got to fly down to Florida tomorrow. The space thing. We designed the guidance system for Shepard's capsule, and George wants me to go down with the engineers, talk to the press if the launch is a success."

"Are they really going to shoot a man into space?" Mary Louise asks.

"That's the plan, honey."

"Well, you don't give me much notice," Kitty says, smiling. "But I suppose I can pack a few summer dresses, and get anything else I need down there."

"Sorry, Kit. This trip is just business. No wives."

"No, only to Grand Rapids. Never to Florida." Kitty says, frowning. She takes a long sip of her drink. "So how long will you be gone?"

"Five days, maybe a week. If things go well, Jim and I are going to drive down to Palm Beach and get some golf in."

"I see. Just business." Kitty drums her lacquered fingernails on the tablecloth. "I guess that means I have to call Barb and Mitchell, too. Or had you forgotten my sister's birthday dinner next Tuesday?" Kitty scowls down the table at her husband, who shrugs and takes a bite of his chop.

Kitty drains her drink. The table is silent for a minute, and then she says, "Mary Louise! Don't put your dirty fork on the tablecloth. Put it on the edge of your plate if you're done. Would you like to be excused?"

"Yes, ma'am," says Mary Louise.

⌒

As soon as she is excused, Mary Louise goes down to the basement to wait. When Ruby is working it smells like a cave full of soap and warm laundry.

A little after seven, Ruby comes down the stairs carrying a brown paper lunch sack. She puts it down on the ironing board. "Well, Miss Mouse. I thought I'd see you down here when I got done with the dishes."

"I don't like eating in the dining room," Mary Louise says. "I want to eat in the kitchen with you."

"I like that, too. But your stepmomma says she got to teach you some table manners, so when you grow up you can eat with nice folks."

Mary Louise makes a face, and Ruby laughs.

"They ain't such a bad thing, manners. Come in real handy someday, when you're eatin with folks you *want* to have like you."

"I guess so," says Mary Louise. "Will you tell me a story?"

"Not tonight, Miss Mouse. It's late, and I gotta get home and give my husband his supper. He got off work half an hour ago, and I told him I'd bring him a pork chop or two if there was any left over." She gestures to the paper bag. "He likes my pork chops even more than your daddy does."

"Not even a little story?" Mary Louise feels like she might cry. Her stomach hurts from having dinner with all the forks.

"Not tonight, sugar. Tomorrow, though, I'll tell you a long one, just to make up." Ruby takes off her white Keds and lines them up next to each other under the big galvanized sink. Then she takes off her apron, looks at a brown gravy stain on the front of it, and crumples it up and tosses it into the pink plastic basket of dirty laundry. She pulls a hanger from the line that stretches across the ceiling over the washer and begins to unbutton the white buttons on the front of her uniform.

"What's that?" Mary Louise asks. Ruby has rucked the top of her uniform down to her waist and is pulling it over her hips. There is a green string pinned to one bra strap. The end of it disappears into her left armpit.

"What's what? You seen my underwear before."

"Not that. That string."

Ruby looks down at her chest. "Oh. That. I had my auntie make me up a conjure hand."

"Can I see it?" Mary Louise climbs down out of the chair and walks over to where Ruby is standing.

Ruby looks hard at Mary Louise for a minute. "For it to work, it gotta stay a secret. But you good with secrets, so I guess you can take a look. Don't you touch it, though. Anybody but me touch it, all the conjure magic leak right out and it won't work no more." She reaches under her armpit and draws out a small green flannel bag, about the size of a walnut, and holds it in one hand.

Mary Louise stands with her hands clasped tight behind her back so she won't touch it even by accident and stares intently at the bag. It doesn't look like anything magic. Magic is gold rings and gowns spun of moonlight and silver, not a white cotton uniform and a little stained cloth bag. "Is it really magic? Really? What does it do?"

"Well, there's diff'rent kinds of magic. Some conjure bags bring luck. Some protects you. This one, this one gonna bring me money. That's why it's green. Green's the money color. Inside there's a silver dime, so the money knows it belong here, a magnet — that attracts the money right to me — and some roots, wrapped up in a two-dollar bill. Every mornin I gives it a little drink, and after nine days, it gonna bring me my fortune." Ruby looks down at the little bag fondly, then tucks it back under her armpit.

Mary Louise looks up at Ruby and sees something she has never seen on a grown-up's face before: Ruby believes. She believes in magic, even if it is armpit magic.

"Wow. How does — "

"Miss Mouse, I *got* to get home, give my husband his supper." Ruby steps out of her uniform, hangs it on a hanger, then puts on her blue skirt and a cotton blouse.

Mary Louise looks down at the floor. "Okay," she says.

"It's not the end of the world, sugar." Ruby pats Mary Louise on the back of the head, then sits down and puts on her flat black shoes. "I'll be back tomorrow. I got a big pile of laundry to do. You think you might come down here, keep me company? I think I can tell a story and sort the laundry at the same time." She puts on her outdoor coat, a nubby burnt-orange wool with chipped gold buttons and big square pockets, and ties a scarf around her chin.

"Will you tell me a story about the magic bag?" Mary Louise asks. This time she looks at Ruby and smiles.

"I think I can do that. Gives us both somethin to look forward to. Now scoot on out of here. I gotta turn off the light." She picks up her brown paper sack and pulls the string that hangs down over the ironing board. The light bulb goes out, and the basement is dark except for the twilight filtering in through the high single window. Ruby opens the outside door to the concrete stairs that lead up to the driveway. The air is warmer than the basement.

"Nitey nite, Miss Mouse," she says, and goes outside.

"G'night Ruby," says Mary Louise, and goes upstairs.

When Ruby goes to vacuum the rug in the guest bedroom on Thursday morning, she finds Mary Louise sitting in the window seat, staring out the window.

"Mornin, Miss Mouse. You didn't come down and say hello."

Mary Louise does not answer. She does not even turn around.

Ruby pushes the lever on the vacuum and stands it upright, dropping the gray fabric cord she has wrapped around her hand. She walks over to the silent child. "Miss Mouse? Somethin wrong?"

Mary Louise looks up. Her eyes are cold. "Last night I was in bed, reading. Kitty came home. She was in a really bad mood. She told me I read too much and I'll just ruin my eyes – more – reading in bed. She took my book and told me she was going to throw it in the 'cinerator and burn it up." She delivers the words in staccato anger, through clenched teeth.

"She just bein mean to you, sugar." Ruby shakes her head. "She tryin to scare you, but she won't really do that."

"But she *did!*" Mary Louise reaches behind her and holds up her fairy tale book. The picture on the cover is soot-stained, the shiny coating blistered. The gilded edges of the pages are charred and the corners are gone.

"Lord, child, where'd you find that?"

"In the 'cinerator, out back. Where she said. I can still read most of the stories, but it makes my hands all dirty." She holds up her hands, showing her sooty palms.

Ruby shakes her head again. She says, more to herself than to Mary

Louise, "I burnt the trash after lunch yesterday. Must of just been coals, come last night."

Mary Louise looks at the ruined book in her lap, then up at Ruby. "It was my favorite book. Why'd she do that?" A tear runs down her cheek.

Ruby sits down on the window seat. "I don't know, Miss Mouse," she says. "I truly don't. Maybe she mad that your daddy gone down to Florida, leave her behind. Some folks, when they're mad, they just gotta whup on somebody, even if it's a little bitty six-year-old child. They whup on somebody else, they forget their own hurts for a while."

"You're bigger than her," says Mary Louise, snuffling. "You could – whup – *her* back. You could tell her that it was bad and wrong what she did."

Ruby shakes her head. "I'm real sorry, Miss Mouse," she says quietly, "But I can't do that."

"Why not?"

"'Cause she the boss in this house, and if I say anything crosswise to Miz Kitty, her own queen self, she gonna fire me same as she fire all them other colored ladies used to work for her. And I needs this job. My husband's just workin part-time down to the Sunoco. He tryin to get work in the Ford plant, but they ain't hirin right now. So my paycheck here, that's what's puttin groceries on our table."

"But, but – " Mary Louise begins to cry without a sound. Ruby is the only grown-up person she trusts, and Ruby cannot help her.

Ruby looks down at her lap for a long time, then sighs. "I can't say nothin to Miz Kitty. But her bein so mean to you, that ain't right, neither." She puts her arm around the shaking child.

"What about your little bag?" Mary Louise wipes her nose with the back of her hand, leaving a small streak of soot on her cheek.

"What 'bout it?"

"You said some magic is for protecting, didn't you?"

"Some is," Ruby says slowly. "Some is. Now, my momma used to say, 'an egg can't fight with a stone.' And that's the truth. Miz Kitty got the power in this house. More'n you, more'n me. Ain't nothin to do 'bout that. But conjurin – " She thinks for a minute, then lets out a deep breath.

"I think we might could put some protection 'round you, so Miz Kitty can't do you no more misery." Ruby says, frowning a little. "But I ain't sure quite how. See, if it was your house, I'd put a goopher right under the front door. But it ain't. It's your daddy's house, and she married to him legal, so ain't no way to keep her from comin in her own house, even if she is nasty."

"What about my room?" asks Mary Louise.

"Your room? Hmm. Now, that's a different story. I think we can goopher it so she can't do you no harm in there."

Mary Louise wrinkles her nose. "What's a *goopher?*"

Ruby smiles. "Down South Carolina, where my family's from, that's just what they calls a spell, or a hex, a little bit of rootwork."

"Root – ?"

Ruby shakes her head. "It don't make no never mind what you calls it, long as you does it right. Now if you done cryin, we got work to do. Can you go out to the garage, to your Daddy's toolbox, and get me nine nails? Big ones, all the same size, and bright and shiny as you can find. Can you count that many?"

Mary Louise snorts. "I can count up to *fifty*," she says.

"Good. Then you go get nine shiny nails, fast as you can, and meet me down the hall, by your room."

When Mary Louise gets back upstairs, nine shiny nails clutched tightly in one hand, Ruby is kneeling in front of the door of her bedroom, with a paper of pins from the sewing box, and a can of Drano. Mary Louise hands her the nails.

"These is just perfect," Ruby says. She pours a puddle of Drano into its upturned cap, and dips the tip of one of the nails into it, then pokes the nail under the edge of the hall carpet at the left side of Mary Louise's bedroom door, pushing it deep until not even its head shows.

"Why did you dip the nail in Drano?" Mary Louise asks. She didn't know any of the poison things under the kitchen sink could be magic.

"Don't you touch that, hear? It'll burn you bad, cause it's got lye in it. But lye the best thing for cleanin away any evil that's already been here. Ain't got no Red Devil like back home, but you got to use what you got. The nails and the pins, they made of iron, and iron keep any new evil away from your door." Ruby dips a pin in the Drano as she talks and repeats the poking, alternating nails and pins until she pushes the last pin in at the other edge of the door.

"That oughta do it," she says. She pours the few remaining drops of Drano back into the can and screws the lid on tight, then stands up. "Now all we needs to do is set the protectin charm. You know your prayers?" she asks Mary Louise.

"I know 'Now I lay me down to sleep.'"

"Good enough. You get into your room and you kneel down, facin the hall, and say that prayer to the doorway. Say it loud and as best you can. I'm goin to go down and get the sheets out of the dryer. Meet me in Miz Kitty's room when you done."

Mary Louise says her prayers in a loud, clear voice. She doesn't know how this kind of magic spell works, and she isn't sure if she is supposed to say the God Blesses, but she does. She leaves Kitty out and adds Ruby. "And help me to be a good girl, amen," she finishes, and hurries down to her father's room to see what other kinds of magic Ruby knows.

The king-size mattress is bare. Mary Louise lays down on it and rolls over and over three times before falling off the edge onto the carpet. She is just getting up, dusting off the knees of her blue cotton pants, when Ruby appears with an armful of clean sheets, which she dumps onto the bed. Mary Louise lays her face in the middle of the pile. It is still warm and smells like baked cotton. She takes a deep breath.

"You gonna lay there in the laundry all day or help me make this bed?" Ruby asks, laughing.

Mary Louise takes one side of the big flowered sheet and helps Ruby stretch it across the bed and pull the elastic parts over all four corners so it is smooth everywhere.

"Are we going to do a lot more magic?" Mary Louise asks. "I'm getting kind of hungry."

"One more bit, then we can have us some lunch. You want tomato soup?"

"Yes!" says Mary Louise.

"I thought so. Now fetch me a hair from Miz Kitty's hairbrush. See if you can find a nice long one with some dark at the end of it."

Mary Louise goes over to Kitty's dresser and peers at the heavy silver brush. She finds a darker line in the tangle of blond and carefully pulls it out. It is almost a foot long, and the last inch is definitely brown. She carries it over to Ruby, letting it trail through her fingers like the tail of a tiny invisible kite.

"That's good," Ruby says. She reaches into the pocket of her uniform and pulls out a scrap of red felt with three needles stuck into it lengthwise. She pulls the needles out one by one, makes a bundle of them, and wraps it round and round, first with the long strand of Kitty's hair, then with a piece of black thread.

"Hold out your hand," she says.

Mary Louise holds out her hand flat, and Ruby puts the little black-wrapped bundle into it.

"Now, you hold this until you get a picture in your head of Miz Kitty burnin up your pretty picture book. And when it nice and strong, you spit. Okay?"

Mary Louise nods. She scrunches up her eyes, remembering, then spits on the needles.

"You got the knack for this," Ruby says, smiling. "It's a gift."

Mary Louise beams. She does not get many compliments, and stores this one away in the most private part of her thoughts. She will visit it regularly over the next few days until its edges are indistinct and there is nothing left but a warm glow labeled RUBY.

"Now put it under this mattress, far as you can reach." Ruby lifts up the edge of the mattress and Mary Louise drops the bundle on the box spring.

"Do you want me to say my prayers again?"

"Not this time, Miss Mouse. Prayers is for protectin. This here is a sufferin hand, bring some of Miz Kitty's meanness back on her own self, and it need another kind of charm. I'll set this one myself." Ruby lowers her voice and begins to chant:

> Before the night is over,
> Before the day is through.
> What you have done to someone else
> Will come right back on you.

"There. That ought to do her just fine. Now we gotta make up this bed. Top sheet, blanket, bedspread all smooth and nice, pillows plumped up just so."

"Does that help the magic?" Mary Louise asks. She wants to do it right, and there are almost as many rules as eating in the dining room. But different.

"Not 'zactly. But it makes it look like it 'bout the most beautiful place to sleep Miz Kitty ever seen, make her want to crawl under them sheets and get her beauty rest. Now help me with that top sheet, okay?"

Mary Louise does, and when they have smoothed the last wrinkle out of the bedspread, Ruby looks at the clock. "Shoot. How'd it get to be after one o'clock? Only fifteen minutes before my story comes on. Let's go down and have ourselves some lunch."

In the kitchen, Ruby heats up a can of Campbell's tomato soup, with milk, not water, the way Mary Louise likes it best, then ladles it out into two yellow bowls. She puts them on a metal tray, adds some saltine crackers and a bottle of ginger ale for her, and a lunchbox bag of Fritos and a glass of milk for Mary Louise, and carries the whole tray into the den. Ruby turns on the TV and they sip and crunch their way through half an hour of *As the World Turns*.

During the commercials, Ruby tells Mary Louise who all the people are, and what they've done, which is mostly bad. When they are done with their soup, another story comes on, but they aren't people Ruby knows, so she turns off the TV and carries the dishes back to the kitchen.

"I gotta do the dustin and finish vacuumin, and ain't no way to talk over that kind of noise," Ruby says, handing Mary Louise a handful of Oreos. "So you go off and play by yourself now, and I'll get my chores done before Miz Kitty comes home."

Mary Louise goes up to her room. At 4:30 she hears Kitty come home, but she only changes into out-to-dinner clothes and leaves and doesn't get into bed. Ruby says good-bye when Mrs. Banks comes at 6:00, and Mary Louise eats dinner in the kitchen and goes upstairs at 8:00, when Mrs. Banks starts to watch *Dr. Kildare*.

On her dresser there is a picture of her mother. She is beautiful, with long curls and a silvery white dress. She looks like a queen, so Mary Louise thinks she might be a princess. She lives in a castle, imprisoned by her evil stepmother, the false queen. But now that there is magic, there will be a happy ending. She crawls under the covers and watches her doorway, wondering what will happen when Kitty tries to come into her room, if there will be flames.

———

Kitty begins to scream just before nine Friday morning. Clumps of her hair lie on her pillow like spilled wheat. What is left sprouts from her scalp in irregular clumps, like a crabgrass-infested lawn. Clusters of angry red blisters dot her exposed skin.

By the time Mary Louise runs up from the kitchen, where she is eating a bowl of Kix, Kitty is on the phone. She is talking to her beauty salon. She is shouting, "This is an emergency! An emergency!"

Kitty does not speak to Mary Louise. She leaves the house with a scarf wrapped around her head like a turban, in such a hurry that she does not even bother with lipstick. Mary Louise hears the tires of her T-bird squeal out of the driveway. A shower of gravel hits the side of the house, and then everything is quiet.

Ruby comes upstairs at ten, buttoning the last button on her uniform. Mary Louise is in the breakfast nook, eating a second bowl of Kix. The first one got soggy. She jumps up excitedly when she sees Ruby.

"Miz Kitty already gone?" Ruby asks, her hand on the coffeepot.

"It worked! It worked! Something *bad* happened to her hair. A lot of it fell out, and there are chicken pox where it was. She's at the beauty shop. I think she's going to be there a long time."

Ruby pours herself a cup of coffee. "That so?"

"Uh-huh. " Mary Louise grins. "She looks like a *goopher*."

"Well, well, well. That come back on her fast, didn't it? Maybe now she think twice 'bout messin with somebody smaller'n her. But you, Miss Mouse," Ruby wiggles a semi-stern finger at Mary Louise, "Don't you go jumpin up and down shoutin 'bout goophers, hear? Magic ain't nothin to be foolin around with. It can bring sickness, bad luck, a whole heap of misery if it ain't done proper. You hear me?"

Mary Louise nods and runs her thumb and finger across her lips, as if she is locking them. But she is still grinning from ear to ear.

Kitty comes home from the beauty shop late that afternoon. She is in a very, very bad mood, and still has a scarf around her head. Mary Louise is behind the couch in the den, playing seven dwarfs. She is Snow White and is lying very still, waiting for the prince.

Kitty comes into the den and goes to the bar. She puts two ice cubes in a heavy squat crystal glass, then reaches up on her tiptoes and feels around on the bookshelf until she finds a small brass key. She unlocks the liquor cabinet and fills her glass with brown liquid. She goes to the phone and makes three phone calls, canceling cocktails, dinner, tennis on Saturday. "Sorry," Kitty says. "Under the weather. Raincheck?" When she is finished she refills her glass, replaces the key, and goes upstairs. Mary Louise does not see her again until Sunday.

Mary Louise stays in her room most of the weekend. It seems like a good idea, now that it is safe there. Saturday afternoon she tiptoes down to the kitchen and makes three peanut butter and honey sandwiches. She is not allowed to use the stove. She takes her sandwiches and some Fritos upstairs and touches one of the nails under the carpet, to make sure it is still there. She knows the magic is working, because Kitty doesn't even try to come in, not once.

At seven-thirty on Sunday night, she ventures downstairs again. Kitty's door is shut. The house is quiet. It is time for Disney. *Walt Disney's Wonderful World of Color*. It is her favorite program, the only one that is not black-and-white, except for *Bonanza*, which comes on after her bedtime.

Mary Louise turns on the big TV that is almost as tall as she is, and sits in the middle of the maroon leather couch in the den. Her feet stick out in front of her, and do not quite reach the edge. There is a commercial for Mr. Clean. He has no hair, like Kitty, and Mary Louise giggles, just a little. Then there are red and blue fireworks over the castle where Sleeping Beauty lives. Mary Louise's thumb wanders up to her mouth, and she rests her cheek on the soft nap of her Bankie.

The show is Cinderella, and when the wicked stepmother comes on, Mary Louise thinks of Kitty, but does not giggle. The story unfolds and Mary Louise is bewitched by the colors, by the magic of television. She does not hear the creaking of the stairs. She does not hear the door of the den open, or hear the rattle of ice cubes in an empty crystal glass. She does not see the shadow loom over her until it is too late.

It is a sunny Monday morning. Ruby comes in the basement door and changes into her uniform. She switches on the old brown table radio, waits for its tubes to warm up and begin to glow, then turns the yellowed plastic dial until she finds a station that is more music than static. The Marcels are singing "Blue Moon" as she sorts the laundry, and she dances a little on the concrete floor, swinging and swaying as she tosses white cotton panties into one basket and black nylon socks into another.

She fills the washer with a load of whites, adds a measuring cup of Dreft, and turns the dial to Delicate. The song on the radio changes to "Runaway," as she goes over to the wooden cage built into the wall, where the laundry that has been dumped down the upstairs chute gathers.

"As I walk along..." Ruby sings as she opens the hinged door with its criss-cross of green painted slats. The plywood box inside is a cube about three feet on a side, filled with a mound of flowered sheets and white terrycloth towels. She pulls a handful of towels off the top of the mound and lets them tumble into the pink plastic basket waiting on the floor below. "An' I wonder. I wa-wa-wa-wa-wuh-un-der," she sings, and then stops when the pile moves on its own, and whimpers.

Ruby parts the sea of sheets to reveal a small head of carrot-red hair.

"Miss Mouse? What on God's green earth you doin in there? I like to bury you in all them sheets!"

A bit more of Mary Louise appears, her hair in tangles, her eyes red-rimmed from crying.

"Is Kitty gone?" she asks.

Ruby nods. "She at the beauty parlor again. What you *doin* in there? You hidin from Miz Kitty?"

"Uh-huh." Mary Louise sits up and a cascade of hand towels and washcloths tumbles out onto the floor.

"What she done this time?"

"She – she – " Mary Louise bursts into ragged sobs.

Ruby reaches in and puts her hands under Mary Louise's arms, lifting the weeping child out of the pile of laundry. She carries her over to the basement stairs and sits down, cradling her. The tiny child shakes and holds on tight to Ruby's neck, her tears soaking into the white cotton collar. When her tears subside into trembling, Ruby reaches into a pocket and proffers a pale yellow hankie.

"Blow hard," she says gently. Mary Louise does.

"Now scooch around front a little so you can sit in my lap." Mary Louise scooches without a word. Ruby strokes her curls for a minute. "Sugar? What she do this time?"

Mary Louise tries to speak, but her voice is still a rusty squeak. After a few seconds she just holds her tightly clenched fist out in front of her and slowly opens it. In her palm is a wrinkled scrap of pale blue flannel, about the size of a playing card, its edges jagged and irregular.

"Miz Kitty do that?"

"Uh-huh," Mary Louise finds her voice. "I was watching Disney and *she* came in to get another drink. She said Bankie was just a dirty old rag with germs and sucking thumbs was for babies – " Mary Louise pauses to take a breath. "She had scissors and she cut up all of Bankie on the floor. She said next time she'd get bigger scissors and cut off my thumbs! She threw my Bankie pieces in the toilet and flushed, three times. This one fell under the couch," Mary Louise says, looking at the small scrap, her voice breaking.

Ruby puts an arm around her shaking shoulders and kisses her forehead. "Hush now. Don't you fret. You just sit down here with me. Everything gonna be okay. You gotta – " A buzzing noise from the washer interrupts her. She looks into the laundry area, then down at Mary Louise and sighs. "You take a couple deep breaths. I gotta move the clothes in the washer so they're not all on one side. When I come back, I'm gonna tell you a story. Make you feel better, okay?"

"Okay," says Mary Louise in a small voice. She looks at her lap, not at Ruby, because nothing is really very okay at all.

Ruby comes back a few minutes later and sits down on the step next to Mary Louise. She pulls two small yellow rectangles out of her pocket and hands one to Mary Louise. "I like to set back and hear a story with a stick of Juicy Fruit in my mouth. Helps my ears open up or somethin. How about you?"

"I like Juicy Fruit," Mary Louise admits.

"I thought so. Save the foil. Fold it up and put it in your pocket."

"So I have someplace to put the gum when the flavor's all used up?"

"Maybe. Or maybe we got somethin else to do and that foil might could come in handy. You save it up neat and we'll see."

Mary Louise puts the gum in her mouth and puts the foil in the pocket of her corduroy pants, then folds her hands in her lap and waits.

"Well, now," says Ruby. "Seems that once, a long, long time ago, down South Carolina, there was a little mouse of a girl with red, red hair and big blue eyes."

"Like me?" asks Mary Louise.

"You know, I think she was just about 'zactly like you. Her momma died when she was just a little bit of a girl, and her daddy married hisself a new wife, who was very pretty, but she was mean and lazy. Now, this stepmomma, she didn't much like stayin home to take care of no child weren't really her own and she was awful cruel to that poor little girl. She never gave her enough to eat, and even when it was snowin outside, she just dress her up in thin cotton rags. That child was awful hungry and cold, come winter.

"But her real momma had made her a blanket, a soft blue blanket, and that was the girl's favorite thing in the whole wide world. If she wrapped it around herself and sat real quiet in a corner, she was warm enough, then.

"Now, her stepmomma, she didn't like seein that little girl happy. That little girl had power inside her, and it scared her stepmomma. Scared her so bad that one day she took that child's most favorite special blanket and cut it up into tiny pieces, so it wouldn't be no good for warmin her up at all."

"That was really mean of her," Mary Louise says quietly.

"Yes it was. Awful mean. But you know what that little girl did next? She went into the kitchen, and sat down right next to the cookstove, where it was a little bit warm. She sat there, holdin one of the little scraps from her blanket, and she cried, cause she missed havin her real momma. And when her tears hit the stove, they turned into steam, and she stayed warm as toast the rest of that day. Ain't nothin warmer than steam heat, no siree.

"But when her stepmomma saw her all smilin and warm again, what did that woman do but lock up the woodpile, out of pure spite. See, she ate out in fancy rest'rants all the time, and she never did cook, so it didn't matter to her if there was fire in the stove or not.

"So finally that child dragged her cold self down to the basement. It was mighty chilly down there, but she knew it was someplace her stepmomma wouldn't look for her, cause the basement's where work gets done, and her stepmomma never did do one lick of work.

"That child hid herself back of the old wringer washer, in a dark, dark corner. She was cold, and that little piece of blanket was only big enough to wrap a mouse in. She wished she was warm. She wished and wished and between her own power and that magic blanket, she found her mouse self. Turned right into a little gray mouse, she did. Then she wrapped that piece of soft blue blanket around her and hid herself away just as warm as if she was in a feather bed.

"But soon she heard somebody comin down the wood stairs into the basement, clomp, clomp, clomp. And she thought it was her mean old stepmomma comin to make her life a misery again, so she scampered quick like mice do, back into a little crack in the wall. 'Cept it weren't her stepmomma. It was the cleanin lady, comin down the stairs with a big basket of mendin."

"Is that you?" Mary Louise asks.

"I reckon it was someone pretty much like me," Ruby says, smiling. "And she saw that little mouse over in the corner with that scrap of blue blanket tight around her, and she said, "Scuse me Miss Mouse, but I needs to patch me up this old raggy sweater, and that little piece of blanket is just the right size. Can I have it?'"

"Why would she talk to a mouse?" Mary Louise asks, puzzled.

"Well, now, the lady knew that it wasn't no regular mouse, 'cause she weren't no ordinary cleanin lady, she was a conjure woman too. She could see that magic girl spirit inside the mouse shape clear as day."

"Oh. Okay."

Ruby smiled. "Now, the little mouse-child had to think for a minute, because that piece of blue blanket was 'bout the only thing she loved left in the world. But the lady asked so nice, she gave over her last little scrap of blanket for the mendin and turned back into a little girl.

"Well sir, the spirit inside that blue blanket was powerful strong, even though the pieces got all cut up. So when the lady sewed that blue scrap onto that raggy old sweater, what do you know? It turned into a big warm magic coat, just the size of that little girl. And when she put on that magic coat, it kept her warm and safe, and her stepmomma never could hurt her no more."

"I wish there really was magic," says Mary Louise sadly. "Because she *did* hurt me again."

Ruby sighs. "Magic's there, sugar. It truly is. It just don't always work the way you think it will. That sufferin hand we put in Miz Kitty's bed, it work just fine. It scared her plenty. Trouble is, when she scared, she get mad, and then she get mean, and there ain't no end to it. No tellin what she might take it into her head to cut up next."

"My thumbs," says Mary Louise solemnly. She looks at them as if she is saying good-bye.

"That's what I'm afraid of. Somethin terrible bad. I been thinkin on this over the weekend, and yesterday night I call my Aunt Nancy down in Beaufort, where I'm from. She's the most powerful conjure woman I know, taught me when I was little. I ask her what she'd do, and she says, 'sounds like you all need a Peaceful Home hand, stop all the angry, make things right.'"

"Do we have to make the bed again?" asks Mary Louise.

"No, sugar. This is a wearin hand, like my money hand. 'Cept it's for you to wear. Got lots of special things in it."

"Like what?"

"Well, first we got to weave together a hair charm. A piece of yours, a piece of Miz Kitty's. Hers before the goopher, I think. And we need some dust from the house. And some rosemary from the kitchen. I can get all them when I clean today. The rest is stuff I bet you already got."

"I have magic things?"

"I b'lieve so. That piece of tinfoil from your Juicy Fruit? We need that. And somethin lucky. You got somethin real lucky?"

"I have a penny what got run over by a train," Mary Louise offers.

"Just so. Now the last thing. You know how my little bag's green flannel, cause it's a money hand?"

Mary Louise nods.

"Well, for a Peaceful Home hand, we need a square of light blue flannel. You know where I can find one of those?"

Mary Louise's eyes grow wide behind her glasses. "But it's the only piece I've got left."

"I know," Ruby says softly.

"It's like in the story, isn't it?"

"Just like."

"And like in the story, if I give it to you, Kitty can't hurt me ever again?"

"Just like."

Mary Louise opens her fist again and looks at the scrap of blue flannel for a long time. "Okay," she says finally, and gives it to Ruby.

"It'll be all right, Miss Mouse. I b'lieve everything will turn out just fine. Now I gotta finish this laundry and do me some housework. I'll meet you in the kitchen round one-thirty. We'll eat and I'll fix up your hand right after my story."

At two o'clock the last credits of *As the World Turns* disappear from the TV. Ruby and Mary Louise go down to the basement. They lay out all the ingredients on the padded gray surface of the ironing board. Ruby assembles the hand, muttering under her breath from time to time. Mary Louise can't hear the words. Ruby wraps everything in the blue flannel and snares the neck of the walnut-sized bundle with three twists of white string.

"Now all we gotta do is give it a little drink, then you can put it on," she tells Mary Louise.

"Drink of what?"

Ruby frowns. "I been thinkin on that. My Aunt Nancy said best thing is to get me some Peaceful oil. But I don't know no root doctors up here. Ain't been round Detroit long enough."

"We could look in the phone book."

"Ain't the kind of doctor you finds in the Yellow Pages. Got to know someone who knows someone. And I don't. I told Aunt Nancy that, and she says in that case, reg'lar whiskey'll do just fine. That's what I been givin my money hand. Little bit of my husband's whiskey every mornin for six days now. I don't drink, myself, 'cept maybe a cold beer on a hot summer night. But whiskey's strong magic, comes to conjurin. Problem is, I can't take your hand home with me to give it a drink, 'long with mine."

"Why not?"

"'Cause once it goes round your neck, nobody else can touch it, not even me, else the conjure magic leak right out." Ruby looks at Mary Louise thoughtfully. "What's the most powerful drink you ever had, Miss Mouse?"

Mary Louise hesitates for a second, then says, "Vernor's ginger ale. The bubbles are *very* strong. They go up my nose and make me sneeze."

Ruby laughs. "I think that just might do. Ain't as powerful as whiskey, but it fits, you bein just a child and all. And there's one last bottle up in the Frigidaire. You go on up now and fetch it."

Mary Louise brings down the yellow and green bottle. Ruby holds her thumb over the opening and sprinkles a little bit on the flannel bag, mumbling some more words that end with "father son and holy ghost amen." Then she ties the white yarn around Mary Louise's neck so that the bag lies under her left armpit, and the string doesn't show.

"This bag's gotta be a secret," she says. "Don't talk about it, and don't let nobody else see it. Can you do that?"

Mary Louise nods. "I dress myself in the morning, and I change into my jammies in the bathroom."

"That's good. Now the next three mornings, before you get dressed, you give your bag a little drink of this Vernor's, and say, 'Lord, bring an end to the evil in this house, amen.' Can you remember that?"

Mary Louise says she can. She hides the bottle of Vernor's behind the leg of her bed. Tuesday morning she sprinkles the bag with Vernor's before putting on her t-shirt. The bag is a little sticky.

But Mary Louise thinks the magic might be working. Kitty has bought a blond wig, a golden honey color. Mary Louise thinks it looks like a helmet, but doesn't say so. Kitty smiles in the mirror at herself and is in a better mood. She leaves Mary Louise alone.

Wednesday morning the bag is even stickier. It pulls at Mary Louise's armpit when she reaches for the box of Kix in the cupboard. Ruby says this is okay.

By Thursday, the Vernor's has been open for too long. It has gone flat and there are no bubbles at all. Mary Louise sprinkles her bag, but worries that it will lose its power. She is afraid the charm will not work, and that Kitty will come and get her. Her thumbs ache in anticipation.

When she goes downstairs Kitty is in her new wig and a green dress. She is going out to a luncheon. She tells Mary Louise that Ruby will not be there until noon, but she will stay to cook dinner. Mary Louise will eat in the dining room tonight, and until then she should be good and not to make a mess. After she is gone, Mary Louise eats some Kix and worries about her thumbs.

When her bowl is empty, she goes into the den, and stands on the desk chair so she can reach the tall books on the bookshelf. They are still over her head, and she cannot see, but her fingers reach. The dust on the tops make her sneeze; she finds the key on a large black book called *Who's Who in Manufacturing 1960*. The key is brass and old-looking.

Mary Louise unlocks the liquor cabinet and looks at the bottles. Some are brown, some are green. One of the green ones has Toto dogs on it, a black one and a white one, and says SCOTCH WHISKEY. The bottle is half-full and heavy. She spills some on the floor, and her little bag is soaked more than sprinkled, but she thinks this will probably make up for the flat ginger ale.

She puts the green bottle back and carefully turns it so the Toto dogs face out, the way she found it. She climbs back up on the chair and puts the key back on top of *Manufacturing*, then climbs down.

The little ball is cold and damp under her arm, and smells like medicine. She changes her shirt and feels safer. But she does not want to eat dinner alone with Kitty. That is not safe at all. She thinks for a minute, then smiles. Ruby has shown her how to make a *room* safe.

There are only five nails left in the jar in the garage. But she doesn't want to keep Kitty *out* of the dining room, just make it safe to eat dinner there. Five is probably fine. She takes the nails into the kitchen and opens the cupboard under the sink. She looks at the Drano. She is not allowed to touch it, not by Kitty's rules, not by babysitter rules, not by Ruby's rules. She looks at the pirate flag man on the side of the can. The poison man. He is bad, bad, bad, and she is scared. But she is more scared of Kitty.

She carries the can over to the doorway between the kitchen and the dining room and kneels down. When she looks close she sees dirt and salt and seeds and bits of things in the thin space between the linoleum and the carpet.

The can is very heavy, and she doesn't think she can pour any Drano into the cap. Not without spilling it. So she tips the can upside down three times, then opens it. There is milky Drano on the inside of the cap. She carefully dips in each nail and pushes them, one by one, under the edge of the dining room carpet. It is hard to push them all the way in, and the two in the middle go crooked and cross over each other a little.

"This is a protectin' hand," she says out loud to the nails. Now she needs a prayer, but not a bedtime prayer. A dining room prayer. She thinks hard for a minute, then says, "For what we are about to receive may we be truly thankful amen." Then she puts the Drano back under the sink and washes her hands three times with soap, just to make sure.

Ruby gets there at noon. She gives Mary Louise a quick hug and a smile, and then tells her to scoot until dinnertime, because she has to vacuum and do the kitchen floor and polish the silver. Mary Louise wants to ask Ruby about magic things, but she scoots.

Ruby is mashing potatoes in the kitchen when Kitty comes home. Mary Louise sits in the corner of the breakfast nook, looking at the comics in the paper, still waiting for Ruby to be less busy and come and talk to her. Kitty puts her purse down and goes into the den. Mary Louise hears the rattle of ice cubes. A minute later, Kitty comes into the kitchen. Her glass has an inch of brown liquid in it. Her eyes have an angry look.

"Mary Louise, go to your room. I need to speak to Ruby in private."

Mary Louise gets up without a word and goes into the hall. But she does not go upstairs. She opens the basement door silently and pulls it almost shut behind her. She stands on the top step and listens.

"Ruby, I'm afraid I'm going to have to let you go," says Kitty. Mary Louise feels her armpits grow icy cold and her eyes begin to sting.

"Ma'am?"

"You've been drinking."

"No, ma'am. I ain't – "

"Don't try to deny it. I know you coloreds have a weakness for it. That's why Mr. Whittaker and I keep the cabinet in the den locked. For your own good. But when I went in there, just now, I found the cabinet door open. I cannot have servants in my house that I do not trust. Is that clear?"

"Yes, ma'am."

Mary Louise waits for Ruby to say something else, but there is silence.

"I will pay you through the end of the week, but I think it's best if you leave after dinner tonight." There is a rustling and the snap of Kitty's handbag opening. "There," she says. "I think I've been more than generous, but of course I cannot give you references."

"No ma'am," says Ruby.

"Very well. Dinner at six. Set two places. Mary Louise will eat with me." Mary Louise hears the sound of Kitty's heels marching off, then the creak of the stairs going up. There is a moment of silence, and the basement door opens.

Ruby looks at Mary Louise and takes her hand. At the bottom of the stairs she sits, and gently pulls Mary Louise down beside her.

"Miss Mouse? You got somethin you want to tell me?"

Mary Louise hangs her head.

"You been in your Daddy's liquor?"

A tiny nod. "I didn't *drink* any. I just gave my bag a little. The Vernor's was flat and I was afraid the magic wouldn't work. I put the key back. I guess I forgot to lock the door."

"I guess you did."

"I'll tell Kitty it was me," Mary Louise says, her voice on the edge of panic. "You don't have to be fired. I'll tell her."

"Tell her what, Miss Mouse? Tell her you was puttin your daddy's whiskey on a conjure hand?" Ruby shakes her head. "Sugar, you listen to me. Miz Kitty thinks I been drinkin, she just fire me. But she find out

I been teachin you black juju magic, she gonna call the po-lice. Better you keep quiet, hear?"

"But it's not fair!"

"Maybe it is, maybe it ain't." Ruby strokes Mary Louise's hair and smiles a sad smile, her eyes as gentle as her hands. "But, see, after she talk to me that way, ain't no way I'm gonna keep workin for Miz Kitty anyhow. It be okay, though. My money hand gonna come through. I can feel it. Already startin to, maybe. The Ford plant's hirin again, and my husband's down there today, signin up. May be when I gets home, he's gonna tell me good news. May just be."

"You can't *leave* me!" Mary Louise cries.

"I got to. I got my own life."

"Take me with you."

"I can't, sugar." Ruby puts her arms around Mary Louise. "Poor Miss Mouse. You livin in this big old house with nice things all 'round you, 'cept nobody nice to you. But angels watchin out for you. I b'lieve that. Keep you safe til you big enough to make your own way, find your real kin."

"What's kin?"

"Fam'ly. Folks you belong to."

"Are you my kin?"

"Not by blood, sugar. Not hardly. But we're heart kin, maybe. 'Cause I love you in my heart, and I ain't never gonna forget you. That's a promise." Ruby kisses Mary Louise on the forehead and pulls her into a long hug. "Now since Miz Kitty already give me my pay, I 'spect I oughta go up, give her her dinner. I reckon you don't want to eat with her?"

"No."

"I didn't think so. I'll tell her you ain't feelin well, went on up to bed. But I'll come downstairs, say good-bye, 'fore I leave." Ruby stands up and looks fondly down at Mary Louise. "It'll be okay, Miss Mouse. There's miracles every day. Why, last Friday, they put a fella up in space. Imagine that? A man up in space? So ain't nothin impossible, not if you wish just hard as you can. Not if you believe." She rests her hand on Mary Louise's head for a moment, then walks slowly up the stairs and back into the kitchen.

Mary Louise sits on the steps and feels like the world is crumbling around her. This is not how the story is supposed to end. This is not happily ever after.

She cups her tiny hand around the damp, sticky bag under her arm and closes her eyes and thinks about everything that Ruby has told her. She wishes for the magic to be real.

And it is. There are no sparkles, no gold. This is basement magic, deep and cool. Power that has seeped and puddled, gathered slowly, beneath the notice of queens, like the dreams of small awkward girls. Mary Louise believes with all her heart, and finds the way to her mouse self.

Mouse sits on the bottom step for a minute, a tiny creature with a round pink tail and fur the color of new rust. She blinks her blue eyes, then scampers off the step and across the basement floor. She is quick and clever, scurrying along the baseboards, seeking familiar smells, a small ball of blue flannel trailing behind her.

When she comes to the burnt-orange coat hanging inches from the floor, she leaps. Her tiny claws find purchase in the nubby fabric, and she climbs up to the pocket, wriggles over and in. Mouse burrows into a pale cotton hankie that smells of girl tears and wraps herself tight around the flannel ball that holds her future. She puts her pink nose down on her small pink paws and waits for her true love to come.

Kitty sits alone at the wide mahogany table. The ice in her drink has melted. The kitchen is only a few feet away, but she does not get up. She presses the buzzer beneath her feet, to summon Ruby. The buzzer sounds in the kitchen. Kitty waits. Nothing happens. Impatient, she presses on the buzzer with all her weight. It shifts, just a fraction of an inch, and its wire presses against the two lye-tipped nails that have crossed it. The buzzer shorts out with a hiss. The current, diverted from its path to the kitchen, returns to Kitty. She begins to twitch, as if she were covered in stinging ants, and her eyes roll back in her head. In a gesture that is both urgent and awkward, she clutches at the tablecloth, pulling it and the dishes down around her. Kitty Whittaker, a former

Miss Bloomfield Hills, falls to her knees and begins to howl wordlessly at the moon.

Downstairs, Ruby hears the buzzer, then a crash of dishes. She starts to go upstairs, then shrugs. She takes off her white uniform for the last time. She puts on her green skirt and her cotton blouse, leaves the white Keds under the sink, puts on her flat black shoes. She looks in the clothes chute, behind the furnace, calls Mary Louise's name, but there is no answer. She calls again, then, with a sigh, puts on her nubby orange outdoor coat and pulls the light string. The basement is dark behind her as she opens the door and walks out into the soft spring evening.

Intelligent Design

"If one could conclude as to the nature of the Creator
from a study of creation, it would appear that God
has an inordinate fondness for stars and beetles."
— J. B. S. HALDANE, 1951

GOD COCKED HIS THUMB and aimed his index finger at the firmament.

Ka-pow! Pow! Pow! A line of three perfect glowing pinpoints of light appeared in the black void. He squeezed his eyes almost shut and let off a single shot. Ping! The pinprick of light at the far edge of the firmament, just where it touched the rim of the earth, glowed faintly red.

God got bored. Ratatatatatatat! He peppered one corner of the sky with tiny specks of light clustered tight together. Each one glowed steadily. God lay down on his back and looked up at what he'd created. It was okay.

He blinked. The lights flickered in and out. He blinked again. Flicker. Flicker. Flicker. God lay on his back and thought hard for a tiny bit of time, then stopped blinking. The lights continued to shimmer and twinkle up in the firmament. God smiled. That was better.

God's grandmother – she who was before the before, she who created dust out of nothing and the universe out of dust, sculptor of the clay of the world, creator and destroyer – was baking. She peered through the thickening mist that separated that which *is* from that which is becoming, and sighed.

"God," she called out. "Don't you think that's enough of those?" She had thought the night should remain in darkness. It was getting quite light in the firmament.

"Just a couple more?" God said.

"All right. But only a few. Then I need you to come in and help with the animals."

Nanadeus rolled out a sheet of clay while she waited for God to come in out of the void. Now that there was fire, there was much to be done. Systems and cycles and chains of being to set in place. And the oceans, which had turned out to be a little tricky.

The waters had been gathered together, separate from the dry land, and that was fine. But they weren't moving. They just lay there, wet and placid and still. She'd gone out and shifted them back and forth, and they did move, but then they slowed down and lay still again, and that just wouldn't do. They had to keep moving, and she didn't have the time to go out and shake them twice a day. Besides, they were too heavy for her to be lifting all the time. Maybe she had made the deep *too* deep? Where was God? If he could help make some of the simpler creatures, she'd have time to deal with the oceans.

God lay on the earth, watching the twinkling stars, spraying random corners of the firmament with his outstretched finger, filling in the parts that seemed a little empty. Pow! Powpowpowpow! KAPOW! Ooops. He pursed his lips and drew in a breath, sucking a bit of light from that spot, then another, and another, until there were a few holes in the midst of the stars, blacker than the black of the void.

He sat up and examined a small muddy pebble clinging to his right knee. He put it on the palm of his hand and flicked it with his first finger, as hard as he could. The pebble shot far up into the firmament. God waited for it to fall down again, but it didn't. It wobbled a little, then just hung there. God made a POP! sound with his lips and the pebble began to glow with a bright white light. He grinned and reached for another pebble.

"God. I need you. Now," called Nanadeus.

God dropped the pebble and went in. "What're you making? Can I help?"

Nanadeus smiled and rumpled his hair. "Yes, you can. You can be a big help right now. Watch what I do."

She pulled a tray of tiny brown ovals from the oven. "You need to decorate them while they're still soft," she said, putting one on the counter. She reached into one of the bins that lined the counter. LEGS, said one. WINGS. ANTENNAE.

She stretched the oval a little, added two hair-like feelers and six legs, daubed it with a bit of green pigment, and added two multicolored wings. She held out her palm. The little bug was perfect in every detail, except it was just clay. Its tiny eyes were blank and featureless and it lay still.

"Pay attention," she said. "This is important." She picked up another soft, baked lump and added identical legs and antennae and wings, stretching it in the same way. "You have to make two of each. They can be different colors, if you want, but the very same creature. Okay, God?"

He nodded slowly, his eyes wide and curious.

"Good. Now watch." She pinched a bit of bluish sparkling dust from a stone vat on the counter and sprinkled it over the dark shapes. "This is the fun part." She leaned over the clay figures and breathed on them gently. "Butterfly," she said.

The butterflies' wings quivered, then slowly beat together and out again. They flew onto the edge of the tray, to God's shoulder, and out into the void.

"Wow!" God clapped his hands in delight. "Can I try?"

His grandmother scooped two clay dots from the tray. God stuck his tongue in the corner of his mouth and very carefully put five tiny legs into the warm clay. "Can I make them red?" he asked.

"Yes," laughed Nanadeus. "We'll need a lot of insects, and you may decorate them in any colors you want. Do try for symmetry, though, won't you dear?"

God nodded solemnly and added a sixth leg and two little wings. He painted the round bugs bright red, and after a moment's thought, added some tiny black spots. He held them out to Nanadeus.

"Very nice," she said. She sprinkled and blew onto them. "Ladybug," she said, and they flew away.

"What other kind of bugs can I make?" God asked.

"Use your imagination," she said. "Just don't get carried away. Keep them small."

"Yay!" said God.

"But — " she held up her finger in warning. "Remember. Only two of each kind. They will make more of themselves."

"Okay," said God. He made two red ants, and two tiny green aphids, and a pair of flies with fuzzy flocked legs. Nanadeus had just breathed onto the second fly when there was a shudder, and then silence.

"Oh, God, the seas have stopped," she sighed. "Will you be all right by yourself? I need to start them up. Again."

He nodded. "I like making bugs," he said.

"I thought you might," Nanadeus smiled. "Have fun, but don't sprinkle them. We'll name them all when I come back." She patted him on the cheek and went out to deal with still waters.

God made two brown ants, and a different kind of aphid. Then he looked to make certain that his grandmother was gone, and opened all the other bins.

FANGS. PINCERS. HORNS. ARMOR. STINGERS.

"Cool," said God. He took one of the larger mounds and outfitted it with fierce claws and long fuzzy antennae, painting it bright, bright green. Then he made three hundred dozen dozen more, each more fearsome and garish than the last. Horns, claws, stripes, spots, bristling legs and armored carapaces blazed in every iridescent hue.

Bugs everywhere. God wanted to make even more, but he had run out of counter space. Where could he move them to? Move...? God looked at the vat of shimmering dust. Nanadeus had said to wait for her, but...

He took a handful of the dust and flung it over the trays of inanimate insects.

"Well," said Nanadeus from out in the void. "That was easier than I'd feared." Her voice was small and distant. "The rock you put up there really did the trick. Moon. Tides. Now why didn't I think of that ages ago...."

She was getting closer. God could hear her sensible shoes tramping across the face of the earth.

He looked at the shimmering trays of bugs and blew, hard, over all of them at once. God whispered, as fast as he could:

"Scarab. Scarab, scarab, scarab. Weevil. Tiger beetle. Leaf beetle. Weevil. Weevil. Weevil. Click beetle. Harlequin, palm borer, leaf miner. Firefly. Weevil, weevil, weevil. Jewel beetle. Blister beetle. Bark beetle. Flour beetle. Stag beetle. Potato beetle. Stink beet – "

"God? How are you coming with those insects?" Nanadeus asked from just beyond.

God looked over his shoulder, then quickly back at the last pair of unmoving creatures on the tray. "*DUNG* beetle," he said with a grin. And it was so.

Then he leaned back and began to whistle as if he hadn't done anything at all. Creeping things covered every surface, legs and claws and pincers scuttling and skittering. God saw them and smiled.

They were good.

The Green Glass Sea

IN THE SUMMER OF 1945, Dr. Gordon was gone for the first two weeks in July. Dewey Kerrigan noticed that a lot of the usual faces were missing from the dining hall at the Los Alamos lodge, and everyone seemed tense, even more tense than usual.

Dewey and her father had come to the Hill two years before, when she was eight. When he was sent to Washington, she came to live with the Gordons. They were both scientists, like Papa, and their daughter Suze was about the same age as Dewey. Dewey's mom hadn't been around since she was a baby.

One Sunday night Mrs. Gordon had shooed the girls to bed early, then woke them before dawn for a hike with some of the other wives, many of whom also had jobs and titles other than Mrs. They carried blankets and sandwiches and thermoses of coffee out to a place on the edge of the mesa where they had a clear view of the southern horizon and sat in the still early darkness, smoking and waiting.

Right before sunrise there was a bright light. Dewey thought it might be the sun coming up, except it came from the wrong direction. It lit up the sky for a moment, then disappeared, like the fireworks they'd had in May when the war in Europe ended. There was silence for a minute after the light faded, then Mrs. Gordon and the other women started hugging each other, smiling and talking. They hugged Dewey and Suze too, but Dewey wasn't sure why.

She figured it must have something to do with the gadget. Everything on the Hill had something to do with the gadget. She just wished she knew what the gadget *was*.

That evening, around dinnertime, a caravan of cars full of men returned to the Hill. They looked tired and hot and dusty and were greeted with cheers. Dr. Gordon walked into the apartment about 7:30. He had deep circles under his eyes and he hadn't shaved.

"Well, we did it," he said as he hugged Mrs. Gordon. He hugged

Suze next, and ruffled his hand through Dewey's curls. He didn't say what "it" was. He just ate a ham sandwich, drank two shots of whiskey, and slept until the next afternoon.

On the fourth of August, Dr. Gordon came into the apartment late in the afternoon. He was whistling, his hat tipped back on his head, carrying a pink box from the bakery down in Santa Fe.

He put the box down on the table and opened a bottle of beer. "Got a birthday surprise for you," he said to Suze.

She stopped coloring in Dorothy's dress with her blue crayon and looked up. "Can I open it now, Daddy?"

"Nope. Your birthday's not until the sixth. Besides, it isn't something you can unwrap. It's a trip, a little vacation. I've gotten special passes."

"Where are we going?"

"Well now, that's the surprise."

"Farther than Santa Fe?"

He smiled. "Just a bit." He took a deep swig of beer. "Why don't you go and pack up a few things before supper. You won't need much. Just a change of clothes and your toothbrush. Your Mom left a paper sack for you to put them in."

Suze threw her coloring book onto the table with a thump and ran into the bedroom, her shoes clattering loudly on the linoleum.

Dewey sat on the couch reading a book about Faraday. She ducked her head behind the page and didn't say anything. She was used to people leaving. It was better to stay quiet. She pushed her glasses up on her nose and concentrated on the orderly rows of black type.

"Aren't you going to get your things ready?" asked Dr. Gordon. He had picked up the newspaper and was looking at it without really reading.

Dewey was startled. "Am I coming *with* you?"

He chuckled. "Of course. What did you think? The whole family's going."

From the bedroom there was a loud sigh, then a snap! as Suze unfolded the paper bag.

"Oh," Dewey said slowly. "Family." The Gordons weren't her family, really. Nobody was, not since she'd gotten the Army telegram about Papa and the accident. But they were nice. Mrs. Gordon even tucked her in, some nights, if she wasn't working late at her lab.

"Don't you want to go on an adventure?" Dr. Gordon asked.

"I guess so." Dewey wasn't sure. She liked being on the Hill. She knew where everything was, and when dinner was served at the Lodge. There weren't any surprises. She'd had enough surprises.

But Dr. Gordon seemed to be waiting for an answer. Dewey carefully replaced her bookmark and closed the book. "I'll go pack my things," she said.

The next morning Mrs. Gordon was up early, making stacks of ham and cheese sandwiches that she wrapped in waxed paper. She put the picnic basket and their paper sacks into the big black Ford, and just after eleven they showed their passes to the guard at the East Gate and set off down the long twisting road that led to the highway several thousand feet below. The temperature climbed as they descended.

Dewey and Suze sat in the back seat, a foot or so of black serge between them. Suze had the road map spread out across her lap. Los Alamos wasn't on the map, of course, but a thin blue line trickled down from the mesa through Pojoaque. When it became a fatter red line, Highway 285, in Santa Fe, Dr. Gordon turned right and they headed south.

Dewey stared out the window. She had never been anywhere in New Mexico except the Hill, not since she and Papa had arrived two years before, and then it had been night. She'd imagined that everything looked like the mesa, just more of it. But now outside the window the land was flat and endless, bounded by craggy brown mountain canyons on one side and distant dusky blue ridges on the far horizons.

Close up, everything that went by the window was brown. Brown dirt, brown fences, brown tumbleweeds, brown adobe houses. But all the distances were blue. Crystal blue, huge sky that covered everything for as far as she could see until the earth curved. Faraway slate blue, hazy blue mountains and mesas, ledges of blue land stretching away from the road, blurring into the sky at the edges. Blue land. She had never seen anything like that before.

Dr. Gordon had gas coupons from the Army, and he filled up the tank when they crossed Route 66. They stopped for a late lunch on the banks of a trickle of river a few miles farther south, eating their sandwiches and drinking Orange NEHI in the shade of a piñon pine. The summer sun was bright and the air smelled like dust and resin.

"How much farther are we going?" Suze asked, putting the bottle caps in her pocket.

"Another three, maybe four hours. We'll spend the night in a little town called Carrizozo," Dr. Gordon said.

Dewey watched as Suze bent over the map and her finger found Carrizozo. It was a very small dot, and other than being a place where two roads crossed, there didn't seem to be anything interesting nearby.

Suze looked puzzled. "Why are we going *there?*"

"We're not. It's just the closest place to spend the night, unless you want to sleep in the car. I certainly don't." He lit his pipe, leaned back against the tree, and closed his eyes, smiling.

It was the most relaxed Dewey had ever seen him.

After lunch, the land stayed very flat and the mountains stayed far away. There was nothing much to see. Beyond the asphalt the land was parched brown by the heat, and there were no trees, just stubby greasewood bushes and low grass, with an occasional spiky yucca or flat cactus.

Dewey's eyes closed and she slept, almost, just aware enough to hear the noise of the car wheels and the wind. When the car slowed and bumped over a set of railroad tracks, she opened her eyes again. They were in Carrizozo, and it was twilight. The distant blues had turned to purples and the sky was pale and looked as if it had been smeared with bright orange sherbet. Dr. Gordon pulled off onto the gravel of the Crossroads Motor Court.

They walked a few blocks into town for dinner. Carrizozo was not much more than the place where the north-south highway heading toward El Paso crossed the east-west road that led to Roswell. There was a bar called the White Sands, a Texaco station, and some scattered stores and houses between the railroad tracks and the one main street.

Through the blue-checked curtains of the café Dewey could see mountains to the east. "Are we going into the mountains in the morning?"

"Nope," said Dr. Gordon, spearing a piece of meatloaf. "The other direction."

Dewey frowned. She had spent most of the day looking over Suze's shoulder at the map. There wasn't anything in the other direction. It was an almost perfectly blank place on the map. White Sands was a little bit west, but almost 100 miles to the south. If they'd been going there, Dewey thought, it would have made more sense to stay in Alamogordo.

"But...," Dewey said, and Mrs. Gordon smiled. "You're confused, my little geographer. That's because where we're going isn't *on* the map. Not yet, anyway."

That didn't make a lot of sense either. But when Mrs. Gordon smiled at her with warm eyes, Dewey felt like everything would be okay, even if she didn't understand.

It was barely light when Mrs. Gordon woke them the next morning. Dr. Gordon had gotten two cups of coffee in paper cups from the café, and Cokes for the girls, even though it was breakfast. The air was still and already warm, and everything was very quiet.

They drove south, and then west for about an hour, the rising sun making a long dark shadow in front of the car. There was nothing much to see out the window or on the map. At an unmarked dirt road, Dr. Gordon turned left.

Thin wire ran from wooden fence posts, separating the pale brown of the road from the pale beige of the desert. A few straggly yucca plants, spiky gray-green balls with stalks of yellow flowers, were the only color forever. The car raised plumes of dust so thick that Dewey could see where they were going, but no longer where they'd been.

After half an hour, they came to a gate with an Army MP. He seemed to be guarding more empty desert. The Gordons both showed their passes and their Los Alamos badges. The guard nodded and waved the car through, then closed the gate behind them.

Dr. Gordon pulled the car off to the side of the road a mile later and turned off the engine. It ticked slowly in the hot, still air.

"Daddy? Where *are* we?" Suze asked after a minute.

They didn't seem to be anywhere. Except for a small range of low mountains to the west, where they'd stopped was the middle of a flat, featureless desert, scattered with construction debris – pieces of wooden crates, lengths of wire and cable, flattened sheets of metal.

Dr. Gordon took her hand. "It's called Trinity," he said. "It's where I was working last month. Let's walk."

They started across the dirt. There were no plants, not even grass or yucca. Just reddish-beige, sandy dirt. Every few yards there was a charred greasewood bush. Each bush was twisted at the same odd angle, like a little black skeleton that had been pushed aside by a big wind.

They kept walking. The skeletons disappeared and then there was nothing at all. It was the emptiest place Dewey had ever seen.

After about five minutes, Dewey looked down and saw burned spots that looked like little animals, like a bird or a desert mouse had been stenciled black against the hard flat ground. She looked over at Mrs. Gordon. Mrs. Gordon had stopped walking.

She stood a few yards back from the others, her lips pressed tight together, staring down at one of the black spots. "Christ," she said to the spot. "What *have* we done?" She lit a Chesterfield and stood there for almost a minute, then looked up at Dr. Gordon. He walked back to her.

"Phillip? How safe is this?" She looked around, holding her arms tight across her chest, as if she were cold, although the temperature was already in the 80s.

He shrugged. "Ground zero's still pretty hot. But Oppie said the rest is okay, as long as we don't stay out too long. Fifteen minutes. We'll be fine."

Dewey didn't know what he was talking about. Maybe sunburn. There wasn't any shade. There wasn't any anything.

Mrs. Gordon nodded without smiling. A few minutes later she reached down and took Suze's hand and held it tight.

They kept walking through the empty place.

And then, just ahead of them, the ground sloped gently downward into a huge green sea. Dewey took a few more steps and saw that it wasn't water. It was glass. Shiny jade-green glass, everywhere, coloring the bare, empty desert as far ahead as she could see. It wasn't smooth, like a Pyrex bowl, or sharp like a broken bottle, but more like a giant candle had dripped and splattered green wax everywhere.

Dr. Gordon reached down and broke off a piece about as big as his hand. It looked like a green, twisted root. He gave it to Suze.

"Happy birthday, kiddo," he said. "I really wanted you to see this. The boys are calling it trinitite."

Suze turned the glass over and over in her hand. It was shiny on the top, with some little bubbles in places, like a piece of dark green peanut brittle. The bottom was pitted and rough and dirty where it had been lying in the sand. "Is it very, very old?" she asked.

He shook his head. "Very, very new. Three weeks today. It's the first new mineral created on this planet in millions of years." He sounded very pleased.

Dewey counted back in her head. Today was August 6th. Three weeks ago was when they got up early and saw the bright light. "Did the gadget make this?" Dewey asked.

Dr. Gordon looked surprised. He tipped his hat back on his head and thought for a minute. "I suppose it's all right to tell you girls now," he said. "Yes, the gadget did this. It was so hot that it melted the ground. Over 100 million degrees. Hotter than the sun itself. It fused seventy-five acres of this desert sand into glass."

"How is that going to win the war?" Dewey asked. It was strange to finally be talking about secret stuff out loud.

"It'll melt all the Japs!" Suze said. "Right, Daddy?"

Mrs. Gordon winced. "Well, if cooler heads prevail," she said, "we'll never have to find out, will we, Phillip?" She gave Dr. Gordon a look, then took a few steps away and stared out toward the mountains.

"You girls go on, take a walk around," he said. "But when I call, you scamper back pronto, okay?"

Dewey and Suze agreed and stepped out onto the green glass sea. The strange twisted surface crunched and crackled beneath their feet as if they were walking on braided ice. They walked in from the edge until all they could see was green: splattered at their feet, merging into solid color at the edges of their vision.

"I didn't know war stuff could make anything pretty," Suze said. "It looks like we're on the planet Oz, doesn't it?"

Dewey was as amazed by the question as by the landscape. Suze usually acted like she didn't exist. "I guess so," she nodded.

"This is probably what they made the Emerald City out of." Suze reached down and picked up a long flat piece. "I am the Wicked Witch of the West. Bow down before my powerful magic." She waved her green glass wand in the air, and a piece of it broke off, landing a few feet away. She giggled.

"I'm going to take some pieces of Oz home," she said. She pulled the bottom of her seersucker blouse out to make a pouch and dropped in the rest of the piece she was holding.

Suze began to fill up her shirt. Dewey walked a few feet away with her head down, looking for one perfect piece to take back with her. The glassy surface was only about half an inch thick, and many of the pieces Dewey picked up were so brittle they crumbled and cracked apart in her hands. She picked up one odd, rounded lump and the thin glass casing on the outside shattered under her fingers like an eggshell, revealing a lump of plain dirt inside. She finally kept one flat piece bigger than her hand, spread out. Suze had her shirttails completely filled.

Dewey was looking carefully at a big piece with streaks of reddish brown when Dr. Gordon whistled. "Come on back. Now," he called.

She looked at Suze, and the other girl smiled, just a little. They walked slowly back until they could see brown dirt ahead of them again. At the edge, Dewey turned back for a minute, trying to fold the image into her memory. Then she stepped back onto the bare, scorched dirt.

They walked back to the car in silence, holding their new, fragile treasure.

Dr. Gordon opened the trunk and pulled out a black box with a round lens like a camera. He squatted back on his heels. "Okay, now hand me each of the pieces you picked up, one by one," he said.

Suze pulled a flat piece of pebbled glass out of her shirt pouch. When Dr. Gordon put it in front of the black box, a needle moved over a bit, and the box made a few clicking sounds. He put that piece down by his foot and reached for the next one. It was one of the round eggshell ones, and it made the needle go all the way over. The box clicked like a cicada.

He put it down by his other foot. "That one's too hot to take home," he said.

Suze pulled out her next piece. "This one's not hot," she said, laying her hand flat on top of it.

Her mother patted Suze's head. "It's not temperature, sweetie. It's radiation. That's a geiger counter."

"Oh. Okay." Suze handed the piece to her father.

Dewey knew what a geiger counter was. Most of the older kids on the Hill did. She wasn't quite sure what it measured, but it was gadget stuff, so it was important.

"Did Papa help make this?" she asked, handing her piece over to Dr. Gordon.

Mrs. Gordon made a soft sound in her throat and put her arm around Dewey's shoulders. "He certainly did. None of this would have been possible without brave men like Jimmy – , like your Papa."

Dewey leaned into Mrs. Gordon and nodded silently.

Dr. Gordon made Suze leave behind two eggshell pieces. He wrapped the rest in newspaper and put them into a shoebox, padded with some more newspaper crumpled up, then put out his hand for Dewey's.

Dewey shook her head. "Can I just hold mine?" She didn't want it to get mixed up with Suze's. After a glance at his wife, Dr. Gordon shrugged and tied the shoebox shut with string and put it in the trunk. They took off their shoes and socks and brushed all the dust off before they got into the car.

"Thanks, Daddy," Suze said. She kissed him on the cheek and climbed into the back seat. "I bet this is the best birthday party I'll ever, ever have."

Dewey thought that was probably true. It was the most wonderful place *she* had ever been. As they drove east, she pressed her face to the window, smiling out at the desert. She closed her eyes and felt the comforting weight of the treasure held tight against her chest. One last present from Papa, a piece of the beautiful green glass sea.

Clip Art

TRANSCRIPT of "Clip Art" segment of Bravo's *Behind the Office Door* series.

First aired October 23, 2006

Voice Over: September, 1939

[*Grainy newsreel photos of Nazi tanks*]

Hitler's army invades Poland, beginning a war that will transform Europe into a bloody battlefield. And in faraway Kokomo, Indiana, a young girl named Frances Tipton Hunter is given a birthday gift that will transform her from a dull, drab, ordinary child into the owner of one of the most fabulous collections the world has ever seen.

[*Photo of small child in pigtails, holding a shiny, blurry object in her hand*]

She is given her first paper clip.

In this interview, made just weeks before her death, Miss Hunter recalls that momentous day.

[*"Talking Head" {TH} shot of a wrinkled old woman with flaming dyed red hair*]

Frances: Well, it wasn't just any clip, you know. If it had been a common Gothic or the like, I guess I would have said a nice 'Thank-you, ma'am,' and that would have been that. But it wasn't. It was a 1936 Clarkson Tri-Fold In-and-Out. Have you ever seen one? Oh, they're lovely. They were only made that one year, just up north, in Chicago.

I guess that's how my mother found it, Chicago being so close. She worked nights down on Slocum, sweeping up the executive washrooms. Found it on the floor, by the drain, and gave it to me for my twelfth birthday. I'd never seen anything quite so beautiful. Right then, I knew I had to have more.

[*TH shot of a very, very old woman in a wheelchair.*]

Caption: Mrs. Edith Hunter, mother. Age 102.

Edith: My lands, I can still see her, afternoons, running home with her grubby fist clenched around some new geegaw. Franny'd check out all the dustbins along Slocum Avenue – that was the business section – and when she'd find a new one, lordy, how she'd carry on. Mister Petroski down to the stationery store gave her one every week, for sweeping the floors on Friday nights. I never saw the point of it, myself. Paper clips? When I was a girl, I had paper *dolls*, but not my Franny. She never did take after me much, except for the sweeping.

[*TH shot, elderly, balding man*]

Caption: Howard Finsterman, Kokomo High School Biology Teacher, retired.

Howard: Frances Hunter? She was a keen one for organizing, I'll say that. Fifteen years old and she already had an impressive collection, mounted and sorted by class and phylum. Well, brand name and style, but it's the same skill, when you come down to it. By the end of the year, she'd filled up six lab books with specimens, dates noted, all arranged neat as a pin. Or as a paper clip, you might say. (*Chuckles.*)

[*TH shot, woman with cigarette dangling from her lip. She has big hair and electric blue eye shadow.*]

Caption: Olive DeSerria, classmate

Olive: Geez, that takes me back. Franny was a character. Her and her paper clips. We was in secretarial school together. Miss Helvetica's Academy of Ladies Business Skills. I had to staple my assignments, on account of Franny would pocket any clips in a New York minute. Her handbag rattled like a junk cart.

(*Pauses for a long drag on her cigarette, coughs.*) I don't think she never did graduate. But she done okay, huh? Otherwise why this fancy TV interview and everything?

[*TH shot, man in tweed jacket. He has a thick, bristling mustache.*]

Caption: Martin St. James Andrews, librarian

Martin: An impressive woman, Frances. Knew her clips, she did. Give her a jumbled drawer, hundreds of them tangled round each other, and Bob's your uncle! She'd have separated out the Banjo Gems and the Marcel Dual-Ds and swept the rest into the rubbish where they belonged. Without her, we'd still be in the dark ages when it comes to the office supply sciences. Take her cataloging of the two-bend spring clip. A masterpiece. We'll not see the likes of her again.

V.O.: Through the business-as-usual 1950s, Frances Hunter's career flourished. Her collection increased to more than 17,000 clips. But the introduction of photocopiers into the offices of America threatened to banish her beloved fastener. Would the paper jam defeat the paper clip?

[*TH shot, thin young man with glasses held together with black tape.*]

Caption: Ronald Landers, Technical Writer, Apple Computer

Ronald: Oh yeah. I was the go-to guy when it came to getting paper clips out of the Xerox machine. I had a whole pile of 'em on my desk. One afternoon, Danny in the next cubicle was working on our first floppy drive, the 3½-incher, and the disk kept getting stuck. I straightened out one of the mangled clips on my desk and said, 'Here, try one of these.' He stuck it in the eject hole, and — zowie! The disk popped right out. So paper clips made it into the manual.

V.O.: The computer revolution introduced the small steel wonder to a new generation of aficionados. Frances was honored to cut the ribbon at the 1993 opening of the Frances Tipton Hunter retrospective at the Museum of Bureaucratic Necessities. Curator Milton S. Gestetner recalls the event.

[TH shot of a man with a goatee and a florid ascot]

Milton: It took me five years of negotiations to acquire the Hunter collection. The Smithsonian wanted it, but Miss Hunter spoke up on our behalf and tipped it our way. Quite a feather in my cap. The highlights? Oh, dear. There are so many. I suppose the Reddy-Clip Four-Oh-Seven. One of only two known to have survived the Blitz in London. The other is in private hands. Went for nearly thirty thousand pounds at auction last year. Naturally, we've had to beef up security.

V.O.: Frances Tipton Hunter

[TH shot, Miss Hunter]

Frances: My favorite? Well, there's a very cunning copper one, sent to me by the Bureau of Yak-Binding in Kathmandu. Crafted by monks. Making them is a meditation, their life's work. But if I could only have *one*, it would have to be this. It's never been exhibited.

(*Holds out an ordinary-looking paper clip, slightly bent, on the palm of her hand.*)

It was 1962, at the Cartapagological Society's annual dinner at the Statler Hotel in St. Louis. I was the keynote speaker, and sitting

next to me on the dais was Cornelius Brosnan himself. Imagine!
The man whose 1899 patent established the first modern paper clip.
Of course he was very old by then, all shaky and sunken. But after
the fish course, he pulled a bit of wire from a little leather case in his
pocket, and with his gnarled, spotted fingers, he bent this Konaclip
for me. Right there at the table. (*Looks at it fondly.*)

A hand-made triple S-bend! At 97! He dropped it into my hand and
said, 'For you, Frances. You've transformed my little gadget into a
work of art.' I nearly wept. And I've kept it with me, all these years,
in a small rosewood box in my writing desk.

V.O.: From that first birthday gift to the dedication of the Hunter
Chair for the Study of Bent Metal Fasteners at M.I.T. just weeks
before her death, her life was dedicated to the glory of one of our most
common – and most overlooked – household objects.

Frances Tipton Hunter earned the affection and respect of millions of
secretaries, clerks, and editors, for whom she will always be, simply,
"The First Lady of the Paper Clip."

[*Head Shot of Frances, backlit dramatically, with an Art Deco–like
fan of paper clips forming an arc behind her.*]

V.O.: Few have done so much with so little.

[*Hold for four seconds, fade to credits*]

Triangle

MICHAEL CONNOLLY put his papers down on top of the podium and looked out over his audience. The meeting room was only about half full, which didn't surprise him. As a junior professor, he wasn't exactly a big-name draw, and since he was the last speaker at the Trends in 19th-Century Studies conference, he suspected a lot of people had ducked out early. He wiped the flop sweat off his forehead with the back of his hand and began.

In the middle of the second page he saw Simon walk in the side door and take a seat near the back of the room. Michael faltered, then recovered, but Emily Dickinson and the iambic quatrain went on auto-pilot as his mind raced to figure out how he was going to get off the podium and out to his rental car without talking to Simon.

The night before, nervous about delivering today's paper, he'd gone down to the bar for a nightcap. After the third scotch, it had seemed a fine idea to go back to Simon's room. He shuddered at the idea of talking to the man again.

Michael wished, for the hundredth time, that he had just swallowed his pride and called Willy at his mother's condo in Boca Raton. Willy would have reassured him that the paper was good, that he'd do fine. But they'd had an argument on the flight out to Miami. Willy was offering him advice on the presentation, what to wear, who to schmooze with, and Michael had snapped at him. Said he could do it on his own, thank you, and didn't need any coaching from the renowned Dr. William Cline.

He'd regretted it as soon as he'd said it, but didn't take it back. Willy had looked at him, hurt, then shrugged and opened his book. The rest of the flight had been tense and silent. Michael tried to say something when they landed, patch things up before they split for the weekend, but Willy's mother had met him at the gate, and there hadn't been time.

Michael paused to take a drink of water from the glass at his elbow and returned his focus to the 19th century. The audience applauded politely at the end of the paper, and the chair of the English department rose from his seat in the first row. Michael could see Simon making his way toward the front through the exiting crowd. He stepped down from the podium and offered his hand to Dr. Bourne.

"A fine lecture, Michael," the older man said. "Are you going to the Norton cocktail party? I'd like to hear more about your thoughts on Dickinson's use of the standard hymnal."

Michael shook his head. "I'd love to, but I have to catch a plane. If you'd like to walk out to my car with me, we could talk for a few minutes, though."

Out of the corner of his eye, he saw Simon gesture, but Michael pretended he hadn't seen him, and walked out of the lecture hall with Dr. Bourne.

Michael peeled off his poplin jacket as soon as he was in the rental car. He was sick of South Florida. Its still, cloying air seemed to cling to everything like an invisible film. He wanted to be home, sitting on the back deck with Willy, watching the cool fog roll over Twin Peaks. He wanted this whole weekend to be over.

He looked at his watch. It was just after 4:00. More than two hours before he needed to be at the airport to meet Willy for their 7:30 flight. A lot of time to kill when you don't want to be somewhere any more. He decided to go shopping, buy Willy a present. A gesture of reconciliation for their fight. And to atone for Simon, take the edge off his guilt, a secret apology for a crime Willy could never know he'd committed.

He'd seen a mall with a huge Barnes and Noble by the freeway. Maybe they'd have the new Andrew Holleran. But just before the turnoff he saw a wooden sign that said Palmetto Antique District, with an arrow pointing to the left. He smiled. Willy's kind of place. He turned and followed the signs.

He parked the white Plymouth Neon in a lot at the back of the first antique mall. The asphalt was hot, even through his shoes; the pavement shimmering at the edges. He stopped to dig the sunscreen out of his carry-on in the trunk. Irish heritage. He was so fair that he freckled after five minutes in the sun and burned after ten. He walked into the mall smelling faintly of coconut.

The air-conditioned mall — 200 DEALERS! — was filled with small stalls, six-by-six cubicles of Depression glass cheek to jowl with Victorian lithographs on one side and vintage TV lunchboxes on the other. A speaker blared scratchy Big Band music. He browsed aimlessly, not really sure what he was looking for, but knowing he hadn't found it yet. Something vintage, something that would tickle Willy's fancy.

He window-shopped at a fairly brisk pace up the north side of Palmetto Avenue. Two out of every three shops specialized in antiquey antiques — delicate porcelain cups, fussy velvet lampshades, windows full of over-dressed dolls with zombie eyes. He stopped in one store to look through a case of hundred-year-old novels, his particular mania, but didn't find anything he couldn't live without.

He'd planned to cross at the corner and check out the shops on the other side. If nothing looked promising, he'd head back to the Barnes and Noble. But as he waited for the light to change, a lone ANTIQUES sign in the next block caught his eye, and he continued on.

The store had no other identity, just a street number in peeling gilt letters on the transom over its front door. A bell chimed overhead as he entered the musty room. It smelled stale. No air-conditioning. The windows were grimy with dust and age; everything that wasn't directly under one of the buzzing fluorescent lights had a sepia tint to it.

He looked around. Wooden cases, some glass-fronted, lined the walls. Above them paintings and a few large, fading photographs covered most of the cracking plaster up to the ceiling. The rest of the room seemed more like an upscale surplus store than an antique shop: cases full of knives, battered metal helmets, swords, uniforms with full regalia.

That might be treasure for some collectors, but definitely not for Willy, who was into retro, collectibles. Michael started to leave, then saw a stack of framed photographs leaning against a cabinet toward the back of the store. Willy adored those old group shots — 1922 graduations and annual picnics at midwestern shoe factories. It was worth checking out. He skirted a glass-topped case of dusty, vaguely distasteful objects: a leather pouch of dental instruments, a photo of a Civil War autopsy, a small, curled whip. He shivered when he saw the first swastika.

A high black cap with silver lightning bolts. A brown uniform shirt with a red armband. Suddenly they were everywhere. Twisted blood-red crosses, vivid against white porcelain cabochons, inlaid into the hilts of daggers; silver swastikas embossed on the corners of photos, more of them on the uniforms of the men with their outstretched, rigid arms.

Michael felt a rising disgust. The atmosphere of the store seemed to surround him like carbon monoxide from a defective furnace, invisible, insidious. He didn't want to be there. But as he turned in the narrow space between cases, he came face-to-face with a locked glass cabinet, its shelves only a few inches deep.

A cracked leather rectangle, the size of a luggage tag, wood-burned with the word CHARLESTON. A typewritten sign below it said "1861. SLAVE AUCTION TAG. $300." Next to it, two scraps of felt were propped up in a paper-lined cigar box. The yellow star, its six points outlined in black, had the word JUDE in the center. The lines and the letters were off-center from the contours of the felt; it had been badly printed or cut. The pale pink triangle was identified by another typewritten sign: "NAZI HOMOSEXUAL BADGE, CA. 1935. $75."

Michael stared at the small piece of pink felt, once worn by a man like him. Or Willy. This one looked like it had never been used. Mint condition. It was perfectly flat, had never conformed to the rounded shape of a human arm. No needle holes pierced its periphery; it had never been sewn onto a sleeve or torn off by a souvenir hunter.

He looked at it appraisingly. Willy taught a Gay Studies course and had books full of black-and-white pictures of these things. And they were all over the Castro, in bright pink neon, on bumper stickers and shot glasses. But Michael had never seen a real one. It had to be rare.

It was an odd present. On the other hand, it was perfect for Willy, and a lot more personal and hand-picked than some book he'd just grabbed at Barnes and Noble. Plus it wouldn't seem too extravagant. It was just a little piece of felt. Seventy-five dollars was lot more than he'd intended to spend, more than he could really afford, but that was good, he thought, under the circumstances.

He walked back to the cash register at the front of the store. When the old guy in the greasy Marlins cap put down his Tom Clancy paperback, Michael handed him a credit card.

———

Coming off the pedestrian walkway in the United terminal, Michael spotted Willy in the cocktail lounge next to Gate 47. A pint of some sort of dark beer was at his elbow, and his laptop was open in front of him. He had his reading glasses on and was staring at the screen, stroking the graying hairs in his dark beard, deep in thought. And he was wearing the Hawaiian shirt that Michael had given him for his birthday. That was a good sign.

Michael stopped and watched him for a minute, smiling affectionately at the familiar face, then took a deep breath. They had some serious talking to do.

He put his carry-on on an empty chair and rested his hand on Willy's shoulder. "Hey."

Willy looked up. "Hey." His voice had a wary tone to it, and he wasn't smiling. "You didn't call me back last night."

"I know. I'm sorry. I got back to the room late and didn't want to wake your mom." He sat down and arranged his jacket on the chair, hoping that his voice hadn't given anything away, buying himself a few seconds to figure out what to say next.

"I'll get you a beer. They've got Redhook ESB on tap." Willy signaled the waitress then fidgeted with his coaster. Neither one of them said anything until the beer arrived.

"Look, I'm really sorry," Michael began. "I was nervous. I shouldn't have bitten your head off."

"I knew you were nervous. I've been there. I was trying to help."

"I know. That was the thing. You've done papers. You're almost finished with your book. Sometimes I feel like you're always one step ahead of me."

"It's not a competition," Willy said quietly.

"Yeah, well, I guess it was for me. I didn't need any help, you know?"

Michael shook his head. "It sounds stupid now, but I wanted to be the big guy."

Willy smiled, just a little. "So, big guy. How did it go?"

Michael's shoulders sagged in relief. Willy was smiling. It was going to be okay. He hadn't realized until just that moment how afraid he was that he'd really blown it.

"It went okay. I was a wreck the night before but..." Michael let his voice trail off. The night before was a minefield. He *had* really blown it there. He could never let Willy know that. He took a sip of beer to regroup. "...but it went well. I got all the way through, and didn't drop anything or swear like a sailor in front of the dean. How was Betty?"

"About the same. She's down to three bridge games a week, and she made me the worst steak I've ever had in my life. Shoe leather with A-1 sauce."

Michael laughed. "We had that at the banquet last night. Must be a local dish."

They looked at each other and Willy reached across the table, covering Michael's hand with his own. "Truce?"

"Truce." Michael added his other hand to the pile and squeezed Willy's gently. "I even brought you a peace offering. I stopped at an antique strip on the way here and found a little something."

"Vintage?"

"Thirties, if it's genuine." He reclaimed his hand and reached into the inside pocket of his jacket.

Willy took the postcard-sized plastic sleeve that held the scrap of pink felt and stared at it for a few seconds, his face paling in recognition. He tipped the felt out onto the palm of his hand.

"Jesus. Where did you *find* this?"

"In a grubby little shop run by a guy who has a penchant for things German. I wandered in because it said 'Antiques.' Creepy place."

"I'll bet." Willy looked down again at the triangle in his hand. Michael couldn't read his expression, but he didn't look too happy.

"It's kind of a weird present, I know, but..."

"No, it's amazing. Really. I'm just a little stunned. It's so...ordinary. Maybe it's because I know what people did with it."

Michael shuddered. He'd never heard Willy's voice sound like that. Willy saw his expression and nodded.

"Want the five-minute lecture? Himmler started sending gay men to Dachau in the early '30s. He had the power to arrest a man for almost anything. If I smiled at you. If you had my phone number in your address book. If you subscribed to the wrong magazine, the Gestapo came to collect you. No trial. You'd be loaded into a cattle car, sent to a camp, and you disappeared. No one would dare ask what happened to you. That was just inviting the Gestapo to knock again. One book estimates that more than fifty thousand of us died in the camps."

"Gas chambers, right?"

Willy shook his head. "That would have been kinder. Getting a pink triangle meant slave labor in a quarry or the cement works, until you starved to death. But I think I'd choose that over being the guinea pig for the castration experiments. The Nazi doctors thought they could eliminate homosexuality by making sure we'd never breed. They tried anything: surgery without anesthetics, lethal doses of hormones, carbolic acid injected directly into testicles. Almost no one survived."

"God, I had no idea." Michael felt nauseated by what he'd heard. He pushed away his half-empty beer glass.

"Not very many people do."

They both stared in silence at the piece of felt resting on the tabletop. "We should go," Willy said finally. "They'll be boarding our flight in a few minutes." He slipped the triangle back into the plastic sleeve.

"If I'd known all that, I wouldn't have bought it." Even in the plastic atmosphere of the airport bar, the thing gave Michael the creeps, and he suddenly realized he didn't want to take it home. He reached for it, but Willy pulled it away, just an inch.

"No," he said. "When we get back, I'll donate it to the Gay Historical Society, if that's all right with you. Maybe it'll remind people how much we take for granted, how lucky we are."

Michael thought for a minute, then nodded. Willy slid the plastic sleeve into a zippered pocket in his black nylon laptop case and laid a ten-dollar bill on the table for the beers.

The red-eye back to San Francisco was only about half full. Michael had a window seat and Willy stretched his six-foot-three inch frame out into the aisle as they waited for take-off.

"Grab me a pillow and a blanket?" Michael asked, yawning.

"Tired?"

"Yeah, 6:30 breakfast meeting." He'd actually been up all night, tossing and turning, unable to sleep after he'd left Simon's room around midnight. He propped the pillow behind his head. "You don't mind?"

"Nah. I've got a book. And some notes to type up." He patted Michael's arm, a gentle reassurance that made Michael smile and his stomach churn with fresh guilt.

He managed to stay awake long enough to have a Beck's from the drink cart and decline both the chicken and the lasagna entrees. He fell asleep somewhere over Mississippi to the rhythmic sound of Willy's fingers clicking on the keyboard.

———

It's cold. Bitter, bone-numbing cold. The wind tears through the cotton ticking of his pants, and wet snow seeps through the thin cardboard soles of his shoes. It's after midnight. They are standing in the parade ground, hundreds of thin, shivering men in striped jackets, in lines outside the wooden barracks. No one knows why. No one asks. No one says a word, moves a muscle.

Last night a man named Stefan stumbled out of line when his leg fell asleep. The Hauptscharführer hit him with the butt of a rifle, knocking him to the ground, then kicked him to death, his blood melting a small patch of snow around his head.

Michael was once horrified by these things, but no more. Now they are common. Now he is only glad he is not Stefan, and he is not certain of that. Stefan is gone, but Stefan may be warm, somewhere. Stefan's bowels are not liquid, Stefan's stomach is not in constant spasms from hunger, from dysentery, from fear.

The Obersturmführer arrives, wrapped in his long wool coat, his thick gloves. He walks along the line of men, his high black leather boots crunching in the snow. As he walks, he looks at a typewritten list, points with his stick, sneering out the names: "Ass-fucker Rudi Bucher.

Ass-fucker Horst Mueller. Ass-fucker Josef Dorfen."

Michael waits motionless, watching the emaciated men step slowly out of line, begin to shuffle through the snow. He watches as the capo shoves them to the left, not toward the railroad siding and the quarry, but toward the medical building.

He was afraid before. Now he is terrified. He has heard the screams in the night. Silently he prays to a god he no longer believes in to spare him. Take someone else. Anyone. Not him. Not him.

And then he hears the Obersturmführer call out, "Ass-fucker Wilhelm Klein." Michael starts, as if it were his own name, and watches helplessly as Willy steps out of the line. His head is shaved, like all the others, and his eyes are deep, dark circles sunken into his face. He looks so naked without his beard.

He shuffles by, looking at the ground. When he passes, Michael wants to reach out, but doesn't move. He lowers his own eyes and cannot look at him.

Willy stumbles and the Obersturmführer hits him on the shoulders with his stick. Michael can see Willy's face contort with pain. In that same moment, he sees him look up, and the light from the open door of the medical building illuminates his widened eyes for just a moment.

Michael hears Willy shout "No!" and watches him break out of the line and begin to run clumsily toward the fence and the barbed wire and the dogs. The silent air is shattered with a single shot. Willy falls face down into the snow.

Three more shots. The prone body jumps with the impact of each bullet. Michael wants to run over and cradle Willy's head in his lap. *I'm sorry. I'm sorry. I'm sorry.* But he doesn't move. Doesn't shift his feet or blink his eyes or cry out, even when the capos come and drag Willy's body to the ditch, tossing it on top of the others.

Michael woke from his nightmare with his heart racing and his nails digging into the seat rest. His eyes stung with tears. He reached over to take Willy's hand, but the seat was empty. No Willy. No laptop. No carry-on.

He tasted bile in his throat, panic. Calm down, he told himself.

Willy's just gone to the bathroom. He'll be back in a minute. But why would he take his stuff?

Five minutes passed. Ten. He'd never felt so scared, so alone. He unbuckled his seat belt, tumbled the blanket onto Willy's empty seat, and walked down the aisle to the bathrooms. The plane was dark, just a few scattered reading lights. Most people were sleeping. A few looked up, annoyed, as he passed by. One bathroom was empty, the other had its OCCUPIED sign engaged. He tapped on the closed door, and whispered loudly. "Willy?"

There was no answer for a second, then the door opened and a blonde woman in a United uniform stepped out.

"Can I help you, sir?"

He tried to sound calm. "I woke up from a nap, and my friend's not in his seat. I thought he might be back here."

The stewardess shook her head. "I haven't seen anyone."

He felt his panic rising, and tried to control his voice. "Could you page him? Willy Cline?"

"Is it an emergency, sir? Everyone's asleep."

Michael didn't know how to answer.

"Why don't you return to your seat. I'll check with the other flight attendant. After all, people don't just disappear from a 737." She smiled professionally, then took his arm and walked him back to his seat.

She continued up to the front of the cabin. He could see her talking, watched the another woman consult a list, shake her head. Michael broke into a cold sweat.

The stewardess walked slowly back to his row. Her brow was furrowed. Annoyed or confused. Michael couldn't tell. She leaned over Willy's empty seat and spoke in a whisper.

"Sir? I'm afraid Seat 13-C was never assigned. There's no one named Cline booked on this flight. Are you all right?"

Michael couldn't answer.

"Well, why don't you just go back to sleep?" she said, then walked slowly back up the aisle.

Michael watched her retreating back. There was some mistake. The list was wrong. She'd missed the name, misspelled it as Kline, with a

K. People did that all the time. "Wait, wait," he called, but if she heard him, she didn't turn around.

Michael's shoulders sagged helplessly. He turned to the window and looked out into the black, featureless night. No clouds. No lights below. As if the world had disappeared completely.

He pressed his face against the cold plastic. "Willy?" he whispered softly, and began to cry.

Without turning his head, he groped for the edge of the blanket to wipe his eyes. His fingers touched the seat cushions, felt a scrap of fabric. He pulled it into the light and stared at it, shivering uncontrollably.

The pink felt triangle was dirty, stained with patches of dried blood. And perforating its edges were ragged holes, as if it had once been sewn on with a large, blunt needle.

The Feed Bag

DAD BOWLED on Monday nights
and Mom was a lousy cook
    (she knew it)
      so we'd go out
to the Feed Bag:
    Red vinyl booths
    Chrome napkin holders and
    Texas Tommies
       the food that I eat at twilight
       on picnics in my dreams.

The menus were wooden signs,
    faux western saloon,
    with hand-painted anthropomorphic food.
Texas Tommy was a six-gun shootin'
    sheriff-star wearin'
    son-of-a-gun
    of a hot dog.

A hot dog that was grilled
    split, sizzling
inside a bun
    buttered, crispy.
In the groove of the meat
    cheese was yellow and molten.
Spiraled all around with bacon,
    pinned to the dog with wooden toothpicks
      that had no frills.

I loved the Feed Bag.
It was a diner
    in the Twilight Zone,
    six blocks from my house.
And so, so creepy noir that it's in black and white
    in my memory
    even though I was there in person.

The hairy man behind the counter in his white paper hat
    glared as he cooked.
We never sat at the counter.
We sat in a booth.
    Or sometimes,
        once or twice,
    in the empty back room with chrome-rimmed tables
        linoleum floor
        buzzing lights
        and a secret passage to the underworld.

The Feed Bag shared a basement with the barber shop next door.
Down six steps, up six steps.
Feed Bag. Barber Shop.
At the bottom was a narrow hall to the bathroom
    single bulb
    concrete floor.
    Door to the left, painted green
        hook-and-eye latch.

One night
I had to pee so hard I couldn't sit still
    couldn't finish my Texas Tommy.
My mother drank her coffee and pointed.
She said not to touch anything.
That was when I knew to be afraid.
I went by myself,
    down six steps

turn to the left
green peeling wooden door
sharp smell like a dog had been there.
The hook and eye were not enough.

I did not sit down.
Not all the way.
I squatted and leaked a little.
The toilet paper roll was wooden and squeaked.
An almost-naked lady on a calendar over the toilet
    watched me.
I was eight.

But at the bottom of the stairs I did not go up
    to the Feed Bag
    to my mother.
I went up the other way, to the barber shop.
The door was open a crack.
It wasn't *shut.*
Outside the street was night.
The shop was empty.

Cold lights shone on metal chairs
    brushes in blue water
    gleaming sharp steel man things.
The clock on the back wall was rimmed
    with pink neon.
    It was a scary color,
        pink.
It glared down on the steel things
and I could feel the old men
    hairy men
    gangsters
    men who got shaves
who belonged here when it was daytime.

I ran back to my world then,
    six steps down
    six steps up.
When I sat down at the table
    I felt older.

I had a second Texas Tommy,
For the comfort of the cheese.

Flying Over Water

SPRING VACATION. Kritter sits in the hotel's restaurant, uncomfortable in the dress she had to wear on the plane. She edges her chair another inch toward the balcony, and stares out at the water, trying to look like she is not with her family. It is just a seating error.

When they were flying over the water, in the plane, her father said that the dark blue color means there are reefs – rocks and coral just a few feet under the surface. He told her there are fish under there. Kritter stares out at the water, wondering about the fish. There are bluegills in the pond on Grandad's farm, but the water is a milky, solid green, even on a sunny day.

This water is amazingly blue – turquoise. No, turquoise is a good word for the shirt on the man at the next table or the stones surrounding his heavy gold wristwatch. But they're as dull as the gray March sky back home compared to this water. The colors blend in and out of each other without edges. Pale, clear green to deepest blue. If her best friend Annie were here, it would be a good place to have an adventure. They could pretend to be pirates in search of treasure, or rich people who are sailing around the world to exotic places like Pago Pago or Rangoon. They would –

"Kristine, I think that's just about enough of those chips," her mother says, interrupting her train of thought. "I know we're on vacation, but that doesn't mean you can forget about your diet all week."

Kritter – only her parents and teachers call her anything else – winces and pulls her hand away from the basket of thick, warm tortilla chips. She slowly and deliberately eats the chip in her hand, and watches her mother's lips tighten in disapproval. She says nothing but Kritter doesn't take another chip. A standoff.

Her mother is a slender, delicate woman with pale blue eyes. When her blond hair is pulled back into a ponytail – for tennis or on Fridays before her hair appointment – she looks like Barbie.

Kritter knows no one would make a doll like her. When she was younger, she heard people say she was built like her father, a sturdy child. She liked that. It sounded strong, and durable, like the pioneers. Puberty is softening her – adding hips and breasts to the solid rectangle of her torso – without changing her shape. She is becoming a woman, her mother says. But Kritter can tell it is not the sort of woman her mother had in mind, and feels responsible, as if she had been leafing through the body catalog and chosen the wrong one.

She looks longingly at the basket of chips, but moves her chair another fraction of an inch away and says nothing.

The next morning, after breakfast, a bright blue ferry pulls up at the dock in front of the hotel. Her father walks up the small, swaying gangplank. They are on vacation, but he is here on business. He will be at a hotel on the mainland for meetings all week and will come back and join them on Friday.

They wave good-bye, and when the sound of the ferry's motor is just a tiny buzz, her mother turns and says, "Well, now it's just us girls." She says it brightly, as if it is a special treat. Kritter would rather be on the boat.

Other than her sister Beth Ann, who is eight and therefore not very interesting, the people at the hotel who aren't grown-ups are all older kids. At least high school. The girls are all wearing bikinis and the boys show off until the girls giggle. Kritter is the only one of her kind.

They have a two-room bungalow with a porch right on the white sand beach of a small lagoon. Kritter unpacks her snorkel – a neon-yellow plastic tube with a bright pink rubber mouthpiece – and lays it on the left side of the invisible line on the dresser that divides her things from Beth Ann's heap of Nancy Drew books and tiny Malibu Skipper beachwear.

She unpacks her new bathing suit last, moving it aside to remove first socks, then sandals, t-shirts, and the paperback copy of *Travels with Charley* that she is supposed to read over vacation. Finally the suit is the only thing left – a crumpled mass of flowered nylon in the corner of the green Samsonite.

Kritter glares at it. She likes swimming. It is the only "sport" she doesn't feel clumsy and awkward at. For as many summers as she can remember, she and Annie have worn matching black Speedo tank suits. Last month, like most springs, when she tried on her suit, she had outgrown it.

But when her mother took her down to Nickerson's, they walked right by the Girls' department and its rack of Speedos and into Young Miss. Kritter knows she is not a Young Miss. She shudders with the memory.

The saleslady has glasses on a beaded chain and smells like hairspray. She has a yellow tape measure draped around her shoulders, and she pulls it around Kritter's waist, then her chest. "Let's see about the bust," she says. She talks only to Kritter's mother, as if Kritter wasn't there. A few minutes later she comes back to the dressing room with an armload of bathing suits.

"Try this one," she says, handing Kritter a hanger. "Then come out and show us how it looks." Her mother gives Kritter a quick pat on the shoulder and pushes the louvered door shut with a click.

Kritter stares at the pile of bathing suits on the bench. None of them are black. They are pastels – pinks and greens and pale blues – and all of them have flowers. When she pulls the top suit off its white plastic hanger, she sees that there are buttons on the straps. The front of the suit looks like there's someone already in it. She thinks it's newspaper, the way purses and knapsacks are stuffed so you'll know how they'll look full of Kleenex and keys and things. But it isn't newspaper. It's stiff white fabric – a bra – sewn right into the suit. She throws it on the floor. No one could *swim* in something like that.

She pulls each flowered monstrosity off its hanger: they are all the same. She wants to throw them over the top of the door and run as hard as she can. Out of the dressing room, out of Nickerson's, out of her life. But she is trapped. Her mother is outside the door, waiting. A tear of frustration rolls down Kritter's cheek. Her only hope is that when her mother sees her in the suit she will know that it is ridiculous, and they will buy a black Speedo and go home.

"Krissy?" Her mother knocks on the door. "We're waiting."

"Just a sec." Kritter wipes the wetness from her cheek with the back of her wrist. She picks up a suit from the heap on the floor and tugs it on, pulling hard, hoping it will rip. But it doesn't. The straps dig into the flesh of her shoulders and the white cups are larger than her breasts, which are not much more than swellings with soft, pink centers. She pokes a finger at her chest and when she pulls it away, a crater remains in one rounded volcano.

She feels like she is wearing armor. Stiff, flowered armor. She opens the door.

"That one looks nice," her mother says.

The saleslady nods her head in agreement. "Come here, hon. Let's see how it fits." Without waiting for Kritter's answer, the saleslady turns to her mother. "I think that's the right size, don't you?"

Her mother nods and smiles. "Is that the color you want?" she asks Kritter.

She has to be kidding. Kritter tries to save herself. "Not really. I was thinking more of a black Speedo. Like last year."

Her mother sighs. She and the saleslady exchange glances. "Do you think that a dark color might be a little more...slimming?" The saleslady peers at Kritter, then nods and bustles over to another rack.

"Mom, I can't swim in this," Kritter says desperately. "I want a Speedo so I –"

"No," her mother says. "Now that you're getting a figure, well, things are different." She is using her this-conversation-is-over (young lady) tone of voice, and Kritter knows then that she is doomed.

The saleslady returns with another suit. It is black, but it has a flared polka-dotted white skirt around the waist. Kritter says nothing. There is nothing to say. She walks over to the heap of bathing suits and, without looking, picks one up and puts it on the counter.

Her mother smiles at the saleslady. "Charge it, please."

When Kritter emerges from the bathroom of the bungalow, a white towel covering as much of her bathing suit as possible, her mother is sitting on the porch with a glass of iced tea and a thick paperback book. Beth Ann is digging in the sand at the edge of the beach.

"There you are," her mother says, looking up over the rims of her sunglasses. "You look very nice. I think those are good colors on you."

Kritter says nothing. She has no idea what she looks like. She avoids mirrors, seeing enough through her mother's eyes.

"Can I go swimming now?" she asks after a minute.

"Yes, you *may*, as long as I'm watching. Just stay inside the lagoon. The ocean's too rough. It's dangerous. Okay?"

Kritter nods silently and walks down to the edge of the water. The lagoon is a tranquil blue oval sparkling in the hot morning sun. Its perimeter is rocky – two parentheses of jagged dark slabs with a white sand beach at one end. Fifty yards out, its narrow mouth funnels into the open sea. There are large rocks on either side, and as she watches, a wave crashes onto one of them, sending spray and mist ten feet into the air.

She puts her towel down on the sand and attaches her snorkel to the strap of the yellow rubber mask the way she has been shown, hoping it will be worth the effort. Before they left home, her mother signed her up for a snorkeling class at the Y. An entire Saturday afternoon. She learned to spit in her mask and put the equipment on. Big deal. She could see underwater, sharp and clear, but what was there to see? The black lines on the bottom of the pool. A penny by the drain. Her legs, magnified, disturbingly white and fat.

She shakes the sand out of her mask and puts the snorkel in her mouth, then stands up. The flippers make it impossible to walk normally, so she walks backwards through the sand, feeling clumsier than usual as she wades out into the water.

Even when she is up to her waist in it, the water is still turquoise. In art class she has rinsed out brushes, watching the paint swirl off the ends of the bristles, coloring the water in the empty peanut butter jar a rich, deep blue. That is what it feels like, standing in the lagoon. Like she is in the water where someone, some god, has rinsed out all the turquoise brushes in the world.

She lifts her arm, half expecting it to be tinted a pale blue-green. But on her skin, it is just clear water. It glistens in the sunlight and beads up on the tiny hairs of her forearms. She readjusts the mask a fraction, then turns and falls forward.

When she puts her face in the water, the world as she knows it disappears. She is alone in a cool, liquid place where there is no sound other than her own breathing. She watches, fascinated, as an endless web of shifting, shimmering sunlight dances across the flat sandy bottom. She puts her foot down and watches the pattern play across her leg like electric lace.

A single kick of her flippers sends her gliding through the water, and she finds she doesn't even need to use her arms. She pulls them in to her sides, hands fluttering at her waist like vestigial fins. Air bubbles rush down her body as she moves forward. Airstream, she thinks. Jetstream. Streamlined, sleek and powerful.

Halfway across the lagoon, Kritter comes to the first reef. Gliding over the angled rocks stretching a few feet below her, she peers into miniature canyons. It looks like Wyoming did from the plane – hundreds of shades of brown, dappled with sunlight. She feels like she is flying, flying over a sunken western landscape where an occasional canyon wall is bright with pink and pale green anemones that would be monstrous if they were to appear outside Cheyenne.

And then she sees the fish. Her first tropical fish. It is thin, nearly transparent, a tapering glass rod with shoebutton eyes. It floats a few feet below the surface, becoming visible, then invisible again in the shifting light. She follows it for a while, swaying back and forth in the gentle current with it, then notices others along the edges of the reef. Flat dark fish like wet, black velvet with a lemon yellow line along their backs, and dozens of tiny guppy-sized blips an iridescent, electric blue. Near the mouth of the lagoon she sees hundreds of fish float sideways as a wave breaks, all of them together, like fallen leaves skittering in formation.

Kritter finds it hard to believe that any of these fish are real, that no one puts them into the lagoon every morning and scoops them up or turns them off when the beach path is roped shut at dusk each night. No one decided on what colors they should be and ordered them by the case, stocking the lagoon the way Disneyland is stocked with pirates.

She smiles at that thought a few minutes later when she is surrounded by a school of cartoon-colored fish. Huge dusty pink fish with bright blue-green lips, doting aunt expressions. Fish the size of small collies. She reaches out to touch one but it darts away easily.

Kritter follows the school, enchanted by the way their colors shift from pink to blue-green and back again in the shimmering light. They circle her, playing tag, almost close enough to touch, close enough that she can feel a feathery brush of moving water as they swim by.

She could swim with them forever. It is so different from swimming in a pool. Here she feels, for the first time in her life, graceful. She moves as if she is as liquid as the water surrounding her. Everything is so beautiful, and as she thinks that, she feels uncomfortable. Beauty stuff is for girls, and she will never be a *girl*. She kicks the thought away with a powerful thrust of her flippers, and dives a foot or two beneath the surface, skirting the edge of a shelf of sharp coral.

When she comes up to blow the water out of her snorkel, she sees her mother waving for her to swim back. Reluctantly Kritter heads toward shore, and when the water is shallow enough, she stands up. Gravity is a rude shock. Her body becomes heavy again. She can feel the fluidness leave her as she leaves the water – waist deep, knee deep, ankle deep through the surf – until she is plodding through the sand.

She looks toward the porch of the bungalow. Her mother has the movie camera up to her face, the red light indicating that it's on, recording Kritter's – no, Kristine's – every awkward footfall. She knows she will relive this moment again, watching herself on screen in the third person. As she takes off her mask her eyes are stinging, and she can't tell if it's the salt water or the memory of the graceful creature the camera and her mother cannot see.

⌒

"We really should have salads," her mother says, scanning the menu of the hotel restaurant. "But your dad says it's not safe to eat anything raw down here, even in the hotel. I think I'll try the grilled chicken. *Nosotros no quiermos, gracias,*" she says to the waiter, waving the basket of chips away.

Kritter sinks down into her chair and doesn't look at the waiter. Her mother has been learning Spanish from cassettes, playing them on the tape deck in the station wagon. After two months she sounds exactly like the woman on the tape – *Bweh-noz Dee-ahz*. She says when you travel you should make an effort to fit in. She frowns at the people at the bar who order their drinks in fractured Spanglish, "Uno more Margarita, okay?" and tells Kritter they are Ugly Americans. But Kritter

is more embarrassed by her mother's textbook Spanish. Her conso-
nants are too precise; she sounds like she is reciting a lesson instead of
talking to real people.

After they have ordered, her mother pulls a guidebook out of her
book bag. "While we're waiting for our food, why don't you show us
what you saw in the lagoon." She puts the book in the middle of the
table.

Kritter makes no move to pick it up. "Just fish and stuff," she shrugs,
but inwardly her stomach squirms. She doesn't want to talk about the
lagoon.

"You want to learn about what you're seeing, don't you, Krissy?"

Her mother says it in a soft voice, but it's a loaded question. If Kritter
says anything but yes, lunch – maybe even the rest of the afternoon –
will become an unspoken lecture. She sighs wordlessly and opens the
book.

As she turns the pages, pretending to look for something familiar,
she stops at random and points out interesting-looking fish and shells.
"What's that one?" Beth Ann asks, and her mother smiles and puts her
arm around the younger girl's shoulder. They pull the book between
them and read the text out loud. Kritter looks away.

"Krissy, look! This one looks just like your bathing suit," Beth Ann
says excitedly. "I wish I could see one of those!"

Kritter turns and is startled by a full-page photo of one of the pink
and blue-green fish that played tag. She reaches to turn the page,
quickly, before her fish can be identified and captured. Her mother puts
a red-nailed hand down and keeps the page open.

"It's called a parrotfish. *Scarus guacamaia.*" She pronounces the Latin
name in the same precise, textbook tones. "Such pretty colors. And,
look, it has an overbite."

Kritter feels her face flush and waits, emotionally braced for the
inevitable "just like yours," but her mother says nothing aloud. She just
smiles and looks at Kritter, who squirms again, the unspoken words
hanging in the air around her like a toxic cloud that dissipates only
when the waiter arrives with their food and gives her mother something else to focus on.

Each day their routine is the same. An hour after breakfast, they all change into their bathing suits. Kritter goes immediately into the lagoon to swim with the parrotfish. Beth Ann plays in the shallow water while their mother watches from the shade of the porch. She doesn't like to be in the sun, and she never goes into the water, except to wash the sand off her feet. She just sits on a lounge chair in her bathing suit with her iced tea and her book. Kritter wonders why she would want to come all the way to a resort like this to do the same things she does at home.

After lunch, her mother always announces "*Es el tiempo por una siesta.*" She seems to think this is a wonderful custom. Kritter hates it. She isn't tired, but she isn't allowed to go swimming alone or explore the island by herself. Until her mother gets up from "resting her eyes," Kritter is trapped on the porch of the bungalow, alone except for *Travels with Charley*.

On the fourth afternoon, she lays her groundwork all through lunch – pretending to be interested in the history of some historic church on the island that her mother wants to go see. Being a good girl. When the check has been signed and they are gathering up their things, she makes her move.

"Mom, while you're taking your – *siesta* – is it okay if I stay up here by the pool and read?"

Her mother looks surprised. "You don't want to come back to the bungalow with us?"

"I, uh, I thought I'd swim some laps in the pool. For the exercise?" She doesn't have any intention of swimming laps, but she thinks it's a nice touch. Her mother approves of exercise. Especially for Kritter.

"Oh, Krissy, that's a wonderful idea!"

The response is a little too enthusiastic for Kritter's comfort, but it's a Yes. They'll meet back at the bungalow at 3:30. Her mother hands her three two-peso coins so that she can get a soda from the bar if it gets too hot. "Diet Coke, remember," she says. *Una cola dietetica.* It sounds even more like a punishment in Spanish.

Kritter nods dutifully at every instruction, and can hardly contain her excitement. When her mother and Beth Ann leave, she walks over to the pool, but it is full of the bikini-girls and their boyfriends. She could swim and ignore them, but they will ignore her first and she is not in the mood for that.

She hesitates for a few minutes, then goes over to the pool bar and orders a Coke – a regular Coke – and a basket of chips, because her mother isn't here. She runs the Spanish words together just a little, trying to match the accent and the cadence of the waiters.

The bartender smiles and nods. *"Cinco pesos, por favor."*

She hands him the three coins, and when he proffers the single peso in change, she waves her hand in a gesture she has seen her mother make. It is the first time she has ever tipped anyone, and she feels incredibly sophisticated and worldly.

Miguel, the towel boy who is sometimes a waiter, gives her a second towel, and she lays it down on one of the white plastic lounge chairs, adjusting the back so she can sit up and look out over the ocean. The other towel she drapes over her body. From her beach bag she pulls the pair of leopard-spotted sunglasses that she bought at Mitchell's Drugs back home the week before. Her mother forbid her to pack them because they were cheap and tacky. Kritter puts them on and feels like a grown-up.

The hotel and the pool terrace are built on top of a sheer bluff. One side overlooks a string of bungalows on a wide, white sand beach, the other the enclosed oval of the lagoon. There is a huge rock formation, an irregular, flat triangle out in the ocean, a short distance from the mouth of the lagoon, but invisible from their beach. With her father's binoculars Kritter can see that the rock is studded with sea lions sleeping in the afternoon sun. As she watches, one of them slides into the water, a brown animal sleek as an oiled puppy.

She wishes she could show them to Annie. They would laugh and talk with accents, and tell each other that it's a boring little island, but they are only here for a few days while their ship is being repaired. Taking on supplies before moving on to Rangoon. Kritter has no idea where Rangoon is, but she likes the sound of it. She says it quietly, but out loud: "We're sailing for Rangoon at the end of the week."

Their ship is sleek and white, with blue canvas tarps and brass fittings. She and Annie will pat the sea lions on their way out to sea, and by nightfall they will be far from Diet Cokes and impending orthodontists. They have a crew to do the complicated parts of sailing, of course, but they work the lines themselves. Kritter wears a black Speedo and a pair of cutoffs so soft and faded they are barely blue anymore. She is tan and lean, and her straight brown hair has turned golden in the sun. Windblown and tousled. It is cut very short because she cannot be bothered.

The sun is hot, and they often stop in mid-afternoon to swim, then tell each other stories until the sun sets red and flaming at the horizon. The crew has names like Pete and One-Eyed Sal and Old Rusty. They call her Cap'n.

When the clock at the bar says 3:30, Cap'n throws her beach bag over her shoulder, salutes the bewildered Miguel, and sets off down the path to the lagoon, whistling a sea chantey — actually the theme from *Gilligan's Island* — and walking with a bit of a pirate swagger.

She is thinking about monkeys and coconuts and rumors of long-buried treasure, so she is halfway across the sand before she sees her mother in front of the porch. The red eye of the camera winks in the tropical sunlight. Cap'n tightens her grip on the bag and continues her march across the sand.

When she is ten feet from the bungalow, the winking eye goes dark and her mother lowers the camera with an audible sigh. "Kristine? Do you have to walk that way? You look like a duck. Go back and start over, by the stairs. Daddy will splice this part out later."

Cap'n vanishes. Kritter stands motionless, her face burning with embarrassment, her feet burning on the hot sand.

"C'mon, Krissy," her mother coaxes. "I bet you'll be glad when we watch the movies later."

It is not a good bet. Kritter knows that she will never sit in front of the screen without also seeing this unfilmed scene. After a minute she drops her beach bag and walks woodenly over to the stairs, then woodenly back.

"That was much better, honey," her mother says encouragingly. "Let's try it one more time, okay?"

Kritter will not be in her mother's movie. At the end of her second promenade, she puts on her snorkeling gear and escapes into the water without another word.

When she reaches the rocks by the mouth of the lagoon, she hesitates, then with a defiant series of kicks, tries to swim through the opening, toward the rock with the sea lions. The ocean is choppy. She struggles again and again, but each time the breaking waves buffet her back into the lagoon.

She is treading water, catching her breath, the stinging salt water trickling into her mouth from around the rubber seal of the snorkel, when she feels something bump her from behind. Another bump, and then another. She turns and the cartoon bodies of the parrotfish shimmer all around her, playing tag. Kritter reaches out and finally touches one of the cool, firm bodies.

"You're it," she thinks, and then her pale white arms begin to pulse with color. She watches in amazement as her hands wisp and filigree, fanning out to fins. Her legs and feet become a broad, translucent tail. She is delighted to feel her soft body thicken and grow compact, muscular and sturdy. The pastel flowers of the hideous bathing suit dissolve into a delicate rainbow of iridescent pink and turquoise scales.

When Kritter is ready, the lead parrotfish motions, and the whole school turns as one and swims below the crashing waves. Beneath the surface, the water is calmer, and the school leaves the lagoon easily. The fish that is Kritter flexes her powerful, streamlined body and dives deep, breathing easily through the slits above her fins.

They travel through a rocky crevasse studded with starfish and waving lavender anemones, blue crabs scuttling into crevices, and rich red-shelled abalone clinging to rock faces. Everything is in constant, gentle motion. They dive deeper and the sunlight becomes a bright haze far above them. As the world loses color and form and becomes light and shadow, Kritter and her new friends turn to follow the current, swimming away toward Rangoon.

Möbius, Stripped of a Muse

TOM O'HARA WATCHED the light wink out in the window of the tenement apartment, then mopped his chiseled brow and walked cautiously up to the old brownstone stoop. He lit a match in front of the row of tarnished brass mailboxes.

Janet Abramowitz. Apartment 4-D.

He swore softly. Twelve years of searching for the double-crossing redhead who'd sent his best friend to the chair, and she'd been here all along. Just a few blocks away from where it had all gone so tragically wrong.

He unholstered his .45 automatic, and stepped into the dank hallway. He heard the click a fraction of a second before he dove for the floor. The slug tore into the plaster an inch from where his head had been.

"Drop the gun, Tom," said a sultry voice from the darkness above. "Drop it now and come up nice and slow. I've been waiting for this a long time."

He dropped the .45, heard it clatter on the stairs. The noise masked the rustle of fabric as he eased the .38-special out of his waistband.

"Why'd you do it, Janet?" he asked as he thumbed the safety off. "The night you and Lucky– "

"Be a good boy, and I'll tell you," she said. "Right before you die. But first you've got to – "

Got to *what*? Damnit, John Cameron thought. He stared at the blinking lights of his Write-O-Matic 3000. How the hell was he going to get O'Hara out of this one? Can't kill him off – the bastard – or Janet, either. Two more books in the series. He'd backed himself into a corner.

Frowning, he pulled the lever marked "TYPE PAGES," and walked into the galley as the keys began to clatter.

"Beer," he said to the vid screen. "Space City Amber."

The ship's sensor blinked once and a cold bottle of beer appeared in the steel receptacle, beads of condensation forming on its brown plexi surface.

"Peanuts?" asked the ship.

"Not today, thanks." Cameron snapped his fingers at the sensor panel and the screen went blank.

John Cameron took a long swig of his beer as he walked over to the perspex slit in the curved metal wall of his module. He looked out at the black, star-studded sky. Two days until the ship was in range for his transmission to Earth, and he still didn't have an ending. The trip had seemed like such an opportunity, in the beginning. The First Novelist in Space. What publicity there had been. The books had sold millions, and he had enough credits to live like a king when he got back to Earth. *If* he got back to Earth. Two more years. He never should have agreed to a four-book contract.

Would he last another 730 more days in this glorified tin can? He wasn't sure. Okay, he had everything he'd ever desired – any meal, any drink, any movie – all at the flick of a switch. But he couldn't think of anything he really wanted, anymore. Not a thing. Zero. Zilch. Zipola. Nothing much, really.

"Nothing?" said Norman Hays out loud. "Great. I've created a future full of *nothing*." He sighed, ripped the page out of his typewriter, crumpling it and tossing it in the vicinity of his wastebasket. The ink from the carbon paper stained his fingers like the dark shadow he felt hanging over him.

John Cameron, Galactic Scribe was just not working out. It was original, a new idea. None of the hacks at *Ripping Yarns of Science* or *Cosmic Thrills* had done a heroic space writer. They were still churning out potboilers about Captain Prime, and Dr. Logic and the Tenderizer. Sure, they were selling. But John Cameron was his ticket out of the pulps and into the big time. Two cents a word. Maybe even three? Three cents and 1938 would be a great year.

Norman climbed out onto his fire escape and leaned against the brick wall. He lit a Lucky Strike, exhaling the blue smoke into the warm night air. Across the river, the lights of New York twinkled like jewels, and high overhead he could hear the faint drone of motors as a zeppelin moved slowly through the sky on its way to Lakehurst.

"Tsk. *Lake*hurst? That simply screams cliché," said Professor Atwood, looking up from the thin sheaf of manuscript pages. "Don't tell me. Don't even tell me. It's the *Hindenburg*, right?"

Elizabeth Norris bit her lip, then nodded.

"Trite. Entirely predictable." He dismissed the pages with a wave of his manicured hand. "Not your best work, Elizabeth."

"You haven't given it a chance," she said. "Just read a little farther. See, in this universe, it's not *really* the Hindenburg. It's an alien spaceship, and it's drawn to Earth when it intercepts Orson Welles's *War of the Worlds* broadcast, which it interprets as an SOS from another ship in its fleet. So instead of exploding, when it docks in New Jersey, battle robots come pouring out. They look like cats, except with tentacles, and they have kind of ray-gun eyes that hypnotize Earth people into becoming their slaves, so that they can – "

"Stop," Atwood said. "Just stop. This is supposed to be a creative literature class. There are no rocket ships in *literature*, Elizabeth. If you want a passing grade, you're going to have to try and salvage something readable out of this." He licked his thumb and leafed quickly through the pages.

"Now here's a promising bit. Where your protagonist is trying to decide whether to pawn his typewriter to buy his aged mother some cheese. It's not much, but it has the potential for a poignant little character sketch. Have you read the sketch chapter in my book, *Prose for the Heartstrings?*"

Elizabeth shook her head.

"Ah, well, you must. It's out of print, sadly, but I can lend you one of my copies. I only live a few blocks away. You could over this evening. Say around seven?" He smiled at her suggestively.

"Oh, please. Not the smile." Marcia Browne made a face and threw the manuscript of "Writers Writing, Always" back onto the slush pile. Why would anyone in their right mind think there was a market for stories like that? She hadn't read anything original all week, and Dan MacDaring, her boss, and the editor of *Romantic Quarks*, was expecting her in his office at four sharp. She had to find *something* to impress him. Marcia had ambitions. She was going to be an editor herself someday. Someday soon. Really soon.

Janet Abramowitz typed the word "soon" again then hit DELETE and turned out her light. She stared out the tenement window. In the darkness four stories below, she saw the brief, bright flare of someone lighting a match. She watched the afterimage for a moment, then smiled and picked the revolver up off her bookshelf. She walked to the doorway of Apartment 4-D and waited, plotting a better future.

Time Gypsy

Friday, February 10, 2006. 5:00 p.m.

As soon as I walk in the door, my officemate Ted starts in on me. Again. "What do you know about radiation equilibrium?" he asks.

"Nothing. Why?"

"That figures." He holds up a faded green volume. "I just found this insanely great article by Chandrasekhar in the '45 *Astrophysical Journal*. And get this – when I go to check it out, the librarian tells me I'm the first person to take it off the shelf since 1955. Can you believe that? Nobody reads anymore." He opens the book again. "Oh, by the way, Chambers was here looking for you."

I drop my armload of books on my desk with a thud. Dr. Raymond Chambers is the chairman of the Physics department, and a Nobel Prize winner, which even at Berkeley is a very, very big deal. Rumor has it he's working on some top-secret government project that's a shoo-in for a second trip to Sweden.

"Yeah, he wants to see you in his office, pronto. He said something about Sara Baxter Clarke. She's that crackpot from the '50s, right? The one who died mysteriously?"

I wince. "That's her. I did my dissertation on her and her work." I wish I'd brought another sweater. This one has holes in both elbows. I'd planned a day in the library, not a visit with the head of the department.

Ted looks at me with his mouth open. "Not many chick scientists to choose from, huh? And you got a post-doc here doing that? Crazy world." He puts his book down and stretches. "Gotta run. I'm a week behind in my lab work. Real science, you know?"

I don't even react. It's only a month into the term, and he's been on my case about one thing or another – being a woman, being a dyke, being close to thirty – from day one. He's a jerk, but I've got other things to worry about. Like Dr. Chambers, and whether I'm about to

87

lose my job because he found out I'm an expert on a crackpot.

Sara Baxter Clarke has been my hero since I was a kid. My pop was an army technician. He worked on radar systems, and we traveled a lot – six months in Reykjavik, then the next six in Fort Lee, New Jersey. Mom always told us we were gypsies, and tried to make it seem like an adventure. But when I was eight, Mom and my brother Jeff were killed in a bus accident on Guam. After that it didn't seem like an adventure any more.

Pop was a lot better with radar than he was with little girls. He couldn't quite figure me out. I think I had too many variables for him. When I was ten, he bought me dresses and dolls, and couldn't understand why I wanted a stack of old physics magazines the base library was throwing out. I liked science. It was about the only thing that stayed the same wherever we moved. I told Pop I wanted to be a scientist when I grew up, but he said scientists were men, and I'd just get married.

I believed him, until I discovered Sara Baxter Clarke in one of those old magazines. She was British, went to MIT, had her doctorate in theoretical physics at twenty-two. At Berkeley, she published three brilliant articles in very, very obscure journals. In 1956, she was scheduled to deliver a controversial fourth paper at an international physics conference at Stanford. She was the only woman on the program, and she was just twenty-eight.

No one knows what was in her last paper. The night before she was supposed to speak, her car went out of control and plunged over a cliff at Devil's Slide – a remote stretch of coast south of San Francisco. Her body was washed out to sea. The accident rated two inches on the inside of the paper the next day – right under a headline about some vice raid – but made a small uproar in the physics world. None of her papers or notes were ever found; her lab had been ransacked. The mystery was never solved.

I was fascinated by the mystery of her the way other kids were intrigued by Amelia Earhart. Except nobody'd ever heard of my hero. In my imagination, Sara Baxter Clarke and I were very much alike. I spent a lot of days pretending I was a scientist just like her, and even more lonely nights talking to her until I fell asleep.

So after a master's in Physics, I got a Ph.D. in the History of Science — studying her. Maybe if my obsession had been a little more practical, I wouldn't be sitting on a couch outside Dr. Chambers's office, picking imaginary lint off my sweater, trying to pretend I'm not panicking. I taught science in a junior high for a year. If I lose this fellowship, I suppose I could do that again. It's a depressing thought.

The great man's secretary finally buzzes me into his office. Dr. Chambers is a balding, pouchy man in an immaculate, perfect suit. His office smells like lemon furniture polish and pipe tobacco. It's wood-paneled, plushly carpeted, with about an acre of mahogany desk. A copy of my dissertation sits on one corner.

"Dr. McCullough." He closes his laptop and waves me to a chair. "You seem to be quite an expert on Sara Baxter Clarke."

"She was a brilliant woman," I say nervously, and hope that's the right direction for the conversation.

"Indeed. What do you make of her last paper, the one she never presented?" He picks up my work and turns to a page marked with a pale green Post-It. "'An Argument for a Practical Tempokinetics?'" He lights his pipe and looks at me through the smoke.

"I'd certainly love to read it," I say, taking a gamble. I'd give anything for a copy of that paper. I wait for the inevitable lecture about wasting my academic career studying a long-dead crackpot.

"You would? Do you actually believe Clarke had discovered a method for time travel?" he asks. "Time travel, Dr. McCullough?"

I take a bigger gamble. "Yes, I do."

Then Dr. Chambers surprises me. "So do I. I'm certain of it. I was working with her assistant, Jim Kennedy. He retired a few months after the accident. It's taken me fifty years to rediscover what was tragically lost back then."

I stare at him in disbelief. "You've perfected time travel?"

He shakes his head. "Not perfected. But I assure you, tempokinetics is a reality."

Suddenly my knees won't quite hold me. I sit down in the padded leather chair next to his desk and stare at him. "You've actually done it?"

He nods. "There's been a great deal of research on tempokinetics in the last fifty years. Very hush-hush, of course. A lot of government money. But recently, several key discoveries in high-intensity gravitational field theory have made it possible for us to finally construct a working tempokinetic chamber."

I'm having a hard time taking this all in. "Why did you want to see *me?*" I ask.

He leans against the corner of his desk. "We need someone to talk to Dr. Clarke."

"You mean she's alive?" My heart skips several beats.

He shakes his head. "No."

"Then — ?"

"Dr. McCullough, I approved your application to this university because you know more about Sara Clarke and her work than anyone else we've found. I'm offering you a once in a lifetime opportunity." He clears his throat. "I'm offering to send you back in time to attend the 1956 International Conference for Experimental Physics. I need a copy of Clarke's last paper."

I just stare at him. This feels likes some sort of test, but I have no idea what the right response is. "Why?" I ask finally.

"Because our apparatus works, but it's not practical," Dr. Chambers says, tamping his pipe. "The energy requirements for the gravitational field are enormous. The only material that's even remotely feasible is an isotope they've developed up at the Lawrence Lab, and there's only enough of it for one round trip. I believe Clarke's missing paper contains the solution to our energy problem."

After all these years, it's confusing to hear someone taking Dr. Clarke's work seriously. I'm so used to being on the defensive about her, I don't know how to react. I slip automatically into scientist mode — detached and rational. "Assuming your tempokinetic chamber is operational, how do you propose that I locate Dr. Clarke?"

He picks up a piece of stiff ivory paper and hands it to me. "This is my invitation to the opening reception of the conference Friday night, at the St. Francis Hotel. Unfortunately I couldn't attend. I was back east that week. Family matters."

I look at the engraved paper in my hand. Somewhere in my files is a xerox copy of one of these invitations. It's odd to hold a real one. "This will get me into the party. Then you'd like me to introduce myself to Sara Baxter Clarke, and ask her for a copy of her unpublished paper?"

"In a nutshell. I can give you some cash to help, er, convince her if necessary. Frankly, I don't care how you do it. I *want* that paper, Dr. McCullough."

He looks a little agitated now, and there's a shrill undertone to his voice. I suspect Dr. Chambers is planning to take credit for what's in the paper, maybe even hoping for that second Nobel. I think for a minute. Dr. Clarke's will left everything to Jim Kennedy, her assistant and fiancé. Even if Chambers gets the credit, maybe there's a way to reward the people who actually did the work. I make up a large, random number.

"I think $30,000 should do it." I clutch the arm of the chair and rub my thumb nervously over the smooth polished wood.

Dr. Chambers starts to protest, then just waves his hand. "Fine. Fine. Whatever it takes. Funding for this project is not an issue. As I said, we only have enough of the isotope to power one trip into the past and back – yours. If you recover the paper successfully, we'll be able to develop the technology for many, many more excursions. If not – " he lets his sentence trail off.

"Other people *have* tried this?" I ask, warily. It occurs to me I may be the guinea pig, usually an expendable item.

He pauses for a long moment. "No. You'll be the first. Your records indicate you have no family, is that correct?"

I nod. My father died two years ago, and the longest relationship I've ever had only lasted six months. But Chambers doesn't strike me as a liberal. Even if I was still living with Nancy, I doubt if he would count her as family. "It's a big risk. What if I decline?"

"Your post-doc application will be reviewed," he shrugs. "I'm sure you'll be happy at some other university."

So it's all or nothing. I try to weigh all the variables, make a reasoned decision. But I can't. I don't feel like a scientist right now. I feel like a ten-year-old kid, being offered the only thing I've ever wanted – the chance to meet Sara Baxter Clarke.

"I'll do it," I say.

"Excellent." Chambers switches gears, assuming a brisk, business-like manner. "You'll leave a week from today at precisely 6:32 a.m. You cannot take anything — underwear, clothes, shoes, watch — that was manufactured after 1956. My secretary has a list of antique clothing stores in the area, and some fashion magazines of the times." He looks at my jeans with distaste. "Please choose something appropriate for the reception. Can you do anything with your hair?"

My hair is short. Nothing radical, not in Berkeley. It's more like early Beatles — what they called a pixie cut when I was a little girl — except I was always too tall and gawky to be a pixie. I run my fingers self-consciously through it and shake my head.

Chambers sighs and continues. "Very well. Now, since we have to allow for the return of Clarke's manuscript, you must take something of equivalent mass — and also of that era. I'll give you the draft copy of my own dissertation. You will be also be supplied with a driver's license and university faculty card from the period, along with packets of vintage currency. You'll return with the manuscript at exactly 11:37 Monday morning. There will be no second chance. Do you understand?"

I nod, a little annoyed at his patronizing tone of voice. "If I miss the deadline, I'll be stuck in the past forever. Dr. Clarke is the only other person who could possibly send me home, and she won't be around on Monday morning. Unless — ?" I let the question hang in the air.

"Absolutely not. There is one immutable law of tempokinetics, Dr. McCullough. You cannot change the past. I trust you'll remember that?" he says, standing.

Our meeting is over. I leave his office with the biggest news of my life. I wish I had someone to call and share it with. I'd settle for someone to help me shop for clothes.

Friday, February 17, 2006. 6:20 a.m.
The supply closet on the ground floor of LeConte Hall is narrow and dimly lit, filled with boxes of rubber gloves, lab coats, shop towels. Unlike many places on campus, the Physics building hasn't been remodeled in the last fifty years. This has always been a closet, and it isn't likely to be occupied at 6:30 on any Friday morning.

I sit on the linoleum floor, my back against a wall, dressed in an appropriate period costume. I think I should feel nervous, but I feel oddly detached. I sip from a cup of lukewarm 7-11 coffee and observe. I don't have any role in this part of the experiment – I'm just the guinea pig. Dr. Chambers's assistants step carefully over my outstretched legs and make the final adjustments to the battery of apparatus that surrounds me.

At exactly 6:28 by my antique Timex, Dr. Chambers himself appears in the doorway. He shows me a thick packet of worn bills and the bulky, rubber-banded typescript of his dissertation, then slips both of them into a battered leather briefcase. He places the case on my lap and extends his hand. But when I reach up to shake it, he frowns and takes the 7-11 cup.

"Good luck, Dr. McCullough," he says formally. Nothing more. What more would he say to a guinea pig? He looks at his watch, then hands the cup to a young man in a black t-shirt, who types in one last line of code, turns off the light, and closes the door.

I sit in the dark and begin to get the willies. No one has ever done this. I don't know if the cool linoleum under my legs is the last thing I will ever feel. Sweat drips down between my breasts as the apparatus begins to hum. There is a moment of intense – sensation. It's not sound, or vibration, or anything I can quantify. It's as if all the fingernails in the world are suddenly raked down all the blackboards, and in the same moment oxygen is transmuted to lead. I am pressed to the floor by a monstrous force, but every hair on my body is erect. Just when I feel I can't stand it any more, the humming stops.

My pulse is racing, and I feel dizzy, a little nauseous. I sit for a minute, half-expecting Dr. Chambers to come in and tell me the experiment has failed, but no one comes. I try to stand – my right leg has fallen asleep – and grope for the light switch near the door.

In the light from the single bulb, I see that the apparatus is gone, but the gray metal shelves are stacked with the same boxes of gloves and shop towels. My leg all pins and needles, I lean against a brown cardboard box stenciled Bayside Laundry Service, San Francisco 3, California.

It takes me a minute before I realize what's odd. Either those are very old towels, or I'm somewhere pre–zip code.

I let myself out of the closet, and walk awkwardly down the empty hallway, my spectator pumps echoing on the linoleum. I search for further confirmation. The first room I peer into is a lab – high stools in front of black slab tables with bunsen burners, gray boxes full of dials and switches. A slide rule at every station.

I've made it.

Friday, February 17, 1956. 7:00 a.m.

The campus is deserted on this drizzly February dawn, as is Telegraph Avenue. The streetlights are still on – white lights, not yellow sodium – and through the mist I can see faint lines of red and green neon on stores down the avenue. I feel like Marco Polo as I navigate through a world that is both alien and familiar. The buildings are the same, but the storefronts and signs look like stage sets or photos from old *Life* magazines.

It takes me more than an hour to walk downtown. I am disoriented by each shop window, each passing car. I feel as if I'm a little drunk, walking too attentively through the landscape, and not connected to it. Maybe it's the colors. Everything looks too real. I grew up with grainy black-and-white TV reruns and '50s technicolor films that have faded over time, and it's disconcerting that this world is not overlaid with that pink-orange tinge.

The warm aromas of coffee and bacon lure me into a hole-in-the-wall café. I order the special – eggs, bacon, hash browns, and toast. The toast comes dripping with butter, and the jelly is in a glass jar, not a little plastic tub. When the bill comes it is 55¢. I leave a generous dime tip, then catch the yellow F bus and ride down Shattuck Avenue, staring at the round-fendered black Chevys and occasional pink Studebakers that fill the streets.

The bus is full of morning commuters – men in dark jackets and hats, women in dresses and hats. In my tailored suit I fit right in. I'm surprised that no one looks '50s – retro '50s – the '50s that filtered down to the next century. No poodle skirts, no DA haircuts. All the men remind me of my Pop. A man in a gray felt hat has the *Chronicle*, and I read over his shoulder. Eisenhower is considering a second term. The San Francisco police chief promises a crackdown on vice. *Peanuts* tops the comics page and there's a Rock Hudson movie playing at the Castro Theatre. Nothing new there.

As we cross the Bay Bridge I'm amazed at how small San Francisco looks – the skyline is carved stone, not glass-and-steel towers. A green Muni streetcar takes me down the middle of Market Street to Powell. I check into the St. Francis, the city's finest hotel. My room costs less than I've paid for a night in a Motel 6.

All my worldly goods fit on the desktop – Chambers's manuscript; a brown leather wallet with a driver's license, a Berkeley faculty card, and twenty-three dollars in small bills; the invitation to the reception tonight; and 30,000 dollars in banded stacks of fifty-dollar bills. I pull three bills off the top of one stack and put the rest in the drawer, under the cream-colored hotel stationery. I have to get out of this suit and these shoes.

Woolworth's has a toothbrush and other plastic toiletries, and a tin "Tom Corbett, Space Cadet" alarm clock. I find a pair of pleated pants, an Oxford-cloth shirt, and wool sweater at the City of Paris. Macy's Men's Shop yields a pair of "dungarees" and two t-shirts I can sleep in – 69 cents each. A snippy clerk gives me the eye in the Boys department, so I invent a nephew, little Billy, and buy him black basketball sneakers that are just my size.

After a shower and a change of clothes, I try to collect my thoughts, but I'm too keyed up to sit still. In a few hours I'll actually be in the same room as Sara Baxter Clarke. I can't distinguish between fear and excitement, and spend the afternoon wandering aimlessly around the city, gawking like a tourist.

Friday, February 17, 1956. 7:00 p.m.
Back in my spectator pumps and my tailored navy suit, I present myself at the doorway of the reception ballroom and surrender my invitation. The tuxedoed young man looks over my shoulder, as if he's expecting someone behind me. After a moment he clears his throat.

"And you're Mrs. – ?" he asks, looking down at his typewritten list.

"Dr. McCullough," I say coolly, and give him an even stare. "Mr. Chambers is out of town. He asked me to take his place."

After a moment's hesitation he nods, and writes my name on a white card, pinning it to my lapel like a corsage.

Ballroom A is a sea of gray suits, crew cuts, bow-ties, and heavy black-rimmed glasses. Almost everyone is male, as I expected, and almost everyone is smoking, which surprises me. Over in one corner is a knot of women in bright cocktail dresses, each with a lacquered football helmet of hair. Barbie's cultural foremothers.

I accept a canapé from a passing waiter and ease my way to the corner. Which one is Dr. Clarke? I stand a few feet back, scanning nametags. Mrs. Niels Bohr. Mrs. Richard Feynman. Mrs. Ernest Lawrence. I am impressed by the company I'm in, and dismayed that none of the women has a name of her own. I smile an empty cocktail party smile as I move away from the wives and scan the room. Gray suits with a sprinkling of blue, but all male. Did I arrive too early?

I am looking for a safe corner, one with a large, sheltering potted palm, when I hear a blustery male voice say, "So, Dr. Clarke. Trying the H. G. Wells route, are you? Waste of the taxpayer's money, all that science fiction stuff, don't you think?"

A woman's voice answers. "Not at all. Perhaps I can change your mind at Monday's session." I can't see her yet, but her voice is smooth and rich, with a bit of a lilt or a brogue – one of those vocal clues that says "I'm not an American." I stand rooted to the carpet, so awestruck I'm unable to move.

"Jimmy, will you see if there's more champagne about?" I hear her ask. I see a motion in the sea of gray and astonish myself by flagging a waiter and taking two slender flutes from his tray. I step forward in the direction of her voice. "Here you go," I say, trying to keep my hand from shaking. "I've got an extra."

"How very resourceful of you," she laughs. I am surprised that she is a few inches shorter than me. I'd forgotten she'd be about my age. She takes the glass and offers me her other hand. "Sara Clarke," she says.

"Carol McCullough." I touch her palm. The room seems suddenly bright and the voices around me fade into a murmur. I think for a moment that I'm dematerializing back to 2006, but nothing so dramatic happens. I'm just so stunned that I forget to breathe while I look at her.

Since I was ten years old, no matter where we lived, I have had a picture of Sara Baxter Clarke over my desk. I cut it out of that old physics magazine. It is grainy, black and white, the only photo of her I've ever found. In it, she's who I always wanted to be – competent, serious, every inch a scientist. She wears a white lab coat and a pair of rimless glasses, her hair pulled back from her face. A bald man in an identical lab coat is showing her a piece of equipment. Neither of them is smiling.

I know every inch of that picture by heart. But I didn't know that her hair was a coppery red, or that her eyes were such a deep, clear green. And until this moment, it had never occurred to me that she could laugh.

The slender blond man standing next to her interrupts my reverie. "I'm Jim Kennedy, Sara's assistant."

Jim Kennedy. Her fiancé. I feel like the characters in my favorite novel are all coming to life, one by one.

"You're not a wife, are you?" he asks.

I shake my head. "Post-doc. I've only been at Cal a month."

He smiles. "We're neighbors, then. What's your field?"

I take a deep breath. "Tempokinetics. I'm a great admirer of Dr. Clarke's work." The blustery man scowls at me and leaves in search of other prey.

"Really?" Dr. Clarke turns, raising one eyebrow in surprise. "Well, then we should have a chat. Are you – ?" She stops in mid-sentence and swears almost inaudibly. "Damn. It's Dr. Wilkins and I must be pleasant. He's quite a muckety-muck at the NSF, and I need the funding." She takes a long swallow of champagne, draining the crystal flute. "Jimmy, why don't you get Dr. McCullough another drink and see if you can persuade her to join us for supper."

I start to make a polite protest, but Jimmy takes my elbow and steers me through the crowd to an unoccupied sofa. Half an hour later we are deep in a discussion of quantum field theory when Dr. Clarke appears and says, "Let's make a discreet exit, shall we? I'm famished."

Like conspirators, we slip out a side door and down a flight of service stairs. The Powell Street cable car takes us over Nob Hill into North Beach, the Italian section of town. We walk up Columbus to one of my favorite restaurants – the New Pisa – where I discover that nothing much has changed in fifty years except the prices.

The waiter brings a carafe of red wine and a trio of squat drinking glasses and we eat family style – bowls of pasta with red sauce and steaming loaves of crusty garlic bread. I am speechless as Sara Baxter Clarke talks about her work, blithely answering questions I have wanted to ask my whole life. She is brilliant, fascinating. And beautiful. My food disappears without me noticing a single mouthful.

Over coffee and spumoni she insists, for the third time, that I call her Sara, and asks me about my own studies. I have to catch myself a few times, biting back citations from Stephen Hawking and other works that won't be published for decades. It is such an engrossing, exhilarating conversation, I can't bring myself to shift it to Chambers's agenda. We leave when we notice the restaurant has no other customers.

"How about a nightcap?" she suggests when we reach the sidewalk.

"Not for me," Jimmy begs off. "I've got an 8:30 symposium tomorrow morning. But why don't you two go on ahead. The Paper Doll is just around the corner."

Sara gives him an odd, cold look and shakes her head. "Not funny, James," she says, and glances over at me. I shrug noncommittally. It seems they have a private joke I'm not in on.

"Just a thought," he says, then kisses her on the cheek and leaves. Sara and I walk down to Vesuvio's, one of the bars where Kerouac, Ferlinghetti, and Ginsberg spawned the Beat Generation. Make that *will* spawn. I think we're a few months too early.

Sara orders another carafe of raw red wine. I feel shy around her, intimidated, I guess. I've dreamed of meeting her for so long, and I want her to like me. As we begin to talk, we discover how similar, and lonely, our childhoods were. We were raised as only children. We both begged for chemistry sets we never got. We were expected to know how to iron, not know about ions. Midway through her second glass of wine, Sara sighs.

"Oh, bugger it all. Nothing's really changed, you know. It's still just snickers and snubs. I'm tired of fighting for a seat in the old boys' club. Monday's paper represents five years of hard work, and there aren't a handful of people at this entire conference who've had the decency to treat me as anything but a joke." She squeezes her napkin into a tighter and tighter wad, and a tear trickles down her cheek. "How do you stand it, Carol?"

How can I tell her? I've stood it because of you. You're my hero. I've always asked myself what Sara Baxter Clarke would do, and steeled myself to push through. But now she's not a hero. She's real, this woman across the table from me. This Sara's not the invincible, ever-practical scientist I always thought she was. She's as young and as vulnerable as I am.

I want to ease her pain the way that she, as my imaginary mentor, has always eased mine. I reach over and put my hand over hers; she stiffens, but she doesn't pull away. Her hand is soft under mine, and I think of touching her hair, gently brushing the red tendrils off the back of her neck, kissing the salty tears on her cheek.

Maybe I've always had a crush on Sara Baxter Clarke. But I can't be falling in love with her. She's straight. She's fifty years older than I am. And in the back of my mind, the chilling voice of reality reminds me that she'll also be dead in two days. I can't reconcile that with the vibrant woman sitting in this smoky North Beach bar. I don't want to. I drink two more glasses of wine and hope that will silence the voice long enough for me to enjoy these few moments.

We are still talking, our fingertips brushing on the scarred wooden tabletop, when the bartender announces last call. "Oh, bloody hell," she says. "I've been having such a lovely time I've gone and missed the last ferry. I hope I have enough for the cab fare. My Chevy's over in the car park at Berkeley."

"That's ridiculous," I hear myself say. "I've got a room at the hotel. Come back with me and catch the ferry in the morning." It's the wine talking. I don't know what I'll do if she says yes. I want her to say yes so much.

"No, I couldn't impose. I'll simply – " she protests, and then stops. "Oh, yes, then. Thank you. It's very generous."

So here we are. At 2:00 a.m. the hotel lobby is plush and utterly empty. We ride up in the elevator in a sleepy silence that becomes awkward as soon as we are alone in the room. I nervously gather my new clothes off the only bed and gesture to her to sit down. I pull a t-shirt out of its crinkly cellophane wrapper. "Here," I hand it to her. "It's not elegant, but it'll have to do as a nightgown."

She looks at the t-shirt in her lap, and at the dungarees and black sneakers in my arms, an odd expression on her face. Then she sighs, a deep, achey-sounding sigh. It's the oddest reaction to a t-shirt I've ever heard.

"The Paper Doll would have been all right, wouldn't it?" she asks softly.

Puzzled, I stop crinkling the other cellophane wrapper and lean against the dresser. "I guess so. I've never been there." She looks worried, so I keep talking. "But there are a lot of places I haven't been. I'm new in town. Just got here. Don't know anybody yet, haven't really gotten around. What kind of place is it?"

She freezes for a moment, then says, almost in a whisper, "It's a bar for women."

"Oh," I nod. "Well, that's okay." Why would Jimmy suggest a gay bar? It's an odd thing to tell your fiancée. Did he guess about me somehow? Or maybe he just thought we'd be safer there late at night, since –

My musings – and any other rational thoughts – come to a dead stop when Sara Baxter Clarke stands up, cups my face in both her hands and kisses me gently on the lips. She pulls away, just a few inches, and looks at me.

I can't believe this is happening. "Aren't you – isn't Jimmy – ?"

"He's my dearest chum, and my partner in the lab. But romantically? No. Protective camouflage. For both of us," she answers, stroking my face.

I don't know what to do. Every dream I've ever had is coming true tonight. But how can I kiss her? How can I begin something I know is doomed? She must see the indecision in my face, because she looks scared, and starts to take a step backward. And I can't let her go. Not yet. I put my hand on the back of her neck and pull her into a second, longer kiss.

We move to the bed after a few minutes. I feel shy, not wanting to make a wrong move. But she kisses my face, my neck, and pulls me down onto her. We begin slowly, cautiously undressing each other. I fumble at the unfamiliar garter belts and stockings, and she smiles, undoing the rubber clasps for me. Her slender body is pale and freckled, her breasts small with dusty pink nipples.

Her fingers gently stroke my arms, my thighs. When I hesitantly put my mouth on her breast, she moans, deep in her throat, and laces her fingers through my hair. After a minute her hands ease my head down her body. The hair between her legs is ginger, the ends dark and wet. I taste the salty musk of her when I part her lips with my tongue. She moans again, almost a growl. When she comes it is a single, fierce explosion.

We finally fall into an exhausted sleep, spooned around each other, both t-shirts still crumpled on the floor.

Saturday, February 18, 1956. 7:00 a.m.
Light comes through a crack in the curtains. I'm alone in a strange bed. I'm sure last night was a dream, but then I hear the shower come on in the bathroom. Sara emerges a few minutes later, toweling her hair. She smiles and leans over me – warm and wet and smelling of soap.

"I have to go," she whispers, and kisses me.

I want to ask if I'll see her again, want to pull her down next to me and hold her for hours. But I just stroke her hair and say nothing.

She sits on the edge of the bed. "I've got an eleven o'clock lab, and there's another dreadful cocktail thing at Stanford this evening. I'd give it a miss, but Shockley's going to be there, and he's front runner for the next Nobel, so I have to make an appearance. Meet me after?"

"Yes," I say, breathing again. "Where?"

"Why don't you take the train down. I'll pick you up at the Palo Alto station at half-past seven and we can drive to the coast for dinner. Wear those nice black trousers. If it's not too dreary, we'll walk on the beach."

She picks up her wrinkled suit from the floor where it landed last night, and gets dressed. "Half past seven, then?" she says, and kisses my cheek. The door clicks shut and she's gone.

I lie tangled in the sheets, and curl up into the pillow like a contented cat. I am almost asleep again when an image intrudes – a crumpled Chevy on the rocks below Devil's Slide. It's like a fragment of a nightmare, not quite real in the morning light. But which dream is real now?

Until last night, part of what had made Sara Baxter Clarke so compelling was her enigmatic death. Like Amelia Earhart or James Dean, she had been a brilliant star that ended so abruptly she became legendary. Larger than life. But I can still feel where her lips brushed my cheek. Now she's very much life-size, and despite Chambers's warnings, I will do anything to keep her that way.

Saturday, February 18, 1956. 7:20 p.m.

The platform at the Palo Alto train station is cold and windy. I'm glad I'm wearing a sweater, but it makes my suit jacket uncomfortably tight across my shoulders. I've finished the newspaper and am reading the train schedule when Sara comes up behind me.

"Hullo there," she says. She's wearing a nubby beige dress under a dark wool coat and looks quite elegant.

"Hi." I reach to give her a hug, but she steps back.

"Have you gone mad?" she says, scowling. She crosses her arms over her chest. "What on earth were you thinking?"

"Sorry." I'm not sure what I've done. "It's nice to see you," I say hesitantly.

"Yes, well, me too. But you can't just – oh, you know," she says, waving her hand.

I don't, so I shrug. She gives me an annoyed look, then turns and opens the car door. I stand on the pavement for a minute, bewildered, then get in.

Her Chevy feels huge compared to the Toyota I drive at home, and there are no seatbelts. We drive in uncomfortable silence all through Palo Alto and onto the winding, two-lane road that leads to the coast. Our second date isn't going well.

After about ten minutes, I can't stand it any more. "I'm sorry about the hug. I guess it's still a big deal here, huh?"

She turns her head slightly, still keeping her eyes on the road. "Here?" she asks. "What utopia are you from, then?"

I spent the day wandering the city in a kind of haze, alternately giddy in love and worrying about this moment. How can I tell her where – when – I'm from? And how much should I tell her about why? I count to three, and then count again before I answer. "From the future."

"Very funny," she says. I can hear in her voice that she's hurt. She stares straight ahead again.

"Sara, I'm serious. Your work on time travel isn't just theory. I'm a post-doc at Cal. In 2006. The head of the Physics department, Dr. Chambers, sent me back here to talk to you. He says he worked with you and Jimmy, back before he won the Nobel Prize."

She doesn't say anything for a minute, then pulls over onto a wide place at the side of the road. She switches off the engine and turns toward me.

"Ray Chambers? The Nobel Prize? Jimmy says he can barely do his own lab work." She shakes her head, then lights a cigarette, flicking the match out the window into the darkness. "Ray set you up for this, didn't he? To get back at Jimmy for last term's grade? Well, it's a terrible joke," she says, turning away, "and you are one of the cruelest people I have ever met."

"Sara, it's not a joke. Please believe me." I reach across the seat to take her hand, but she jerks it away.

I take a deep breath, trying deperately to think of something that will convince her. "Look, I know it sounds crazy, but hear me out. In September, *Modern Physics* is going to publish an article about you and your work. When I was ten years old – in 1985 – I read it sitting on the back porch of my father's quarters at Fort Ord. That article inspired me to go into science. I read about you, and I knew when I grew up I wanted to travel through time."

She stubs out her cigarette. "Go on."

So I tell her all about my academic career, and my "assignment" from Chambers. She listens without interrupting me. I can't see her expression in the darkened car.

After I finish, she says nothing, then sighs. "This is rather a lot to digest, you know. But I can't very well believe in my work without giving your story some credence, can I?" She lights another cigarette, then asks the question I've been dreading. "So if you've come all this way to offer me an enormous sum for my paper, does that mean something happened to it — or to me?" I still can't see her face, but her voice is shaking.

I can't do it. I can't tell her. I grope for a convincing lie. "There was a fire. A lot of papers were lost. Yours is the one they want."

"I'm not a faculty member at *your* Cal, am I?"

"No."

She takes a long drag on her cigarette, then asks, so softly I can barely hear her, "Am I — ?" She lets her question trail off and is silent for a minute, then sighs again. "No, I won't ask. I think I prefer to bumble about like other mortals. You're a dangerous woman, Carol McCullough. I'm afraid you can tell me too many things I have no right to know." She reaches for the ignition key, then stops. "There is one thing I must know, though. Was last night as carefully planned as everything else?"

"Jesus, no." I reach over and touch her hand. She lets me hold it this time. "No, I had no idea. Other than finding you at the reception, last night had nothing to do with science."

To my great relief, she chuckles. "Well, perhaps chemistry, don't you think?" She glances in the rearview mirror then pulls me across the wide front seat and into her arms. We hold each other in the darkness for a long time, and kiss for even longer. Her lips taste faintly of gin.

We have a leisurely dinner at a restaurant overlooking the beach in Half Moon Bay. Fresh fish and a dry white wine. I have the urge to tell her about the picture, about how important she's been to me. But as I start to speak, I realize she's more important to me now, so I just tell her that. We finish the meal gazing at each other as if we were ordinary lovers.

Outside the restaurant, the sky is cloudy and cold, the breeze tangy with salt and kelp. Sara pulls off her high heels and we walk down a sandy path, holding hands in the darkness. Within minutes we are both freezing. I pull her to me and lean down to kiss her on the deserted beach. "You know what I'd like?" I say, over the roar of the surf.

"What?" she murmurs into my neck.

"I'd like to take you dancing."

She shakes her head. "We can't. Not here. Not now. It's against the law, you know. Or perhaps you don't. But it is, I'm afraid. And the police have been on a rampage in the city lately. One bar lost its license just because two men were holding hands. They arrested both as sexual vagrants and for being – oh, what was the phrase – lewd and dissolute persons."

"Sexual vagrants? That's outrageous!"

"Exactly what the newspapers said. An outrage to public decency. Jimmy knew one of the poor chaps. He was in Engineering at Stanford, but after his name and address were published in the paper, he lost his job. Does that still go on where you're from?"

"I don't think so. Maybe in some places. I don't really know. I'm afraid I don't pay any attention to politics. I've never needed to."

Sara sighs. "What a wonderful luxury that must be, not having to be so careful all the time."

"I guess so." I feel a little guilty that it's not something I worry about. But Stonewall happened six years before I was born. By the time I came out, in college, being gay was more of a lifestyle than a perversion. At least in San Francisco.

"It's sure a lot more public," I say after a minute. "Last year there were a half a million people at the Gay Pride parade. Dancing down Market Street and carrying signs about how great it is to be queer."

"You're pulling my leg now. Aren't you?" When I shake my head she smiles. "Well, I'm glad. I'm glad that this witch hunt ends. And in a few months, when I get my equipment up and running, perhaps I shall travel to dance at your parade. But for tonight, why don't we just go to my house? At least I've got a new hi-fi."

So we head back up the coast. One advantage to these old cars, the front seat is as big as a couch; we drive up Highway 1 sitting next to each other, my arm resting on her thigh. The ocean is a flat, black void on our left, until the road begins to climb and the water disappears behind jagged cliffs. On the driver's side the road drops off steeply as we approach Devil's Slide.

I feel like I'm coming to the scary part of a movie I've seen before. I'm afraid I know what happens next. My right hand grips the upholstery and I brace myself for the oncoming car or the loose patch of gravel or whatever it is that will send us skidding off the road and onto the rocks.

But nothing happens. Sara hums as she drives, and I realize that although this is the spot I dread, it means nothing to her. At least not tonight.

As the road levels out again, it is desolate, with few signs of civilization. Just beyond a sign that says SHARP PARK is a trailer camp with a string of bare lightbulbs outlining its perimeter. Across the road is a seedy-looking roadhouse with a neon sign that blinks HAZEL'S. The parking lot is jammed with cars. Saturday night in the middle of nowhere.

We drive another hundred yards when Sara suddenly snaps her fingers and does a U-turn.

Please don't go back to the cliffs, I beg silently. "What's up?" I ask out loud.

"Hazel's. Jimmy was telling me about it last week. It's become a rather gay club, and since it's over the county line, out here in the boondocks, he says anything goes. Including dancing. Besides, I thought I spotted his car."

"Are you sure?"

"No, but there aren't that many '39 Packards still on the road. If it isn't, we'll just continue on." She pulls into the parking lot and finds a space at the back, between the trash cans and the ocean.

Hazel's is a noisy, smoky place – a small, single room with a bar along one side – jammed wall-to-wall with people. Hundreds of them, mostly men, but more than a few women. When I look closer, I realize that some of the "men" are actually women with slicked-back hair, ties, and sportcoats.

We manage to get two beers, and find Jimmy on the edge of the dance floor – a minuscule square of linoleum, not more than 10 × 10, where dozens of people are dancing to Bill Haley & the Comets blasting from the jukebox. Jimmy's in a tweed jacket and chinos, his arm around the waist of a young Latino man in a tight white t-shirt and even tighter blue jeans. We elbow our way through to them and Sara gives Jimmy a kiss on the cheek. "Hullo, love," she says.

He's obviously surprised – shocked – to see Sara, but when he sees me behind her, he grins. "I told you so."

"James, you don't know the half of it," Sara says, smiling, and puts her arm around me.

We dance for a few songs in the hot, crowded bar. I take off my jacket, then my sweater, draping them over the railing next to the bottles of beer. After the next song I roll up the sleeves of my button-down shirt. When Jimmy offers to buy another round of beers, I look at my watch and shake my head. It's midnight, and as much as I wanted to dance with Sara, I want to sleep with her even more.

"One last dance, then let's go, okay?" I ask, shouting to be heard over the noise of the crowd and the jukebox. "I'm bushed."

She nods. Johnny Mathis starts to sing, and we slow dance, our arms around each other. My eyes are closed and Sara's head is resting on my shoulder when the first of the cops bursts through the front door.

Sunday, February 19, 1956. 12:05 a.m.

A small army of uniformed men storms into the bar. Everywhere around us people are screaming in panic, and I'm buffeted by the bodies running in all directions. People near the back race for the rear door. A red-faced, heavy-set man in khaki, a gold star on his chest, climbs onto the bar. "This is a raid," he shouts. He has brought reporters with him, and flashbulbs suddenly illuminate the stunned, terrified faces of people who had been sipping their drinks moments before.

Khaki-shirted deputies, nightsticks in hand, block the front door. There are so many uniforms. At least forty men – highway patrol, sheriff's department, and even some army MPs – begin to form a gauntlet leading to the back door, now the only exit.

Jimmy grabs my shoulders. "Dance with Antonio," he says urgently. "I've just met him, but it's our best chance of getting out of here. I'll take Sara."

I nod and the Latino man's muscular arms are around my waist. He smiles shyly just as someone pulls the plug on the jukebox and Johnny Mathis stops in mid-croon. The room is quiet for a moment, then the cops begin barking orders. We stand against the railing, Jimmy's arm curled protectively around Sara's shoulders, Antonio's around mine.

Other people have done the same thing, but there are not enough women, and men who had been dancing now stand apart from each other, looking scared.

The uniforms are lining people up, herding them like sheep toward the back. We join the line and inch forward. The glare of headlights through the half-open back door cuts through the smoky room like the beam from a movie projector. There is an icy draft and I reach back for my sweater, but the railing is too far away, and the crush of people too solid to move any direction but forward. Jimmy sees me shivering and drapes his sportcoat over my shoulders.

We are in line for more than an hour, as the cops at the back door check everyone's ID. Sara leans against Jimmy's chest, squeezing my hand tightly once or twice when no one's looking. I am scared, shaking, but the uniforms seem to be letting most people go. Every few seconds, a car starts up in the parking lot, and I can hear the crunch of tires on gravel as someone leaves Hazel's for the freedom of the highway.

As we get closer to the door, I can see a line of black vans parked just outside, ringing the exit. They are paneled with wooden benches, filled with the men who are not going home, most of them sitting with their shoulders sagging. One van holds a few women with crewcuts or slicked-back hair, who glare defiantly into the night.

We are ten people back from the door when Jimmy slips a key into my hand and whispers into my ear. "We'll have to take separate cars. Drive Sara's back to the city and we'll meet at the lobby bar in your hotel."

"The bar will be closed," I whisper back. "Take my key and meet me in the room. I'll get another at the desk." He nods as I hand it to him.

The cop at the door looks at Sara's elegant dress and coat, barely glances at her outstretched ID, and waves her and Jimmy outside without a word. She pauses at the door and looks back at me, but an MP shakes his head and points to the parking lot. "Now or never, lady," he says, and Sara and Jimmy disappear into the night.

I'm alone. Antonio is a total stranger, but his strong arm is my only support until a man in a suit pulls him away. "Nice try, sweetie," the man says to him. "But I've seen you in here before, dancing with your pansy friends." He turns to the khaki-shirted deputy and says, "He's one of the perverts. Book him." The cop pulls Antonio's arm up between his shoulder blades, then cuffs his hands behind his back. "Time for a little ride, pretty boy," he grins, and drags Antonio out into one of the black vans.

Without thinking, I take a step toward his retreating back. "Not so fast," says another cop, with acne scars across both cheeks. He looks at Jimmy's jacket, and down at my pants and my black basketball shoes with a sneer. Then he puts his hands on my breasts, groping me. "Loose ones. Not all tied down like those other he-shes. I like that." He leers and pinches one of my nipples.

I yell for help and try to pull away, but he laughs and shoves me up against the stack of beer cases that line the back hallway. He pokes his nightstick between my legs. "So you want to be a man, huh, butchie? Well just what do you think you've got in there?" He jerks his nightstick up into my crotch so hard tears come to my eyes.

I stare at him, in pain, in disbelief. I am too stunned to move or to say anything. He cuffs my hands and pushes me out the back door and into the van with the other glaring women.

Sunday, February 19, 1956. 10:00 a.m.

I plead guilty to being a sex offender, and pay the $50 fine. Being arrested can't ruin *my* life. I don't even exist here.

Sara and Jimmy are waiting on a wooden bench outside the holding cell of the San Mateo County jail. "Are you all right, love?" she asks.

I shrug. "I'm exhausted. I didn't sleep. There were ten of us in one cell. The woman next to me – a stone butch? – really tough, Frankie – she had a pompadour – two cops took her down the hall – when she came back the whole side of her face was swollen, and after that she didn't say anything to anyone, but I'm okay, I just – " I start to shake. Sara takes one arm and Jimmy takes the other, and they walk me gently out to the parking lot.

The three of us sit in the front seat of Jimmy's car, and as soon as we are out of sight of the jail, Sara puts her arms around me and holds me, brushing the hair off my forehead. When Jimmy takes the turnoff to the San Mateo bridge, she says, "We checked you out of the hotel this morning. Precious little to check, actually, except for the briefcase.

Anyway, I thought you'd be more comfortable at my house. We need to get you some breakfast and a bed." She kisses me on the cheek. "I've told Jimmy everything, by the way."

I nod sleepily, and the next thing I know we're standing on the front steps of a brown shingled cottage and Jimmy's pulling away. I don't think I'm hungry, but Sara makes scrambled eggs and bacon and toast, and I eat every scrap of it. She runs a hot bath, grimacing at the purpling, thumb-shaped bruises on my upper arms, and gently washes my hair and my back. When she tucks me into bed, pulling a blue quilt around me, and curls up beside me, I start to cry. I feel so battered and so fragile, and I can't remember the last time someone took care of me this way.

Sunday, February 19, 1956. 5:00 p.m.

I wake up to the sound of rain and the enticing smell of pot roast baking in the oven. Sara has laid out my jeans and a brown sweater at the end of the bed. I put them on, then pad barefoot into the kitchen. There are cardboard boxes piled in one corner, and Jimmy and Sara are sitting at the yellow formica table with cups of tea, talking intently.

"Oh good, you're awake." She stands and gives me a hug. "There's tea in the pot. If you think you're up to it, Jimmy and I need to tell you a few things."

"I'm a little sore, but I'll be okay. I'm not crazy about the '50s, though." I pour from the heavy ceramic pot. The tea is some sort of Chinese blend, fragrant and smoky. "What's up?"

"First a question. If my paper isn't entirely – complete – could there possibly be any repercussions for you?"

I think for a minute. "I don't think so. If anyone knew exactly what was in it, they wouldn't have sent me."

"Splendid. In that case, I've come to a decision." She pats the battered brown briefcase. "In exchange for the extraordinary wad of cash in here, we shall send back a perfectly reasonable-sounding paper. What only the three of us will know is that I have left a few things out. This, for example." She picks up a pen, scribbles a complex series of numbers and symbols on a piece of paper, and hands it to me.

I study it for a minute. It's very high-level stuff, but I know enough physics to get the gist of it. "If this really works, it's the answer to the energy problem. It's exactly the piece Chambers needs."

"Very, very good," she says smiling. "It's also the part I will never give him."

I raise one eyebrow.

"I read the first few chapters of his dissertation this afternoon while you were sleeping," she says, tapping the manuscript with her pen. "It's a bit uneven, although parts of it are quite good. Unfortunately, the good parts were written by a graduate student named Gilbert Young."

I raise the other eyebrow. "But that paper's what Chambers wins the Nobel for."

"Son of a bitch." Jimmy slaps his hand down onto the table. "Gil was working for me while he finished the last of his dissertation. He was a bright guy, original research, solid future – but he started having these headaches. The tumor was inoperable, and he died six months ago. Ray said he'd clean out Gil's office for me. I just figured he was trying to get back on my good side."

"We can't change what Ray does with Gil's work. But I won't give him *my* work to steal in the future." Sara shoves Chambers's manuscript to the other side of the table. "Or now. I've decided not to present my paper in the morning."

I feel very lightheaded. I *know* she doesn't give her paper, but – "Why not?" I ask.

"While I was reading the manuscript this afternoon, I heard that fat sheriff interviewed on the radio. They arrested ninety people at Hazel's last night, Carol, people like us. People who only wanted to dance with each other. But he kept bragging about how they cleaned out a nest of perverts. And I realized – in a blinding moment of clarity – that the university is a branch of the state, and the sheriff is enforcing the state's laws. I'm working for people who believe it's morally right to abuse you – or me – or Jimmy. And I can't do that any more."

"Hear, hear!" Jimmy says, smiling. "The only problem is, as I explained to her this morning, the administration is likely to take a very dim view of being embarrassed in front of every major physicist in the country. Not to mention they feel Sara's research is university property." He looks at me and takes a sip of tea. "So we decided it might be best if Sara disappeared for a while."

I stare at both of them, my mouth open. I have that same odd feeling of déjà vu that I did in the car last night.

"I've cleaned everything that's hers out of our office and the lab," Jimmy says. "It's all in the trunk of my car."

"And those," Sara says, gesturing to the boxes in the corner, "are what I value from my desk and my library here. Other than my Nana's teapot and some clothes, it's all I'll really need for a while. Jimmy's family has a vacation home out in West Marin, so I won't have to worry about rent – or privacy."

I'm still staring. "What about your career?"

Sara puts down her teacup with a bang and begins pacing the floor. "Oh, bugger my career. I'm not giving up my *work*, just the university – and its hypocrisy. If one of my colleagues had a little fling, nothing much would come of it. But as a woman, I'm supposed to be some sort of paragon of unsullied Victorian virtue. Just by being *in* that bar last night, I put my 'career' in jeopardy. They'd crucify me if they knew who – or what – I am. I don't want to live that way any more."

She brings the teapot to the table and sits down, pouring us each another cup. "End of tirade. But that's why I had to ask about your money. It's enough to live on for a good long while, and to buy all the equipment I need. In a few months, with a decent lab, I should be this close," she says, holding her thumb and forefinger together, "to time travel in practice as well as in theory. And that discovery will be mine – ours. Not the university's. Not the government's."

Jimmy nods. "I'll stay down here and finish this term. That way I can keep tabs on things and order equipment without arousing suspicion."

"Won't they come looking for you?" I ask Sara. I feel very surreal. Part of me has always wanted to know *why* this all happened, and part of me feels like I'm just prompting the part I know comes next.

"Not if they think there's no reason to look," Jimmy says. "We'll take my car back to Hazel's and pick up hers. Devil's Slide is only a few miles up the road. It's – "

"It's a rainy night," I finish. "Treacherous stretch of highway. Accidents happen there all the time. They'll find Sara's car in the morning, but no body. Washed out to sea. Everyone will think it's tragic that she died so young," I say softly. My throat is tight and I'm fighting back tears. "At least I always have."

They both stare at me. Sara gets up and stands behind me, wrapping her arms around my shoulders. "So that *is* how it happens?" she asks, hugging me tight. "All along you've assumed I'd be dead in the morning?"

I nod. I don't trust my voice enough to say anything.

To my great surprise, she laughs. "Well, I'm not going to be. One of the first lessons you should have learned as a scientist is never assume," she says, kissing the top of my head. "But what a terrible secret for you to have been carting about. Thank you for not telling me. It would have ruined a perfectly lovely weekend. Now let's all have some supper. We've a lot to do tonight."

Monday, February 20, 1956. 12:05 a.m.

"What on earth are you doing?" Sara asks, coming into the kitchen and talking around the toothbrush in her mouth. "It's our last night – at least for a while. I was rather hoping you'd be waiting in bed when I came out of the bathroom."

"I will. Two more minutes." I'm sitting at the kitchen table, rolling a blank sheet of paper into her typewriter. I haven't let myself think about going back in the morning, about leaving Sara, and I'm delaying our inevitable conversation about it for as long as I can. "While we were driving back from wrecking your car, I had an idea about how to nail Chambers."

She takes the toothbrush out of her mouth. "It's a lovely thought, but you know you can't change anything that happens."

"I can't change the past," I agree. "But I *can* set a bomb with a very long fuse. Like fifty years."

"What? You look like the cat that's eaten the canary." She sits down next to me.

"I've retyped the title page to Chambers's dissertation – with your name on it. First thing in the morning, I'm going to rent a large safe deposit box at the Wells Fargo Bank downtown, and pay the rent in advance. Sometime in 2006, there'll be a miraculous discovery of a complete Sara Baxter Clarke manuscript. The bomb is that, after her tragic death, the esteemed Dr. Chambers appears to have published it under his own name – and won the Nobel Prize for it."

"No, you can't. It's not my work either, it's Gil's and – " she stops in mid-sentence, staring at me. "And he really *is* dead. I don't suppose I dare give a fig about academic credit anymore, should I?"

"I hope not. Besides, Chambers can't prove it's *not* yours. What's he going to say – Carol McCullough went back to the past and set me up? He'll look like a total idiot. Without your formula, all he's got is a time machine that won't work. Remember, you never present your paper. Where I come from it may be okay to be queer, but time travel is still just science fiction."

She laughs. "Well, given a choice, I suppose that's preferable, isn't it?"

I nod and pull the sheet of paper out of the typewriter.

"You're quite a resourceful girl, aren't you?" Sara says, smiling. "I could use an assistant like you." Then her smile fades and she puts her hand over mine. "I don't suppose you'd consider staying on for a few months and helping me set up the lab? I know we've only known each other for two days. But this – I – us – Oh, dammit, what I'm trying to say is I'm going to miss you."

I squeeze her hand in return, and we sit silent for a few minutes. I don't know what to say. Or to do. I don't want to go back to my own time. There's nothing for me in that life. My dissertation that I now know isn't true. An office with a black-and-white photo of the only person I've ever really loved – who's sitting next to me, holding my hand. I could sit like this forever. But could I stand to live the rest of my life in the closet, hiding who I am and who I love? I'm used to the 21st century – I've never done research without the Internet, or cooked much without a microwave. I'm afraid if I don't go back tomorrow, I'll be trapped in this reactionary past forever.

"Sara," I ask finally. "Are you sure your experiments will work?"

She looks at me, her eyes warm and gentle. "If you're asking if I can promise you an escape back to your own time someday, the answer is no. I can't promise you anything, love. But if you're asking if I believe in my work, then yes. I do. Are you thinking of staying, then?"

I nod. "I want to. I just don't know if I can."

"Because of last night?" she asks softly.

"That's part of it. I was raised in a world that's so different. I don't feel right here. I don't belong."

She kisses my cheek. "I know. But gypsies never belong to the places they travel. They only belong to other gypsies."

My eyes are misty as she takes my hand and leads me to the bedroom.

Monday, February 20, 1956. 11:30 a.m.

I put the battered leather briefcase on the floor of the supply closet in LeConte Hall and close the door behind me. At 11:37 exactly, I hear the humming start, and when it stops, my shoulders sag with relief. What's done is done, and all the dies are cast. In Palo Alto an audience of restless physicists is waiting to hear a paper that will never be read. And in Berkeley, far in the future, an equally restless physicist is waiting for a messenger to finally deliver that paper.

But the messenger isn't coming back. And that may be the least of Chambers's worries.

This morning I taped the key to the safe deposit box – and a little note about the dissertation inside – into the 1945 bound volume of *The Astrophysical Journal*. My officemate Ted was outraged that no one had checked it out of the Physics library since 1955. I'm hoping he'll be even more outraged when he discovers the secret that's hidden inside it.

I walk out of LeConte and across campus to the coffee shop where Sara is waiting for me. I don't like the political climate here, but at least I know that it will change, slowly but surely. Besides, we don't have to stay in the '50s all the time – in a few months, Sara and I plan to do a lot of traveling. Maybe one day some graduate student will want to study the mysterious disappearance of Dr. Carol McCullough. Stranger things have happened.

My only regret is not being able to see Chambers's face when he opens that briefcase and there's no manuscript. Sara and I decided that even sending back an incomplete version of her paper was dangerous. It would give Chambers enough proof that his tempokinetic experiment worked for him to get more funding and try again. So the only thing in the case is an anonymous, undated postcard of the St. Francis Hotel that says:

"Having a wonderful time. Thanks for the ride."

Be Prepared

CRAIG CLAIBORNE HAD NOT BEEN the first choice for Galaxy Lines' third (and final) "Cooking in Space" cruise. But a week before take-off it was discovered that none of the launch suits could be modified to fit Paul Prudhomme.

Claiborne was in the process of explaining to a tedious woman from Davenport, Iowa, during the second morning's cooking class, that it was just not feasible to attempt a soufflé in zero-gravity, when a band of pirates breached the airlock and took control of the ship.

They captured a dozen or so of the largest, plumpest passengers, Claiborne included, and herded them onto a black ship that hovered a few meters off the stern of the now-doomed *De Gustibus*.

Reluctantly, but encouraged with the use of a sort of electrified spatula, the men and women were taken to a white, tiled chamber, at the end of which was an apparatus that seemed to Claiborne to consist of a series of graduated stewpots – Calphalon, if he wasn't mistaken.

The pirates, who were a sort of dull fennel color with calamari-like appendages, lined their prisoners up single-file. Claiborne was near the end.

He watched as one of the pirates picked up a hose with a turkey-baster-ish nozzle at one end and, with a sound not unlike that of coring a ripe Casaba melon, thrust it into the top of the skull of the unpleasant woman from Iowa. She slumped to the floor, the stewpots clattered, and the contents of a measuring tube at the end of the array rose a fraction of an inch.

Sloppy technique, thought Claiborne. *Drain and pick over the brains to remove the outer membranes, blood, and other extraneous matter.* New York Times Cookbook, *page 207, second edition.*

The line moved forward. The ship's clerk was next. A whistling sound came from one of the stewpots, and a pirate rushed over and adjusted a dial.

Hmmph, Claiborne thought derisively. *Add fresh lemon juice and stir to break up the brains. Ideally, the brains should be mashed at intervals while they are cooking.*

A few minutes later, a pirate turned a small valve below the measuring device, and a bit of pinkish gray liquid trickled into a clear receptacle. He tasted it and pursed what might have been his lips.

Not at all palatable, I'd think. Claiborne grimaced. *Combine olive oil, lemon juice, dill, parsley, oregano, and capers in a saucepan and bring to a boil. Pour over the brains and serve lukewarm.* He furrowed his brow. Perhaps accompanied with a dry Pinot Grigio, or one of the French –

The nozzle was cold.

There would be no dessert.

Travel Agency

MY OLDER SISTER AND HER DAUGHTER, my favorite niece, have come to stay with me in my house outside Boston for a few nights. Marjorie is a frequent flyer; she works for the airlines, in management. She wears stretch jeans and a white sweatshirt with glittery appliquéd gingham teddy bears. This is Emily's first visit. She's almost ten. She gives me an awkward hug, and a shy smile when her mother is not looking.

My guest room is a room that is usually the den. I have cleaned up the day-to-day clutter of papers and books, and put clean sheets on the sofabed. Marjorie frowns when she sees it. It is a little small for two to sleep comfortably.

I tell Emily that she'll be sleeping in the attic, if that's okay. The child's eyes light up as if she'd just been offered a bunk on a pirate ship. They live in a suburb, in a split-level ranch house with white carpeting. But I know from her letters that many of her favorite books seem to involve old houses with great, sometimes magic, attics. Mrs. Piggle-Wiggle's house has an attic, and the Four-Story Mistake. I think there's one in *Half Magic*, too.

Magic rarely happens in a living room, or in a basement, unless it's scary magic, which isn't the kind you want to have surround you at night.

For most of my guests, my attic is a utilitarian place. It's just a room at the top of the house, the place where the luggage lives when it's not traveling, and where the boxes of Christmas ornaments and books without bookshelf space are stored. Winter clothes in the cedar closet in July; bathing suits in plastic boxes in December.

But the child is beside herself, hopping excitedly from one foot to the other, waiting to see my attic. I am a librarian. I am neither blasé about the importance of my offer, nor alarmed at the hopping. I am actually rather delighted. Marjorie puts a hand on Emily's arm and tells her to behave. The child stops hopping and pulls her ears a fraction closer to her shoulders.

The attic door opens off the upstairs hallway, between the guest room and the bathroom. It isn't one of those attics that is reached by pull-down stairs set in the ceiling. It is a proper attic, with a proper doorway and small, twisting, steep stairs. Emily turns to me and smiles when I open the door, her eyes so bright I'm amazed that the narrow stairwell isn't illuminated by them.

At the top of the stairs, we step out into one big slope-ceilinged room. It's finished in the sense that there are paneled walls and not just exposed beams and studs and lath. But it is not wallpapered or carpeted or decorated. Two-thirds of it is full of the usual attic-y jumble of boxes and trunks, lamps that don't match my new couch, and occasional tables whose occasion has come and gone. It is a place for things that no longer belong.

The far end is an open, rectangular space with a small iron cot of the same shape and vintage as the ones in the cabins of my childhood summer camp. A thin mattress lies atop springs that I know will squeak when the child sits down, or when she turns over. I have made it up with some faded green sheets and an equally faded summer-weight quilt.

The cot sits in the middle of an old, threadbare Oriental rug that holds the encroaching boxes at bay. An upturned footlocker stands at the side of the bed, topped with a green glass-shaded lamp. Next to the lamp is an offering of nine-year-old-type books that I have pulled from the dozens of bookcases that line the rest of my house: *The Lilac Fairy Book*, *The Wind in the Willows*, an Enid Blyton schoolgirl book about the fourth form at St. Clare's, and *The Phantom Tollbooth*.

A few feet above the cot, there's a small, round window, filled with the leaves of the neighbor's tall maple. The wall faces west, and the late afternoon light streams golden onto the tiny bed.

Emily stops in her tracks when she sees all of this, stops moving altogether. I'm not even sure if she's breathing.

She looks from her mother to me and then asks, "Do I really get to sleep here?" The wonder in her voice makes one of us smile.

"For two whole nights? Just me? By myself?"

I nod. The child has her own room at home. It's not like she lies shackled to her straw pallet next to the kitchen hearth, deprived of both comfort and privacy. But this is a place that she'll remember. Years from now, she'll be able to close her eyes and recall every detail. She may no longer be able to remember where she'd been, or why, exactly, but she'll remember there was a bed in an attic, and a doting aunt who gave her the chance for a bit of a storybook childhood.

"We're going to go down and start dinner," I say, giving her a wink. "Do you want to stay up here, or come down and have a root beer while we cook?"

It is not a hard choice.

"Here, I think. Maybe I'll kind of unpack." She is already eyeing the books on the bedside table.

So Marjorie and I go downstairs and open a bottle of Chardonnay, and I begin chopping vegetables while she goes on about United, and Donald, and how they plan to landscape the yard next spring. An hour later, I excuse myself and tiptoe back up the narrow stairs.

Dust motes swirl in the last rays of twilight. As I had hoped, the cot is empty, only a small girl-shaped indentation left in the quilt. Enid Blyton is lying face down, pages open. I smile as I close it and tuck it under my arm.

I thought it was what she'd choose. It's a lovely place for a holiday, and the girls in the fourth form are such a lively bunch this year.

A Taste of Summer

MATTIE RODGERS SAT on the tiny sleeping porch of the summer cottage on Indian Lake, halfway reading a Nancy Drew book, and mostly watching her dad and two of her three older brothers try to fix the outboard motor on the dinghy. She was hoping they'd let her help, or at least get it back together soon, so her dad could take her exploring in the other parts of the lake.

She folded over the page of the book and got up out of the chair. Her legs made a slurping sound when she pulled up off the painted wood, because she was sticky hot. The boat lay upside down on the grass near the dock. Her dad was kneeling over the blades. AJ and Mike were doing something to the motor part with a screwdriver. They all had their shirts off and were shiny with sweat and streaks of black grease. She stopped a few feet away.

"Can I help, Daddy?"

He started a little, dropped the wrench, said one of the bad words, not quite in a whisper, then turned around and looked at her over his shoulder.

"No, sweetie. This is guy stuff."

"Are you fixing it?"

"Nope, not yet." His voice wasn't mad, but it sounded like it could change into mad pretty quick. He turned back to the propeller.

Mattie waited a minute, shifting her weight from one foot to the other on the grass. "Daddy? How long do you think it's going to be? Will you take me out for a ride when you're done?"

Her father turned around. "Matts?" He looked surprised that she was still standing there. "Why don't you be a big girl and go play someplace else for a while? We'll be lucky to finish this before dark as it is." He sighed and rubbed his face, leaving a grease mark on his chin.

"There's nobody to play with."

"Where's Danny?"

"Fishing. He says I can't come along because girls scare fish."

"Well then, how about the twins?"

Mattie made a face. She was almost nine and Cindy and Shelley were eleven. They'd always played pirates before, exploring the lake-shore for treasure, but this summer all they wanted to do was read about the Beatles and roll their hair. "They don't want to do anything fun anymore. Can I go swimming?"

Her dad looked over at the weathered gray dock and shook his head. "Nobody's got time to watch you right now. Maybe when your mom gets back from Lake City."

Her mom had gone to get her hair done. Most Saturdays Mattie had to go along, but her birthday was in two days, and her mother had secret shopping to do. Mattie wasn't sure there was anything in Lake City she really wanted, and she hoped it wasn't going to be clothes. She was wearing her favorites — a pair of her brother Mike's hand-me-down cut-offs and a faded green Celtics tank top that came down past her knees and said HAVLICEK in letters that were just barely visible. Her red high-top sneakers were busting out at the toes and her brown hair was ragged over her ears where she'd tried to cut off the annoying parts with her mother's nail scissors earlier that morning.

Mattie's shoulders sagged. "She'll just say we need to start dinner," she said under her breath.

"Look, Matts," her father said after a moment, "The boys and I want to get this back together before it starts to rain. Why don't you go get a popsicle at Miller's." He wiped his hand on his khaki shorts, reached into his pocket, and pulled out a five-dollar bill, three pennies, a dime, and a nickel. He poured all the change into Mattie's hand. "My treat." He reached up and patted her hair, looking at the gathering clouds. "But you'd better scoot on out of here. We'll have rain by supper, and if you come home soaking wet your mom'll have my hide."

Mattie considered her options and decided that a walk with a popsi-cle at the other end was probably the best of them. "Okay, Daddy." She kissed the cleanest part of his cheek and carefully put the coins in the front pocket of her cut-offs.

Their cottage was on a dirt road bordered by thick woods and black-berry bushes, about half a mile from the highway. As she walked, she scuffed her sneakers in the dirt and tried to decide what she wanted most when she got to Miller's. She sometimes had a nickel, or even a dime, but today she had eighteen whole cents, and that could buy just about anything. Maybe a popsicle. Or maybe penny candy. B-B-Bats or Nik-L-Nip wax bottles full of sweet syrup, or an Indian necklace made of pale candy beads strung on elastic just long enough to reach her mouth from around her neck. Maybe one of each. She felt pretty good. Not as good as if she was having a real adventure exploring on the lake, but better than just sitting on the porch watching the boys.

By the time she got to the old farmhouse and the field that was about halfway to the highway, the wind was whipping up dust around her feet. The leaves of the maple trees on the side of the road were turned over upside-down, showing their pale undersides. It was definitely going to rain, and she didn't think it was going to wait until dinnertime. She thought for a minute about going back, but decided that maybe being wet on a sort-of adventure was better than being dry and bored for sure.

The dirt road ended at State Route 42, two lanes of blacktop, an intersection everyone called "the Tee" – a tiny shopping district with a gas station, a grocery store, a bar, a real estate office, and an ice cream parlor.

That summer, Mattie's mother said she was a big girl and could walk down to the Tee by herself, but she wasn't allowed to cross the highway, because there was no stop light and the cars went too fast. Mattie didn't really mind; the only buildings on the other side were the bar and Bingham's Ice Creamery, and even today she didn't have enough money for that. The smallest cone cost a whole quarter.

Mattie walked up to the front door of Miller's Superette. It was on the safe side of the highway, but today its CLOSED sign hung in the big window, even though it was the middle of a Saturday afternoon.

She stood in front of the automatic IN door and jumped up and down on the rubber mat twice, but the glass door stayed closed. She kicked a bottle cap down the sidewalk in frustration, then looked around. Nobody was at the Tee. The real estate office had its blinds shut, and there was only one dusty black Rambler in the parking lot of Pete's Tavern.

The sky had gotten to be a weird color – yellow-green and dark at the horizon, so dark that there was no line between the land and the sky. Three in the afternoon, and it looked like it was almost bedtime. The clouds were so low they seemed to touch the top of the Texaco station, and the whole sky looked like a bruise. The neon beer signs across the highway in the window of the bar were hot red and yellow and green, shining through the darkness like alien jewels.

She stepped to the side of the highway. She could see for more than a mile in each direction – flat east, flat west – and there was no traffic at all. Far to the west, she could just barely see a solitary pair of headlights, tiny, like twin stars in a distant galaxy, glowing side by side.

Her mother said that God was watching her, all the time, and if she did anything bad, He'd know. But Mattie figured that God was probably pretty busy making the storm. It looked like it might be a big one. Big enough that he wouldn't really be paying much attention to one small almost-nine-year-old, even if she was the only person around.

She looked both ways again, just to be sure, then stepped out onto the highway. A shudder went through her whole body when her sneaker touched the blacktop, and she waited for a second, but nothing bad happened. She walked slowly over to the yellow stripe down the middle. She told herself that she wasn't really *crossing* the highway, because crossing meant the other side and she was just in the middle, but she knew it was the same kind of bad.

When they had driven over to Lake City to the restaurant with real tablecloths for her mother's birthday, she'd turned around on the back seat and watched the yellow stripe behind them until her father made her sit down. One thin stripe, unrolling like a ribbon. But standing on it, here on the ground, she could see that it wasn't. It was a lot of small stripes, the yellow paint faded in patches, all strung out one after the other, with big gaps in between them.

They were so far apart she couldn't even jump from the end of one to another. She turned around and walked back on her stripe, tightrope style, her arms out at her sides for balance. It was very dangerous. The yellow was solid ground, a narrow cliff, and the blacktop was a deep, deep canyon on either side. If her foot slipped, she'd tumble down and down. But it didn't, and when she got to the end of the cliff, she turned around and walked back again.

Then a thought came into her head. A thought so wonderful and so very, very bad and dangerous that she was afraid that her brain could even think it. She looked around. No one was watching, and the car didn't seem any closer. She couldn't hear its motor, not even a little. She thought the thought again, and this time it thought itself so hard that it made her mouth smile.

So she leaned down and put her head on the end of the yellow stripe, right in the middle of the highway, and did a somersault over to the next one. She laughed out loud, and tightroped to the end of that stripe, then did another roll, coming up onto her feet. When she straightened up she could hear, just faintly, the hum of the approaching motor. The headlights had grown to the size of marbles. She felt the first fat wet drop of rain splatter on her arm just as a bolt of jagged lightning lit up half the sky.

The rain began to roar down around her. She looked back at the awning of the closed Superette, and then over at Bingham's. The lights were off but the OPEN sign still hung in the window. She hesitated, then crossed the yellow line and ran as fast as she could to the other side of the highway.

She pushed on the battered tin MEADOW DAIRY sign that separated the top and bottom halves of Bingham's screen door. Its colors had faded to the ghosts of red and blue, and it was rusty at the corners. The door hinges squeaked as it opened and she stepped onto the bare wooden floor.

Bingham's smelled like sweetness. Vanilla and sugar cones and butterscotch, mingled with the soft, hot oldness of the wood. Her dad sometimes walked her down after dinner when he came up from Grand Rapids on weekends. He always got coffee fudge. This summer her favorites went back and forth between the butter pecan and the peppermint stick.

But with the lights off and the dark sky outside, it felt to Mattie like no one had been in here in a hundred years. A little bit magic, like it had been forgotten for a very long time.

She walked up to the counter, her sneakers leaving wet tracks on the dusty planks. She stood on tiptoe but saw nothing in the gloom except stacks of glass sundae bowls and clown-covered boxes of pointed cones under the hand-painted board with the names of all the ice creams. "Hello?" she called.

No one answered for a moment, and then from the back room a boy's voice said, "Sorry, we're closed."

Mattie watched the car pass Bingham's window. "It's raining really hard outside," she said after its taillights had disappeared into the downpour.

Silence. And then the voice said, "Okay, hang on. Hang on."

There was the muted clatter of dishes and the sound of water running, just for a minute. She had expected to see Mr. Bingham, the ice cream man, but instead out came a tall skinny boy in a pair of black shorts and a white Daddy shirt with the arms cut off ragged at the shoulders. He had a pair of glasses hanging on a cord around his neck.

The boy shook his head. "Kiddo, what in the world are you doing out in this weather?" he asked. He wiped his hands on a white towel, then tossed it on the back counter.

"I was going to Miller's for candy, but it's closed. Everything's closed but here."

The boy frowned. "I forgot to turn the sign around. Didn't think anybody'd be out because of the storm." He stopped and looked at the screen door like he was waiting for someone else to come in behind her. "You by yourself? Your parents know where you are?"

Mattie shrugged. "Sort of."

"I ought to let them know you're okay. Summer folks?"

Mattie nodded.

"They got a phone?"

She thought for a moment. Her brain told her their phone number really quick, but that was the one at home. Home home. The cottage number had words and numbers. "Indian 769," she said finally.

The boy turned and picked up the black phone on the wall by the cash register. Mattie expected him to dial, but he just listened for a moment and hung up. "No dial tone. Line must be down." He looked out the window at the sheets of rain. "Nobody's going to be driving in that. I guess we'll just have to wait it out. You want an ice cream? On the house. Storm special." He flicked on the light behind the counter.

Mattie made a little surprise sound in the back of her throat and stared. She didn't mean to, and her mother would probably tell her that it wasn't polite, but she couldn't help it. The boy wasn't a boy at all. It was a lady, a grown-up lady dressed in man clothes, with curly hair almost as short as her Dad's, but gray at the sides.

"Do you work for Mr. Bingham?" Mattie asked when she trusted her voice again.

The lady laughed. "Off and on. I'm his sister. Nan Bingham. I come up on weekends to fool around with some new flavors."

Mattie had never seen a lady that looked like that. But she was Mr. Bingham's sister, and Mr. Bingham was really nice. He sometimes gave her a wink and put jimmies on her cone without her even asking. So maybe his sister was nice too. It was hard to tell just by looking. "I'm Mattie," she said. "Did you make the butter pecan? It's my favorite, this week."

"Nope, that's an old standard. Good, though. I could give you some of that, or you could try my newest experiment."

Mattie wasn't sure she liked the word *experiment*. It sounded like chemicals and nothing that might taste good. "Are you a scientist or something?"

Nan nodded. "I'm a flavor chemist at Kellogg's down in Battle Creek."

"Wow." Mattie's eyes got big. "Did you invent Froot Loops?"

"'Fraid not," Nan chuckled. "I worked on the cherry flavor, though."

That was pretty neat. Mattie had never wondered about who thought up cereal tastes. "What other flavors can you make?"

"Well, I just finished mixing up a batch of apple pie à la mode. Fred — my brother — will have it up on the board next week, but you can have a sneak preview, if you want."

"I like apple pie," Mattie said.

Nan smiled. "Me too." She took a glass sundae dish off the stack and scooped a small dollop of ice cream into it from a shiny metal cylinder she pulled up out of the big freezer compartment below the counter. She handed the dish and a spoon to Mattie.

"It just looks like vanilla," Mattie said. It did. It was a pale creamy white. She had expected it to be light brown, the color of applesauce. And it was smooth, no chunks of apple like there were pieces of real candy in the peppermint stick ice cream.

"Taste it."

Mattie dipped the spoon into the edge of the mound of ice cream and sliced off a rounded crescent. It was cold and creamy, but as it melted on her tongue, Mattie tasted baking. She tasted soft, syrupy apples and cinnamon. She tasted crust, golden and flaky, and then a bit of cool, smooth vanilla ice cream.

"There's crust," she said in amazement. She ate another spoonful. "How did you *do* that?"

"Well, the chemist answer is that it's a balance of alpha-enol carbonyls with some soluble acetate esters and a squirt or two of ethyl maltol. But I guess you could say that I – " Nan stopped in mid-sentence as a lightning bolt lit up the room, followed almost instantly by a boom of thunder that rattled the front window and slammed the screen door all the way open with a bang. Nan and Mattie both jumped.

"That was a little too close for comfort," Nan said. "I think maybe we'd better go down to the storm cellar. The radio said earlier there might be a tornado watch. We'll be safer down there."

Mattie wasn't sure if that sounded safe or not. She wasn't sure about this chemistry stuff, or about going down into a basement with a kind of weird stranger, even though she seemed nice so far. But she *knew* that lightning and thunder and tornadoes were bad.

The room behind the shop was full of big refrigerators and boxes and counters, lit by a flickering fluorescent fixture over a big metal sink. At the back screen door, Nan held up her hand like a safety patrol person. "Wait here. It's really coming down, and I've got to open the cellar door. When I holler, run!"

Mattie leaned up against a stack of cardboard boxes. She listened as hard as she could, but the rain made so much noise that it was hard to tell whether she heard Nan's voice. She ran anyway. The screen door banged behind her, and then she was outside in more weather than she'd ever been in before. The trees were all bent over and the rain was bouncing off the parking lot higher than her ankles. It hit her body all over, so hard that it stung.

The storm cellar was a few feet to the left, two big wooden doors that opened out, just like in *The Wizard of Oz*. Mattie had always thought that riding the tornado off to Oz would be really fun, but today, as she fought against the wind to get into the cellar, she thought maybe staying in Kansas – or at least Michigan – wasn't such a bad idea after all.

She clattered down the wooden steps into the cellar, and when she was all the way down, Nan pulled the doors shut and shot the big iron bolt home with a bang. It was pitch dark and the rain sounded very far away. The cellar was cool and smelled like dirt and iron and old vegetables. Mattie knocked over something that rang like metal on the cement floor and was just about to be scared when Nan pulled a chain and a single light bulb lit up the cellar.

Stacked along one wall were more cardboard boxes, some marked GLASS and some marked PERISHABLE and one marked XMAS. Another wall was wooden shelves with glass dishes and jars of canned fruit and a jumble of kitchen utensils and fix-it tools. The last wall looked like a laboratory – a tall stool next to a long, high table with test tubes and burners and flasks. A stainless steel cabinet sat at one end, and a battered old armchair at the other.

Mattie's basketball shirt was soaked through and clung to her body like Saran Wrap, all the way to her knees. Her sneakers made squishy noises when she walked. Nan's hair was plastered to her head and water ran down her face and her legs. Through her sodden white shirt Mattie could see the outline of a bra. That embarrassed her and she looked away quickly.

"Let me see if I can find you a clean towel," Nan said. "It won't help a whole lot, but at least you can dry your hair." She rummaged in a drawer in the lab table and tossed Mattie a pale green hand towel with a blue B embroidered on it. It didn't look like a science kind of towel at all.

Nan rubbed her own hair dry. "Have a seat," she said, pointing to the armchair.

"Is this where you make the flavors of ice cream and cereal and stuff?"

"Sometimes. That's what I do at my job, anyway. But down here I like to play around with flavors that Kellogg's would never use."

"You make yucky flavors?"

"Sometimes it works out that way," Nan laughed. "There are a lot of experiments that just don't end up how I hoped. But what I'm really trying to do is…" She paused for a minute. "I've never tried to explain this to anybody. I guess it's that what I do at work is all science. And what I do here is more of a hobby, like art, like I'm painting with flavors." She paused again and looked at Mattie. "Does that make any sense?"

"Not exactly. Do you mean you use food instead of paint to make pictures? Or like it's a painting you can really eat?"

Nan sighed. "No. It's…" She shook her head. "I can't explain it in words. You have to taste it. Do you want to? It's just flavor. It's not mixed in with ice cream or anything."

"I guess so." Mattie had never heard of anything like tasting pictures, or flavor without ice cream, and her stomach felt funny. It was kind of exciting, but scary too, like jumping off the high diving board at the pool. "But not a yucky one."

"Not yucky at all, I promise. Hold on." Nan went over to the steel cabinet. It opened with a soft hiss. She put on her glasses and looked at a list on the inside of the door for a minute, then picked up a small white cup. "I think you'll like this one," she said.

"What is it?"

"Taste it and see if you can guess." She handed the cup to Mattie.

It was a little paper cup, not a Dixie cup, but the pleated kind that tartar sauce came in at the drive-in. It felt cool in her hand. Inside was puffy stuff that was almost white, but not quite. It looked like a cloud. Mattie put the tip of her finger into it. She expected it to feel like whipped cream, or maybe marshmallow fluff. But it didn't. It didn't feel like anything. It just felt cool, and swirled around her finger like fog.

"Tip the cup, just a little, over your hand," Nan said.

Mattie did, and watched the white stuff start to drift very slowly over the edge. It poured a lot thicker than it looked.

"Now pour it onto your tongue."

Mattie hesitated for a moment, then lifted the rolled edge of the paper cup to her lips. She tipped it and felt something cool, like whipped air, flow onto her tongue. Then there were flavors.

They changed and mixed and separated as the stuff flowed back on her tongue and down her throat. She tasted a fuzzy sweetness, then coconut and a salty tang, then a different, sharper sweet and a bit of burnt and smoke and way in the back of her mind she thought about her father mowing the grass.

The flavors lingered for a minute before fading, bit by bit, until all she could taste was mouth again. She licked her lips and peered into the paper cup. It was empty and just barely damp on the bottom.

Mattie tried to put a name to what she'd tasted, but her brain wouldn't give her a word. "Wow. What flavor *was* that?"

"What did it make you think of?" Nan was sitting up on the table, one foot propped on the stool.

"Lots of things, I guess. Drinking a coke, and going swimming and being too hot and putting on suntan lotion. And then I thought about barbecuing hamburgers and my dad mowing the lawn. You know, summer stuff."

Nan smiled and clapped her hands. Her eyes were shining like she was maybe going to cry, except that she looked too happy. "Turn the cup over," she said.

On the bottom, in pencil, it said SUMMER AFTERNOON.

"But summer's not a flavor," Mattie said.

"You just tasted it, didn't you?"

"Yeah, but…"

"But when you think about flavors, you think chocolate, or strawberry, or maybe barbecue potato chips, right?"

"Yeah. And this was more like a movie that went from my tongue to my brain. It was…" Mattie stopped talking or breathing for a minute, then said, very slowly, "It was what you said. It was like pictures I could taste."

Nan smiled. "Well, that's what I do down here."

"Wow." Mattie looked at Nan with admiration. "How did you figure out how to do that?"

"First I went to school for a long time." Nan leaned back against a bare spot on the wall.

"Chemistry stuff?"

"Mostly. And physiology. How people's bodies work."

"Oh." Mattie rolled that idea around for a minute. "Like taste buds?"

"Yep. And a few other things. What do you know about taste buds?"

Mattie bit her lip. "We had them in school. They're the bumpy parts of your tongue, and they tell your brain what you're eating. Some of them can taste salty, and some can taste sour, and some can taste sweet, and the rest taste stuff like coffee. I don't like coffee."

"Because it tastes yucky to you, right?"

"Yeah." Mattie made a face.

"And yucky things don't make you feel good."

"Of course not."

"See, there you go. But feeling good isn't a taste or a flavor. It's an emotion." Nan looked down at her lap for a minute. "That's what fascinates me about tastes and smells. Each taste bud has about fifty different receptors, and they're all connected with two different parts of your brain. One is the part that thinks and the other is the part that *feels*. So a taste can be just a taste, like the cherry flavor in Froot Loops, but it can also bring up emotions and memories. Like a summer afternoon."

"If you made summer-flavored ice cream, would it taste like the stuff in the little cup?" Mattie asked.

"I suppose. But I don't think Fred would have many customers asking for it."

"I would," Mattie said quickly. "Well, maybe not in the summer, 'cause it's happening then already. And we don't come here in the winter. But if I could get some to go, I'd put it in the freezer at home, and eat summer in the winter, when it's cold and I can't go outside, just to remember."

Nan smiled. "Well, if you want to come back some weekend next month, I'll make up a batch, just for you, to take home."

"I'd like that. It would be like a late birthday present."

"When's your birthday?"

"The day after tomorrow," Mattie said. "I'm going to be nine."

"Nine, huh? Are you going to have a party?"

Mattie shook her head. "Probably not. My dad has to leave tomorrow, on account of working, and he won't be up again until Friday, and by then it won't be my birthday anymore. My mom said that on my real birthday she'll drive me and all three of my brothers to the place with the fried clams, over in Lake City, but that's not exactly a party."

"What about your friends?"

"They're all at home in Grand Rapids. Nobody's my friend on the lake this summer. They're all boys or else they're old."

Nan looked at her for a minute and smiled a sad-looking smile. "I know the feeling. That's kind of how it is for me at work, being a chemist." She stood up and stretched. "I'd guess that I fall into your 'old' category, but I'd be pleased to have you as a friend. If you want."

"Okay," Mattie agreed.

"And if we're friends, then I ought to give you a birthday present, right?"

Mattie nodded. "Summer ice cream."

"No. You've already tried that. Besides, it *is* kind of a waste to eat it in July. For your birthday, I'd like to give you a really special flavor. One that I wouldn't share with just anybody."

"That would be very neat," Mattie said seriously. It was the first birthday present she thought she'd be excited about opening. "But if it's ice cream, then my brothers will probably find it in our freezer and eat it all."

"Don't worry. It's just flavor. I've got some little jars with screw-on lids that I use to take samples back and forth between here and my lab at work. You can put one in your pocket and it'll be your secret. Your brothers will never know."

She rummaged around at the back of the table and came up with a small blue glass jar. She put her glasses on again, picked up a pen, and wrote something on a white label, then licked the back of the paper and stuck it onto the jar. Mattie couldn't see what it said.

Nan opened the cabinet and scanned the list on the door. She reached way back to the back of the top shelf, so far that Mattie could only see her shoulders. Then she emerged again with another white paper cup in her hand. "This is the last of this batch," Nan said. She screwed off the jar lid, and slowly poured out the thick white cloud of flavor until the cup was empty, then screwed the lid back on.

"Happy birthday, Mattie." Nan handed her the jar.

It felt cool in Mattie's hand. The glass was dark blue and reminded her of Vicks. She turned it around and read the label, printed in neat capital letters: MAGIC.

"But…but…" Mattie stared at the jar and then up at Nan.

"What's a scientist know about magic?" Nan shrugged. "Look around, kiddo. The world is an amazing place. The stuff we can explain is what we call science. But all the rest — "

"What does it taste like?"

"I can't really tell you. It will taste like whatever is magic to you. The last time for me was like walking in the door of a kitchen where the most wonderful food I'd ever dreamed of was simmering on the stove, made with spices whose names I didn't know, all jumbled together so there might have been two or three or twenty. There was a little bit of something golden, just on the back of my tongue, mixed with a touch of danger that faded into a warm sweetness, like toffee made on another planet." Nan smiled. "It's different every time."

Mattie looked at the jar in her hand. "This is the best present I've ever gotten in my whole life." She gave Nan a hug and tucked the jar into her pocket.

"Enjoy it, kiddo. I hope — " Nan was interrupted by a loud banging on the cellar door.

"Nan? Nan? Storm's passed on through. You okay down there?" It was Mr. Bingham.

"Just fine, Fred." Nan yelled and went over to push aside the iron bolt. The door was flung open from the outside, and pale afternoon light flooded into the cellar. Outside, little wisps of steam were coming off the pavement, and the air felt soft and clean, as if the earth had just done laundry.

Mattie's mother grabbed her in a tight hug as soon as she was up the stairs. She smelled like hairspray and beauty shop chemicals. "Oh, baby, I was so worried. I waited in Lake City til the storm was over, and when I got home, your dad said he'd told you to go down to Miller's."

"Bob Miller closed up early. But Mattie did the right thing," Nan said. "Saw my OPEN sign and got herself in out of the rain. We went down to the cellar when it really started to let fly."

Mattie wriggled loose from the hug and watched her mother look hard at her new friend, trying to decide if it was okay to like Nan or not. She finally put out her hand. "Well, thank you. I'm Eileen Rodgers. I don't think we've met."

Nan shook hands. "Nan Bingham."

"Nan's my sister. Works down at the Kellogg plant. She's a food chemist." Fred said proudly.

"Oh. Isn't that interesting," Mattie's mother said. There was a moment of awkward silence, then she turned back to Mattie. "Well, let's get you home and out of those wet clothes. The station wagon's parked over at Miller's."

Mattie waved goodbye to Nan and they walked across the parking lot. When they came to the edge of the highway, her mother reached down to take Mattie's hand.

"Mom," Mattie said, shaking her head, "You said I'm a big girl now." Her mother made a face that was half a smile and half a frown, but let her hand drop back to her side. As they crossed the yellow line, Mattie curled her fingers tighter around the jar of magic in her pocket and smiled at the clouds moving off to the east.

Ringing Up Baby

NANNY SAYS that I am spoiled. It comes from being an only child, and not having to share holidays or cakes and always getting to sit by the window. If I had a little brother or sister, I would learn responsibility. More work for her, she sighs, but she is only thinking of my character. Thinking about me is Nanny's job.

Of course, Mother is far too busy to have a baby right now, what with the Henderson case and all. (When I have supper with her, on Wednesdays, she talks about nothing but the Henderson case.) So Nanny has arranged for a nice lady to plant Mother's egg and do all the messy parts, then give the baby to us when it's done.

"What would you like," Nanny asks me over cocoa. "A brother or a sister?"

I have to think for a moment, but only a little, because a brother would be a pest and get into my best things, like Courtney Taylor's brother Robby, who programmed her mobile phone to ring with a nasty farting sound. A sister is someone I can be the boss of.

"A sister, please," I say in my sweet voice. Nanny *loves* my sweet voice.

Nanny touches a box on the wall screen, and it glows bright pink. "Birthday?" she asks, her finger not quite touching the screen, but ready.

My birthday is in June. "October," I say after a minute, because I've had to count in my head, so her party won't get in the way of Christmas, either.

"Excellent," says Nanny. "We can place our order now." She taps her finger on the screen. That box glows red.

"What else can we pick?" There are a lot of boxes. I finish my cocoa and stand right next to Nanny, who smells like Vermont today. A nice cool green smell.

She begins to read to me, scrolling slowly down.

"Hair color?"

"Brown." Mine is honey blond.

"Eyes?"

Mine are blue, so brown again.

"Intelligence?"

I have to think about that. I don't want a sister who's *stupid*, but if she's smarter than me, she will be difficult to boss.

"Above average," Nanny decides. "Good at math?"

Hmm. I'm in second grade, and we're doing the times tables. That could be useful. But it probably isn't something she'll be able to do right away.

So I shrug, which is a mistake, because Nanny is very strict about manners and posture and I have to listen to a lecture before she will tap the bottom of the screen and scroll to the next page of baby parts.

This page is less interesting because the words are very long and I don't know what they mean. Bioimmunity. Cholesterol. Neuro-muscular. I stare at the screen with my eyes very wide so that I don't yawn out loud.

On the side of the screen is a list, like the menu on the Emirate of Toys site, which I used by myself last year for my Christmas wants. The baby list is not very long. Babies only come in about six colors — we're getting one that matches Mother and me. Humans are a lot less interesting than Legos or iBots.

Nanny reads me all the diseases you can ask your baby not to have. Most of them are options, she says, which means we have to pay more. But I think we should pick them all, because a sick sister is not a good thing. Angela Xhobi's sister has asthma, because she was made the old-fashioned way, without a menu, and she gets *all* the attention. I wouldn't like that.

Nanny takes a breath for another lecture, but I am saved when the iVid sings the Phone Call Song. Nanny sighs again and when she says, "Connect," I see that it's her mother, who calls every afternoon. Mrs. Nanny is quite deaf, even with her implants, so Nanny taps SAVE on the baby screen and goes downstairs where she can shout without me hearing all the words. "Little pitchers," she says to her mother as she grays the upstairs iVid. I don't know what that means.

I slump back into my chair, because Nanny isn't here to tell me not to, and because she will be gone a long time. Her mother always has a lot to say. I stare at all the diseases, and then I see a better word at the bottom of the screen. PETS.

We don't harbor animals, because Nanny is allergic. (She was made the old-fashioned way, too.) But I'd like to see what we *could* have. I touch the screen to scroll down for more pets, and a Bubble Man appears to tell me about a special offer. His picture seems to come out of the wall and stand right in front of me.

"Jellyfish DNA on sale," the Bubble Man says. He takes off his top hat, pulls a rabbit out of it, and holds it out toward me. The rabbit's fur glows a soft, bright green.

"Wow," I say.

"Bioluminescence, fifty percent off. Today only. Touch Box 306a to order!" He steps back into the screen and disappears with a little picture of smoke.

It only takes me a minute to find Box 306a and tap it to red. Then I SAVE and scroll back up to the disease boxes. It is good to leave things just the way you found them.

I sit very straight in my chair, humming, because I know a secret. Once I have my baby sister, I will never need my night-light again.

Nanny will be so proud.

Guys Day Out

ANDREW CLEMENS had always wanted a son.

A boy to take fishing, share ice cream right out of the carton, play baseball on a Saturday afternoon.

He got Tommy.

Tommy had a sweet smile, spatulate fingers, soft-focus eyes.

"Mongoloid," the doctor said. "Sorry, Andy. But he's mentally retarded. He may never get beyond simple tasks like dressing himself."

Andrew was silent for a minute. "When can I see him?"

"It's not a good idea." The doctor shook his head. "He should be in an institution, and you don't want to get attached. They're fine places, really. It's 1960, not the dark ages. But it'll be easier on Helen if she doesn't know, if you sign the papers before she comes out of the anesthetic." He patted Andrew on the shoulder. "Give her a few weeks, let her rest, then try again. It's for the best."

"I want to see my son," Andrew said. "I'll take my family home."

⌒

"Are you sure he can handle this?" Helen asked.

"C'mon. He's ten. It's Guys Day Out. He's been excited about it all week. I'm not going to try to teach him to cast or anything. I got him a bamboo pole and a carton of worms."

"What about the hook? He could – "

"Sweetie, he'll be fine." Andrew kissed his wife on the cheek. "I'll put the worm on the hook for him, I'll make sure he keeps his life jacket on the whole time. He's going to have a ball."

"I don't want a ball. I want to see *fish*." Tommy trudged down the stairs in a striped t-shirt and jeans, his wide moon face in a determined grin under his Detroit Tigers baseball cap. A Boy Scout knapsack, insignia faded, weighed down his left shoulder; his soft, stocky body canted in compensation.

"Hey, Buddy," said Andrew. He reached up and swung the boy off the last two steps. "We're going to see fish, all right. You about ready to go?"

Tommy nodded several times. "I packed my backsack with *everything*." He bent over and lifted the flap. "I have my toothbrush and a dime and my lib'ary book and three pens and two green socks." He looked at his mother. "My feet could get wet. I don't like that."

"That's very good planning," she said.

"I know. And I have my radio and some Lifesavers and a banana in case of Amy or David get hungry."

Andrew laughed. "And here I thought it was just going to be the two of us. Are all twenty-six of your invisible friends coming along?"

"Daddy." Tommy put his hands on his hips and rolled his eyes. "They won't *all* fit in there. Just Amy, Cathy, David, Edie, and Frank." He thought for a minute. "And Xner, Yackie, and Zelda, because sometimes they don't get a turn. They're at the end. Brian can *not* come. He was bad again, so he is locked in his room all day with no food."

"Pretty stiff punishment."

"He was *bad*." Tommy pushed the flap of the knapsack closed. "Can we go now?"

"As soon as we get our lunch out of the icebox, we're on the road."

"I get baloney with mustard and no – *pickles*." He stuck out his tongue.

"Absolutely. And Fritos and Hostess cupcakes," his mother said. "Coca-Cola in the green bottles. I know what my fellas like." She lifted up the bill of his cap and kissed his dark hair. "Have a great time, little man. I'll miss you."

"I'm going to see fish." Tommy tugged his cap back into place and picked up his knapsack, slinging it almost over his shoulder. He headed for the garage.

The man at the dock took Andrew's deposit and winched a battered green rowboat down onto the concrete ramp that slanted into the lake.

"I close at 6:30," he said. "It's shallow past the island, on accounta the drought, so don't get stuck."

"I think we can handle that," Andrew said. He put his tackle box, rods, and the plaid thermos cooler into the boat and reached back a hand for Tommy.

"I never rented to one of them before. You ain't gonna let *him* row, are ya?"

"No. I'm not." Andrew bit his lip against saying anything more and lifted his son into the boat. He tugged on the straps of the orange life jacket, pulling them snug, and rested his knuckles, just for a moment, on the pale, smooth skin of the boy's cheek. "Good to go, Buddy?"

Tommy gave him a thumbs-up and grinned. "Let's go see fish."

Andrew pushed off with one oar and sat down, his back to the boat man. He began to row, the rounded haft of the wood rough against his hands until he found his rhythm.

The lake was wide and glass-smooth, the sun glinting on the ripples from the oars. The hum of a distant outboard motor echoed off the trees. Tommy sat with his arms tight at his sides for ten minutes before stretching a tentative hand over the gunwale and letting his fingertips drag through the brown-green water.

"It's cold! I got goose bumps."

"Yep."

"Do fish get goose bumps?"

"I don't think so. Fish are pretty well adapted to living down there."

"That's good," said Tommy. "If they get too cold they swim upside down like the goldfish that died in my class."

Andrew rowed for half an hour until they came to a bank overhung by the roots of a dying oak tree, cicadas buzzing high in the branches. He angled the boat toward the shore. "Let's see how they're biting, okay?"

Tommy jerked his hand out of the water and cradled it in his lap. "I don't want them to bite me."

"No, no, no. Sorry. They don't bite people. Only bugs. That's what they eat."

"*I* eat baloney." Tommy peered into the water but kept his hands in his lap.

Andrew tied a round red-striped bobber onto the line of the bamboo pole, about three feet above the hook. He opened the white cardboard tub of worms, digging through the moss for a thick red tail.

"Eeeeuuuw," said Tommy. "Slimy worms."

"Yeah, but fish eat 'em like candy." Andrew twisted the worm into a loose knot and reached for the hook.

"Worm candy. Ick. Ick. Ick." Tommy scrunched his entire face into a grimace of disgust. "I don't want it." He backed away, huddled against the far side of the boat. "I don't want it, Daddy."

"Okay. You don't have to touch it. See?" Andrew dropped the worm back into the carton with a sigh. "You can watch while I set up my gear." He slid his fiberglass rod from its case and snapped the reel onto the shaft, threading a length of monofilament through the guides. He selected a fly from his tackle box and tied it to the loose end.

"That is not a worm," Tommy said. He scooted closer, his face curious.

"Nope. It's a trout fly. A Royal Coachman. I tied it myself, last weekend."

"People can not make flies."

"You are correct, sir. Not real flies. I make these to fool the fish into *thinking* it's a fly, so they'll try to bite it."

"Can I have one? Instead of a *worm*?"

"Let me see what else I've got." Andrew inventoried his wet flies. "Ah, here we go. Dragonfly. You'll like this one." He held out his palm and showed Tommy an inch-long creation of green and blue feathers wrapped tightly with teal silk floss.

"It looks like a fairy," Tommy said, his eyes wide. "Maybe I can fool *them* and catch a real one." His face creased into a wide grin.

Andrew started to shake his head, stopped. "You can try," he smiled. He clipped the barb off the hook and attached a teardrop-shaped lead sinker to the shaft, tying it a few feet below the bobber. He put the butt of the pole into Tommy's hands.

"Now what?" Tommy grasped the bamboo with a white-knuckle grip.

"Now I throw the bobber into the water." He tossed the plastic sphere with an overhand flick. "Watch. The dragonfl – the fairy – will sink down, but the bobber floats on top."

"I can't see anything. The water is too shiny."

"I forgot." Andrew pulled a pair of sunglasses from the top pocket of his fishing vest. "Polarized, just like mine." He pointed to the green lenses clipped to the frames of his wire-rims. "They let you see what's under the surface."

"They're magic glasses?" Tommy asked, putting his on. They slid down a bit on his small, flat nose.

Andrew thought for a minute before he nodded. "Pretty much." Easier than trying to explain the components of reflected light. He pulled the line up until the dragonfly cleared the water, then let it drop again. The fly was a pale gleam as it sank.

"I can see the fairy swimming!" Tommy shouted. He watched with open-mouthed fascination.

Andrew smiled and picked up his rod. He cast, whipping the line back and forth until the Royal Coachman sailed through the air and touched the water, thirty feet away, with barely a ripple.

He glanced at Tommy between casts. The boy sat unmoving, unwavering, fierce attention focused on the plastic bobber as it drifted gently.

"I need to put down my fishing pole," he said after fifteen minutes.

"Sure. There's a tube on the side of the boat to hold it. You need to stretch, huh?"

"No. Yackie and Zelda want to slide down the string, and I have to have both my hands to get them."

"I didn't know they could swim," Andrew said.

"They can do anything they want because they're b'visible." Tommy set the pole and reached into his knapsack, cupping both hands around a secret cargo, fragile and precious.

"But you can see them."

"Yeah. *I'm* special. Like special ed, you know." Tommy leaned over the side of the boat and submerged both hands next to the bobber. He released his invisible friends and stared into the water for a full minute before straightening up.

"They got down okay. When they are done, I'll pull them up and give them some banana."

"Done with what? What are they going to do down there?"

"Talk to the fairies."

"Oh. What will they talk about?" Andrew made a long, lazy cast. The fly began to drift back as soon as it touched the water.

"Mommy says that fairies make up dreams for me," Tommy said. "Zelda wants some too."

"Fair enough." Andrew pulled his line in. "Speaking of bananas, I'm about ready for a snack. What about you?"

"I have a light snack at four o'clock."

"Right. Then how about lunch now?"

"Lunch is at twelve noon."

Andrew looked at his watch. "It's 11:30, but it's Guys Day Out. No rules. We can eat anytime we want."

"Lunch is at twelve *noon*," Tommy said.

Andrew sighed.

They ate half an hour later.

When Tommy had finished the last of his cupcake, Andrew wiped the ear-to-ear chocolate smears with a damp paper towel. "It's getting hot," he said. "Pull your line up and we'll head down to the other end, see if we can find a shadier spot for the rest of the afternoon."

"Yackie and Zelda are not back yet."

"Well, tell them the boat is leaving in five minutes."

"Daddy, they're not done with — "

"Five minutes, Thomas."

"But the fairies haven't...," Tommy mumbled, his face closing into a pout. He turned away, and Andrew didn't catch the rest. He glanced at his watch. Four and a half minutes later he heard a deep sigh. The boy reached over the side and rapped his knuckles on the bobber, jiggling it. He cupped his hands below the surface, as if waiting for underwater communion, then brought them up, thumbs tight together. He breathed gently into the hollow.

"They are dry now. Can you open my backsack for me?"

Andrew reached across and lifted the khaki canvas flap. "There you go."

Tommy let his invisible passengers tumble from his hands onto the yellow curve of the banana, then wiped his palms on the legs of his jeans. "I didn't catch a fairy."

"Not this time. The fish weren't biting either. Maybe we'll have better luck at the next spot."

Andrew stowed their gear along the side of the rowboat and unshipped the oars. The lake smelled of damp earth and green plants. They stopped again half a mile down the shore, tying the boat up in a shaded inlet, and pulled sweat-beaded Cokes from the melting ice in the bottom of the cooler. Tommy sank the dragonfly again, and watched the bobber intently until his four o'clock snack. Then he yawned and folded into a fetal curl in the bottom of the boat, his head pillowed on his knapsack, his eyelids drooping into sleep.

Andrew tilted the Tigers cap over the boy's nose, already pink from the sun, covered him with a rain poncho, and stepped out onto the riverbank.

A deep, shadowed pool a few yards away looked promising. He threaded a Green Caddis Fly onto his line and fished for two hours, catching a rainbow trout and two small striped bass on barbless hooks. He released each back into the shallows.

When the sun dipped below the trees, casting long shadows across the water, he climbed back into the boat without waking the boy and rowed silently through the growing dusk. The surface dimpled as fish began to feed on the evening hatch, clouds of tiny insects just visible in the fading light. In the fringes of tall weeds and grasses along the bank, the first fireflies rose, twinkling yellow-green.

Tommy turned over and muttered, half-awake.

"Hey, get up, Buddy. You ought to see this."

"Wha – ?" Tommy sat up and pushed his baseball cap off his head, wiping the sleep from the corners of his eyes. He looked around for a moment, his face puckered in confusion, then saw his father and smiled.

"Look over there." Andrew pointed to the flickering lights on the bank. "Lightning bugs."

"Fairies," Tommy said in a matter-of-fact tone. "They have to fly my dreams home before I can go to sleep." He climbed into Andrew's lap and snuggled under his arm. "I had fun. Even if I didn't catch one."

Andrew kissed the top of Tommy's head and rowed back to the dock in awkward joy.

———

They fished every summer. Helen came along a few times, swaddled in long sleeves and sun hat, but mostly it was Guys Day Out. Winter evenings, in his den, Andrew laid out feathers, fur, and gossamer thread and hand-tied artificial creatures – Leadwings and Caddis for trout, elaborate dragonfly variations for Tommy's fairies.

Tommy's voice cracked and deepened; he began to shave. For six months he struggled, stubble patching his cheeks where he had missed spots, or just forgot. Easier to leave it be. Andrew let his own beard grow, like father, like son, and was startled in the mirror by more salt than pepper.

At twenty-two, Tommy graduated from the County Training Center. In the photo on Andrew's desk, Thomas Matthew Clemens is a soft, beaming fireplug of a man with bashful oriental eyes. His arm is draped across the wheelchair of his best friend, Patrick, whose head lolls to one side, his twisted body held upright by a nylon strap in blue and gold – the school colors.

The county found him a job in a restaurant, washing endless tablecloths and napkins in an industrial machine, for minimum wage. After eighteen months, the restaurant went broke. Tommy went home and watched cartoons and *Gilligan's Island* until his caseworker assigned him to another job, and then a third.

The year Helen got sick, he went to work at the McDonald's on Archer Avenue, twenty minutes on the bus. His red nametag said TOM in white letters, his grown-up name. He smiled at every customer, filled the ketchup-packet bin, and wiped tables with green disinfectant that smelled like the hospital he was afraid to visit again.

"Just us now, Buddy," Andrew said after the funeral.

Tommy nodded. "Guys Day Out, every day."

But it wasn't. Every day wasn't fishing. It was waiting for the number 20 bus at 8:53 in his red-and-yellow uniform, home on the number 16, in time for *Scooby Doo*. Every day flowed into every other, until he had been at McDonald's fifteen years, awarded a golden arches to pin beneath his TOM.

Tommy left work one Thursday afternoon and walked to the bus stop. He sat in the shelter, his bus pass in his pocket — Handicapped Adult, Reduced Fare — waiting for the number 16 to come. Number 34. Number 44. No 16. He zipped his windbreaker to his chin when the rain began, and got on the next bus, his white sneakers wet and squeaking on the rubber mats. He rode to the end of the line without seeing his stop, so he rode back again. Nothing looked familiar.

"You gonna get off or what, buddy?" the bus driver growled.

"Only Daddy calls me Buddy," Tommy said.

"Nut case." The driver used his walkie-talkie to call in. The policeman met them at the last stop. He took one look and his face softened. "What's your name, son?"

"Tommy. Tom. Tom Clemens."

"Do you know your phone number, Tom? Is there someone we can call?"

He nodded. "My dad is at my house. It's two-six-nine — " Tommy's face wrinkled in thought. "Two-six-nine — " He closed his eyes. "Two-six-nine — " But he couldn't remember the rest.

"Can't be too many Clemenses at that prefix," the policeman said. "Dispatch can find it." He talked into the radio on his shoulder. Andrew arrived twenty minutes later and took Tommy home.

The next Tuesday, at work, Tommy put mustards in the ketchup bin and went on his lunch break half an hour after he clocked in. Mr. Barnett, his manager, sat him down to have a little chat.

"This isn't like you, Tom. Your one of my most dependable guys. But you're not paying attention. Are you getting enough sleep?"

"I go to bed at 10:30," Tommy said. "Eleven, if it is Saturday."

"Well, be more careful from now on, okay?"

"Okey-dokey." Tommy gave him a thumbs-up and watched very carefully that afternoon when he mopped the entrance floor and filled the napkin dispensers.

A week later, Marcus, the black teenager who worked the drive-up window, bumped into him accidentally. Tommy dropped his Big Mac; lettuce and secret sauce splashed across the floor.

"Fuck you, you fucking fucker," he shouted. He hurled a stack of supersize drink cups at Marcus. They flew onto the warming racks and spattered into the deep fryer. Everyone at the counter stopped and stared. Tommy stood motionless, his arms rigid at his sides, his mouth open and slack, eyes vacant.

The ringing phone woke Andrew from an afternoon nap. "We've got a problem," Mr. Barnett said. "You'll have to come get Tom."

⌣

"Alzheimer's," said Tom's doctor. "I'm sorry, Mr. Clemens. I could run some tests for you, but the symptoms are all there." He ticked them off on his fingers. "Memory loss, confusion, violent outbursts. What we used to call senile dementia."

"I'm seventy-six," Andrew said. "*I* should worry. But he's only forty-three."

The doctor nodded. "It's unfair. But I'm afraid every Down Syndrome adult over forty experiences this sort of premature aging."

Andrew looked at his hands for a long time before he spoke. "So what are the treatment options?"

"There really aren't any. Tom may have four or five years left, but he'll continue to lose function. I can make some calls if you want – facilities with units for the memory-impaired. They're good places. He'll be comfortable."

"No," said Andrew. "I'll take care of my boy. I always have."

⌣

"Dinner's ready, Buddy," Andrew stood in the doorway of the living room. "Meatloaf and your favorite – smashed potatoes."

Tommy sat on the rug, watching *Finding Nemo* for the third time in two days, a thin line of drool silver in the lamplight, a dark stain spreading down the leg of his Dockers.

"Tom? Do you need to take a whizz?"

Tommy looked down at himself. "No. I already did." He turned back to the cartoon.

His father took his hand and led him upstairs. Sponged him off, changed his clothes. After dinner, he drove to the drugstore for a carton of Depends, size extra-large.

Andrew diapered his bearded boy for a week, his tears soaking into the absorbent layers. Tommy lay placid on the bed, 170 pounds of toddler, humming tunelessly to himself.

"Okay, good to go," Andrew said that Friday night. Tommy pulled up his elastic pants and shambled downstairs. A few minutes later the theme song from *The Brady Bunch* blared from the TV. Andrew went to his den and tied half a dozen dragonflies, surprised he still remembered how. Blue feathers, lead shot, gossamer wings, teal silk thread.

"Hey, Buddy," he said, walking into the living room. "Tomorrow's Saturday. Let's go look at fish."

He called the marina at the lake, reserved a dingy with an outboard motor. Just half a day. He made Tommy's favorite lunch – bologna sandwiches, Fritos, cupcakes with fudge-dark icing – and put them in a white foam cooler with a six-pack of Bud Lite.

Mid-afternoon, a blond-haired college boy, State U. sweatshirt cut ragged at the shoulders, drove a trailer down the concrete ramp and slid the boat into the lake.

"There you go, Gramps," he said, handing Andrew the outboard key. "We close at 6:30."

Andrew sat in the stern, hand on the throttle, watching Tommy trail his fingers through the water and eat Fritos from the bag with his other hand. Summer houses crowded the lakeshore now, and it took forty-five minutes before Andrew found an unpopulated inlet.

He anchored the boat and assembled his rod, tied a Royal Coachman on his line. He cast into the shallows for an hour, catching nothing. Tommy sat on the bank, legs sprawled, his back against a willow. He ate three sandwiches, mustard smearing yellow-bright against his beard.

"Uh-oh," he said.

"What?"

"Brian was bad again," Tommy said. "Brian wet himself."

"I'll be right there."

Andrew's eyes blurred with tears. He took two Bud Lites from the cooler, pulling the pop-tops back. Beer, because Tommy liked the way the bubbles tickled, liked to drink what TV men did. Beer because it would mask the taste of the tablets Andrew dropped in, one by one, all twenty-six.

"Drink up, Buddy," he said, climbing slowly up onto the bank. He handed Tom a can.

In the tall grass around them, fireflies began to rise in the twilight, twinkling yellow-green.

"Look. Fairies." Andrew's voice cracked. "Can you count the fairies for me, Tommy? Can you count out loud?"

At thirty-six, Tommy's head began to droop. At forty-one the empty beer can tumbled to the ground.

"Oh." Tommy's eyes opened wide, his face creased into a wide grin. He cupped both hands around a secret, fragile cargo for just a moment, then slid boneless down the willow.

Andrew settled next to him, hugged him tight, and drank the second bitter beer. He kissed his son's cheek one last time and lay the string of dragonflies on Tommy's wrist, bright against the pale, soft flesh.

"Sweet dreams," he whispered, and he closed his eyes.

Portable Childhoods

"That girl I once was? I thought I'd left her behind,
but discover that she travels always with me, both
baggage and treasure chest."
  — W. M. JANEWAY

1 Knuckles

THE FIRST TIME I saw the child, she was bright red and covered with the
pastry cream that no one but the mother and the folks at the hospital
ever get to see. She was squalling her lungs out, and I was too tired to
be anything but relieved that she was finally out and okay and that my
labor was over.

Looking at her now, sitting at the kitchen table, doing her math
homework, the edge of her tongue peeking out of the left side of her
mouth as she tries to concentrate, it's hard to believe that I could once
carry her like a football in the crook of my arm, that I once spent a
whole morning marveling that she had knuckles.

Knuckles.

I never thought about her knuckles before she was born. Her hands,
yes, and those only in the abstract. But there they were, tiny hands
with tiny knuckles. How did I know how to grow knuckles? Much less
how to put them together in the right way so that her little fist could
open and close so tightly around my enormous finger?

She had bright blue eyes then, now darkened to a greenish hazel,
and hair that was auburn, almost reddish; unless she's in the bright sun
for a few hours, it masquerades as brown these days.

She looks up to catch me staring at her. "Why are you looking at me
goofy?"

"I was thinking about the day you were born, and how tiny you were, and what a miracle it was that this person came from me."

"Oh."

No interest at all this afternoon. A few years ago, she went through a phase of endless curiosity about her own beginnings. We looked at baby pictures, some blurry, haphazard videos, a few tiny clothes I keep in the cedar chest, just to remember. But today, this almost-nine-year-old is much more interested in fractions than in my nostalgia for an infant she never knew.

It strikes me as so odd that she never knew the baby, my baby, who somehow became her. I know both of them so well. It's too abstract a thought, too convoluted and philosophical. I get up to start chopping vegetables for dinner.

A neighbor with a green thumb booned me with zucchini and tomatoes and some fresh peas that I'm going to turn into something with pasta. I cut off the ends of the zukes and start chopping them into a coarse dice. It's a rhythmic, unconscious motion, and as my hands work, my mind wanders over to peer at the child and think about the baby.

One and the same. Entirely different. Those first days she seemed so fragile, and I marveled at her strength. Tight-gripping fingers, strong sucking on my pinkie. Great mouth muscles. But that's what she was built for, at that particular time.

My mother, I've been told, didn't see me until I was several hours old. She'd had "twilight sleep" for the birth, and so wasn't really there when I was born. Times were different then, I've also been told. But I can't imagine missing that moment. By the time I saw my mother, felt her arms around me, I'd been bathed and poked and prodded and dressed by strangers. In moments when I feel depressed and disconnected, those first hours loom like Calvinist predestination. How could I ever hope to connect with anyone when my first experience involved being passed from hand to hand by professional, competent strangers?

I put the chopped zucchini into a bowl and pour myself a glass of wine, stealing a look at the child, who is paying no attention. Eventually, she too was poked and prodded by similar strangers; that's what they do. But not until she'd lain on my chest, both of us naked and clammy and crying. I cupped her butt in my hand and kissed the top of her head and we stayed there like that, flesh to flesh, until the nurse took her a few feet away to get her measurements.

I read in the paper about babies who are found abandoned in cardboard boxes or dumpsters, wrapped in a blanket but left to depend on the kindness of strangers, or die. I read about the children who abandoned their baby behind the hotel room where he was born, or the girl who left her newborn in the trash in the ladies room and went back to the prom, hoping no one would notice. I know those babies were not wanted or planned; they were impediments to a happy life, not the cornerstone of one. But I cannot imagine meeting my newborn child and abandoning her.

Okay. Truth. When she was teething, there were weeks when I got no sleep and walked around like a zombie, holding my screaming darling and praying for her to just shut up for half an hour. At those times, I did think seriously about trying to rent her out. I thought longingly of nannies and the great convenience of having a clean, sleepy, well-fed baby come to visit me as I lay on the chaise, wearing my pink satin quilted bed-jacket. I would coo at her for a few minutes and then hand her back to Nurse and return to my novel. It was tempting.

But not part of the deal. For every knuckle-admiring, blissful morning spent with the cherubic outpouring of my loins, there were two more with the squalling child who had an ear infection, bad diaper rash, or a dozen other minor ailments that could only be communicated through loud, frustrated, pain-ridden rage. Inarticulate, language-less, yet so expressive.

I look over at the child again, and ask, "How many more problems do you have?" I'm thinking of her homework, although my brain registers the double meaning.

She looks at the xeroxed handout. "One that I'm doing now, one that I haven't done yet, and one that I'm kinda stuck on."

"How 'bout you finish the one you're on and make a salad for us? I'll help you with the stuck one after dinner, if you want."

She bites her lip in thought, then nods. "Do we have any photons?"

It's what she calls croutons. I laughed for ten minutes the first time it came out of her mouth. She was about five. Now sometimes at the grocery, I have to stop myself from asking a clerk what aisle the photons are on, pause long enough to remember they have another name.

"I'm pretty sure there's a box in the cupboard. If not, write them on the list."

She nods again and goes back to her fractions. After a minute she puts down the pencil, gathers up the scratch paper, and moves everything over to "her" section of the counter. She looks in the cupboard. "Nope, we're out."

She walks over to the little chalkboard by the fridge. As she passes, I reach out and take her wrist, lifting her knuckles to my lips, and kiss them gently.

She gives me a startled, slightly annoyed look, and reclaims her hand. "You know, sometimes you're a little strange," she says, and prints PHOTONS at the bottom of the list.

2 *St. Elmo*

It is the feast day of St. Elmo, the child informs me. We are not Catholic. We're not really anything, belong to no church or synagogue or mosque or coven or prayer group. When she asks, we talk about god or religion, but I don't bring it up. She knows that I have a sort of altar in my room. I don't pray in front of it, but I keep little talismans – a silver dollar from the year I was born, a fire opal in matrix, a tiny dried blowfish – on its too-dusty shelf.

In my office, on another dusty shelf, there are many reference books. As a writer, I need to know odd facts. One of the books is the *Penguin Dictionary of Saints*. The child was in one of her Joan of Arc moods the other night and asked if she could look at it. The *Dictionary of Saints* is far more disturbing and violent than the Brothers Grimm, or even *The Godfather*. The saints were tortured, in hideous – although imaginative – ways. But I let her. She's not prone to nightmares, and we've talked about how it's better not to share some things with kids on the playground.

She asks me if St. Elmo is related to the orange guy on Sesame Street, and I tell her I don't think so. Elmo's other name is Erasmus, she explains, but that's dorky. Elmo is cool. She likes to say the name Elmo.

When I was growing up, there was a St. Erasmus High School, a boys' school, in a nearby city. It showed up on the sports page or on TV when their basketball or football teams did especially well. Both the child and I agree that *we'd* rather have letter jackets that said ELMO across the back.

"St. Elmo is mostly known for St. Elmo's fire," the child reads me from the book. "He's the patron saint of sailors because he died by having his intestines wound out of his body on a windlass." She looks at me questioningly and I point her toward the dictionary. She comes back making a face. "It's a gross way to die," she says. "Like winding up the hose on that reel by the back door, except it's your *guts*." I worry sometimes that the Committee on Sound Parenting is going to find out about these breakfast chats the child and I have.

She turns to the back of the book, where all the feast days are listed. Her birthday was yesterday, June first. She is now nine. Her saints are Justin, who was boring and pious and was merely beheaded, and Pamphilus, who was also boring and beheaded, but has a more interesting name. She sighs when she reads me these pathetic choices, like having to choose between liver and turnips.

I tell her that since we're not Catholic, she doesn't have to have a saint at all, that she's not stuck with Justin and Pamphilus. But she likes the idea of her own personal saint, at least this birthday.

"Why couldn't I have been born a day later?" she asks. "Then I could have had Elmo."

I start to tell her I'm sorry, that June first wasn't really my decision. Entirely her choice at that point. But she gets that glazed look on her face and I can tell that she's hearing sounds, but nothing's getting through. *Blah, blah, blah.*

Then I have an idea. "Will you get me the phone book?"

She looks startled and baffled, begins to ask why, then just shrugs. "White or yellow?"

"White."

When she returns, I flip to the front of the book, where all the odd useful information is, and look up how to call foreign countries. I don't want phone numbers or country codes, just the time zones.

"Look," I say after a minute, "Who's in charge of all this saint stuff?"

She thinks for a moment. "The pope guy, I guess."

"Excellent." I smile at that. The pope guy. "And where does the pope guy live?"

"In Italy, I think. That city that's sort of a country."

"The Vatican. Bingo."

She narrows her eyes at me. "So?"

"So you were born in California, on June first, at seven o'clock at night."

Eyes narrow even more. What a *pain* I am. "I know that."

"But…" I let the 'but' dangle in the air just long enough for her to be curious. "But at the Vatican, it was already the middle of the night. Or very early in the morning. The morning of June second."

The child looks puzzled for a minute, then brightens. "So I *can* have St. Elmo! Because where the pope guy lives, I was born on June second, and he'd say (she lowers her voice to a stately growl) 'This child comes into the world on the feast day of the blessed Elmo.'"

I burst out laughing. "Exactly. So Happy St. Elmo's Day."

She smiles and hugs me then, and asks if we can have fish sticks for dinner – in honor of St. Elmo, the patron of sailors and kids who dote on great odd names.

3 *Shuffling*

It's cold and foggy outside. Typical for San Francisco, but not a good combination for a summer Saturday. The child was cheered by the comics, briefly, but fell into a funk after I made her put her breakfast dishes in the dishwasher.

"Now what can I do?"

I refrain, with great restraint, from pointing out that her room is filled with books, craft stuff, a computer, and enough puzzles and games and other oddments to keep any good Victorian child occupied through a blizzard-filled winter. I say none of that, because I hear it in my head in my mother's voice, and that's usually an omen.

"The Giants game is on at noon. They're playing the Rockies."

This appears to be marginally uplifting. She looks at the clock. "It's only nine-thirty. What can I do until *then?*" This is a whine, a genuine, high-pitched whine, not my favorite tone in the child's repertoire. She doesn't choose to practice it often, but it is her tone of choice this morning. And I'm not really up for it.

I'm doing the Jumble and the crossword, avoiding the laundry and a manuscript that I need to copyedit. I don't have to finish it today, but I do need to make a dent in it for a couple of hours. I was eyeing the Giants game as my break, my reward, but that won't happen unless I can shut myself up in my office in the next half hour.

This requires the child to be self-sufficient and play nicely by herself for a while, and she's not on the program. Her arms are crossed over her chest and her lower lip is sticking out in a not-quite scowl. She's in a seriously pissy mood.

I sigh and try to figure out a plan that will work for both of us.

"Tell you what. I'll put a load in the washer," I say, feeling mildly virtuous that something practical's going to get done on my end. "And after it's going, I'll teach you how to shuffle. Then you can practice while I get some work done, and we can play a little poker during the ball game. Bring me your sheets."

She brightens at the word *shuffle*. It's a skill she's been bugging me to teach her for a couple of weeks. Until very recently, her hands have been just a bit too small to get a good grip on the deck.

"Okay," she says. She comes back with her arms full of dinosaur sheets and a scowl-ette on her face. She's realized that giving me her sheets means she has to remake her bed, which she hates. I've told her that it would be much easier if it wasn't in the corner, but she likes sleeping sheltered on two sides.

She plops the sheets onto the top of the laundry basket with a "see what I have to put up with?" look. Right now she's not my favorite human. I stifle the urge to just turn around, go into my office, shut the door, and let her stew in it. But one of us needs to try to be pleasant. I guess that would be me.

"Thanks. I'll take these downstairs while you go and get an old deck from the drawer in the living room."

"Why can't we use the kitchen deck?"

"You want a deck that's pretty broke in to learn to shuffle, Tex."

That stops her in her tracks. She wasn't expecting Tex. She looks at me in confusion for a minute, and then regroups.

"Well, then, I reckon that's a good idea, Slim," she drawls, and goes off to get the cards.

I'm relieved. Tex was my last resort. Tex and Slim have a much better chance at not yelling at each other this morning than we do. Maybe it'll take some of the edge off. Tex *never* whines.

Once the washing machine is gurgling and whirring, I take my now-lukewarm cup of tea and sit down at the table where the child is waiting. I pick up the deck and give it a good, whiffling shuffle, with a show-off bridge at the end. "You ready, Tex?"

"Yup."

I shuffle a few times, slowing it down, watching what my hands are doing before I say anything. It's such an unconscious, automatic thing, shuffling a deck of cards. A skill my body has had for so long that that I'm not sure I can explain it in words. It's like tying my shoes. I don't really pay attention; I'm not aware of the individual motions involved. It's just one fluid, instant action.

Loop, loop, pull – my shoes are tied. Cut, interlock, whiffle – and the deck is shuffled.

I break the motion apart into steps, walk her through it as much as I can. A few dozen slow-mo shuffles. Not all of them are successful. I tell her that's okay, see, even I can't do it every time. After about ten minutes, my fingers are cramping and I hand her the deck.

She grips it so tightly her knuckles whiten. The cut is easy. Now her face is pure concentration: furrowed brow, tip of her tongue visible as she tries to align the edges of the cards just right so they will riffle instead of merging into solid hunks.

The first few tries are just hunks. And then she does a real riffle and the cards all fall back neatly into place, reordered. She smiles. That's a good thing to see this morning.

We trade back and forth for another fifteen minutes, until she's got it, pretty much. Not every time, but enough that she's not too frustrated.

"Okay, now shuffle and deal a couple of hands," I tell her.

She handles the deal with the same concentration, trying to get enough loft under the pasteboards so that they sail across the table to me, but not so much that they skitter off onto the floor.

"Can we play for real now?" she asks, after pretend-dealing half a dozen hands.

"Nope. Now you get some practice time with nobody watching over your shoulder, and I'm going to go into my office and work for a while." I look at the clock. Remarkably, it's just after 10:00. "I'm going to work until noon, then we can play while the game's on. Okay?"

She nods, cuts the cards without looking at them. "I guess so."

When I emerge from my office, thirty copy-edited pages later, the kitchen floor is littered with cards, scattered like a game of 52-pickup or a Three Stooges Flying Shuffle Explosion.

"Watch!" she says before I can even ask. She picks up an abbreviated deck, maybe twenty cards in it, and with a flair that would make Doc Holliday proud, shuffles it expertly and arches it into a bridge that riffles like the wind.

"That's great. I'm impressed."

"Yeah, isn't it cool?" she says.

She's beaming, grinning from ear to ear. And I decide to keep her.

4 Cursive

The child has a paper due for school on Monday. It has to be two pages long, all written in cursive. They're studying cursive this year, what we used to call script, and the word has come down from on high that printing is only for babies, not big boys and girls. I doubt that Ms. Whiteman phrases it just like that, but that's the message.

It's not true, of course. Part of the path to being a grown-up is figuring out your own handwriting. The days of Spencerian penmanship and the Palmer Method are long gone. My own handwriting is semi-legible on good days – a mix of printed letters and some connected loops that are not really cursive, not the nicely rounded, beautifully connected shapes that ran across the top of the blackboard on long manila strips.

It's also full of a fair number of odd, personal shorthand symbols that even I can't always translate out of context.

If someone were to blow up bits of my journal and put them on an overhead projector and ask a room full of people to decipher them, the guesses would be random and amusing. I doubt if many of them would be correct.

I think, if I put my mind to it, I could probably eke out an entire page in proper, fourth-grade cursive. It would look very much like hers. Mine hasn't changed much since I was nine. I don't use it. Don't practice that particular art form. It's never necessary, and mostly I type. When I have to write a note that I want someone to understand, I print.

I want to explain this to the child, how, once you're out of school no one – really, no one – cares whether you can write cursive. Because you'll either never write much again, except for filling out forms (where you're required to print neatly in the little boxes), or you'll learn to type.

But this is not a truth about the world that Jackson Elementary is ready to have its fourth-graders know. Neither is the fact that no non-teacher adult ever writes a capital Q in cursive. It looks like a mutant 2. Avoid it, I tell her. Just don't write sentences that start with a Q.

I think she appreciates the support. But she's also seen my chicken scratches, has been decoding my grocery lists and scribbled phone messages since she's been able to read. So she knows full well that I have never been a member of the Illustrious Handwriting Guild.

She is just getting to the age where she believes that she has abilities and knowledge that are far superior to mine, and has taken to giving me pitying looks now and then. When she is in full cursive mode, every glance at my handwriting is withering.

She's sitting at the kitchen table now, a stack of blank notebook paper in front of her. Wide-lined, of course. No one in their right mind does a two-page paper on narrow-ruled paper. More lines. More words. More work.

Her paper is on spelunking. It's a nice big word, and she gets to spend about six lines defining it, on the off chance that her teacher doesn't know it. Doubtful, but possible. Ms. Whiteman strikes me as one of those pert, well-meaning women whose teaching credential is mostly a stopgap between college and being a mommy. It's catty of me, but I'm underwhelmed by her pedagogy.

I suspect the child is too, or she wouldn't have told me about the word *spelunking* with such glee.

She's done her research – two different encyclopedias and an old issue of *National Geographic* – and has written out a first draft. The draft pages are scribbled, x'd-out hybrids of printing and cursive, a nascent version of what I suspect will turn out to be her actual handwriting.

But that's not good enough for the report, which is due Monday morning. Tomorrow morning. It's now five o'clock on Sunday, and her bedtime is 8:30. She has not begun copying her first draft, turning it into the finished piece. She has topped off her root beer, and gotten a napkin, so that if the glass sweats she can dry her hands and not smear the ink. She has stacked her blank paper neatly three times, and gone to get another pen – just in case this one runs out in mid-sentence. It's a clear blue Bic; we can both see that the barrel is full. She explains each trip in a flurry of self-justification.

I know exactly what she's doing. I'm a writer. I recognize the intensity of her procrastination. She's at the sit-down-and-write part, the hard part, the butt-to-the-chair-until-it's-done part. And there's no getting around it. Deadline time.

What's worse is that Ms. Whiteman expects two pristine pages of unblotched penmanship. No cross-outs. The child has told me that twice. NO cross-outs. Not a single one. Which means that if she makes a mistake, she has to start over. The whole project is too daunting to even begin.

So I tell her the secret. Do the first page. And when it's done, put it in an envelope, a big one, where it will stay clean and unwrinkled and nothing can happen to it. Then you'll deserve a dinner break. We'll go to McDonald's or Burger King, depending on which one has the better Happy Meal deal this week.

And when we come back, half of it will be done. You can reward yourself again when the second page is safely tucked away. We'll watch *The Simpsons*. Just take it one page at a time.

But you're out of slack, I tell her, rubbing her shoulders. You have to sit down and get that first page out of the way, right now. Because until you do, the task will get bigger and bigger and bigger. Trust me. I'm an old hand at putting things off until they're almost impossible.

5 *School Picture*

Tomorrow is school picture day, the child informs me. She has a xeroxed sheet of instructions about what to wear — or not to wear. The guidelines haven't changed much since I was in fourth grade. No white blouses, unless you have a colorful sweater or cardigan to wear over it.

I'm not sure the child even owns a white blouse, the staple ritual garment of glee-club recitals and other group events of my childhood; everyone matched. White t-shirts were not okay. And at camp, for the council fire on Friday night — a white blouse and blue shorts and a red Camp Fire Girl tie. We would have been indistinguishable from a communist youth group, except for shouting Wo-He-Lo.

The child's school has a dress code so liberal that I'm sure my elementary school principal, Ralph M. Northenberg, would sneer and consider it no dress code at all. She can wear t-shirts, as long as they're clean, in good repair, and have no advertising or offensive slogans on them. But she wore her Milk Duds t-shirt last week, and no one seemed to care, so I don't pay much attention, as long as she leaves the house with shoes on.

A school picture, however, requires a little more thought. "What are you thinking of wearing?"

She shrugs. "What did you wear?"

Seems irrelevant to me, the fashions of 1963 being somewhat out of date. "A red corduroy jumper and a white blouse."

She makes a face. "Sounds dorky. Can I see?"

The album with all my school pictures in it is in the cupboard next to my desk. I bring it out and put it on the kitchen table. In most of the elementary pictures, I am wearing a dress or some sort of sleeveless jumper with a white blouse under it. Many of the garments are plaid.

I think there was some sort of law in the late '50s that required all female schoolchildren under the age of ten to have a wardrobe with a minimum of six plaid items. I remember a red Stewart tartan skirt that had straps with white buttons. They crossed at the back, making it hard, almost impossible, for me to dress myself without help. Today the only plaid item I own is a Black Watch comforter cover.

The child has turned the album page to fourth grade. That year I had moved on to solid-color jumpers. Sure enough, this one is red corduroy, and yes, I'm wearing a short-sleeved white blouse with a Peter Pan collar. It would be a couple of years before I discovered Oxford-cloth button-downs, which I called shirts and my mother still called blouses.

"That's *you?*"

I nod and she shakes her head in disbelief. She cannot imagine me as her peer, any more than, as a child, I could imagine that my own mother had ever been nine.

I'd seen pictures of my mother's childhood too, but they were so overlaid with who she was in my reality that the best I could do was imagine a very small woman who wore her hair in sausage curls but also drank scotch on the rocks when the sun was "over the yardarm."

"Did your mom make you wear that?" She's heard enough stories about my mother, who died before the child's conception, to know that her young life and mine were under very different managements.

"She had final approval."

"So what do you think *I* should wear tomorrow?"

Hmm. This may or may not be a loaded question. "Depends. What look are you going for?"

She wrinkles her face in confusion. "What do you mean?"

"There are probably ten copies of my fourth-grade picture in various family albums. And it was taken forty years ago. Yours will follow you around for a long time, too. So how do you want to remember fourth grade? Are you a geek? A jock? Class clown? Teacher's pet?" As far as I know, the child is not actually any of these, is a fairly balanced composition of many of them. "Those all require different outfits."

"Okay," she says, warming to this game. "Let's say I'm a geek. How would you dress me?"

"Well, first of all, we'd have to go out right now and get some geeky clothes, because I've been trying really hard not to buy you any. Who's the geekiest girl in your class?" This is San Francisco, in the 21st century, so I'm not sure if there even is a truly geeky girl, but the child answers immediately.

"Samantha Richards. She'll wear like a sweater with rosebuds on it, with too-short brown pants, and tell everyone her grandmother made them or something."

I smile. I can see Samantha. "Okay, then I'd dress you in that outfit that Aunt Lindsay sent you for Christmas, if it still fits. The one with the pink puppies chasing each other around the shirt."

The child shudders. "How about if I just want to be me?"

"Just you? I'd say you should dress yourself, Toots. 'Cause if I dressed you, it'd just be *my* idea of you. But if I had to pick, it'd be your black jeans and that pale green t-shirt and maybe your black cotton kimono, to give you that cool look you kind of like."

She looks at me in amazement. "That's exactly what I was thinking!"

It's only been her favorite "kind of dress-up" outfit for two months now. But I score major points.

6 *Columbus Day*

"Tomorrow is Indignant People Day," the child says casually. She has just come home from school, and is making herself a light snack of Wheat Thins and milk. I stifle a smile and hope she'll go on.

"Why is that?" I ask, trying to sound innocent.

"Well, it used to be called Columbus Day, on account of on October 12, 1492, Christopher Columbus came here. Not here, here. But America. Florida, I think. It's got beaches." She pauses to take a bite of Wheat Thin. "Anyway, he discovered America and then sent news back to Spain. That wasn't really where he was from, but he got a job driving the boat for the King and Queen of there." She looks at me to see if I'm following this so far. I nod.

"Except he didn't really discover America. Not like somebody else found it first, but there were already people living here. And they didn't want to belong to Spain. I don't think they even wanted to be Americans, because they were already something else. I don't know what." She eats another Wheat Thin slowly, contemplating all this ancient history. I put the kettle on to make tea.

"It's sort of like if some guy rang our doorbell this morning and said he'd discovered our house, so it belonged to him, and then he called us another name. We wouldn't like that much, so we'd be really mad at him." A long drink of milk.

"Which is pretty much how the Indians felt. Except they weren't even Indians. Columbus just called them that because he thought he was driving the boat to India to get spices. I guess Florida looks a lot like India." She shakes her head. "But the Indians didn't want to be Indians or Americans or Spanish, and they didn't want to have a king, because they already had chiefs. So they were indignant." She looks over at me. "That means p.o.'d for a good reason, right?"

"Pretty much."

"Anyway, it used to be called Columbus Day, the holiday tomorrow. But now we're supposed to call it Indignant People Day, on account of maybe Columbus wasn't such a big hero if he discovered something that was already *there*." She finishes with a great deal of emphasis, then leans back in her chair.

I am having a lot of trouble breathing. I have been biting my cheeks for several minutes and holding my breath, off and on, trying desperately to stifle the guffaw or raging fit of giggles that I know will explode out of me if I drop my vigilance for even a moment. I do not dare to take a sip of tea.

It is one of the most righteous, stone-cold accurate wrong answers I have ever heard. The child has done her homework. She's paid attention, and I'm quite proud. But I feel like I'm raising little Emily Litella, and the punchline is, of course, "that's indigenous, not indignant. Indigenous." Except that I like it better her way.

I waffle. I do not want to make her feel bad. But at the same time, I feel a responsibility to inform her of the actual word, maybe have a small vocabulary lesson. How can I accomplish both at the same time?

I take a sip of tea, the threat of giggles now past, and once it's safely swallowed, take a deep breath. "You know a lot about Columbus and history. I'm impressed."

She looks up from the comics section of the newspaper and smiles.

"We're studying explorers in school. They start with him because most kids have heard of him, and they named a whole big city Columbus. The other foreign guys, like Cadillac, discovered smaller stuff, like rivers and lakes, and just got cars named after them."

I nod. I'm really pretty impressed by the level of information that Ms. Whiteman has managed to include in her curriculum. "That's great," I say, meaning it. "But there's one little thing you should probably know."

The child's eyes widen a little. She is curious. "What's that?" There is wary caution on the rest of her face — a subtle tightening of her mouth as her eyebrows move toward each other, just a fraction.

"The holiday? It's not actually called Indignant People Day."

She looks at me with a mixture of relief and condescension. "I *know* that. Officially it's still Columbus Day. Like on the sign at the bank and the calendar and stuff. But it *should* be Indignant People Day."

I sigh and pull a piece of scratch paper off the pile that lives on the kitchen counter. I carefully print INDIGENOUS on it and hand it to her.

She looks at it, frowns, and then her mouth contracts into the O of sudden comprehension. "That isn't indignant," she says slowly.

"Nope. But I really liked your explanation."

"Yeah. Except for it was wrong." She looks down at her lap.

I put my hands on her shoulders and lean down to nuzzle the top of her head. "It wasn't wrong. You had all the facts right about Columbus, and you are absolutely right that a lot of people *do* feel indignant about the whole thing. Not a wrong answer in the bunch."

"So what does indigenous mean?" She gives it a hard G, like indignant.

"Native, more or less. The people who were born in the place Columbus thought he discovered. He called them Indians, but it's more politically correct these days to call them indigenous people."

She takes all this in. After a few seconds she tilts her head back to look up at me. "But they were indignant, weren't they?"

"Absolutely. Extremely indignant."

"I thought so," she says.

7 Lonny-with-a-Y

The child comes in the door with a friend in tow, a smallish girl with very curly, carrot-red hair. Her name is Lonny. With a Y. The child has talked about this new friend a lot in the last few weeks, but never used a pronoun. For some reason, I'd assumed Lonny was a boy. Never assume.

The two of them are sitting at the kitchen table, drinking Dr. Pepper — the caffeine-free kind — talking about homework and school and other things that I don't much understand. It's nine-year-old shorthand for events and people that are foreign to me.

That it doesn't concern me is something they are making very clear. Neither of them has said anything, but Lonny just gave me a sidelong glance, then looked back at the child as if to say, "She's not listening, is she?" Now the child is grimacing at me, clear body language for "Don't you have something you need to be doing?"

I can take a hint. I grab a can of Diet Coke and go off to my office, where I check my email. Two replies from friends. A message from my editor wanting to know if she can have the galleys back a week earlier than we'd discussed, in order to allow for the copy editor's vacation.

No, she can't. I'm on schedule, more or less. I'll meet the deadline. You deal with the copy editor. I don't say — or type — that. He's a great copy editor, although he tends to be a bit conservative about adjectives, and I love the little buggers. It's just that I'm not willing to bust my butt so he can have a week in Bermuda.

The sounds from the kitchen are giggles — high-pitched, raucous, entirely self-absorbed. In an hour or so, I can legitimately go in there to fix dinner. Actually, as the ranking grown-up, I can just go in there now, if I want, taking over the kitchen by eminent domain and banishing the kids to another room, instead of shutting myself up in exile in my office.

But eminent domain doesn't set well in a two-person household. The fact is, the child is entertaining a guest, and that's a proper use of shared space. So I click on the icon for my guaranteed time-suck — Hearts — and kick back in my chair with my soda. I space out for a while in the contemplative yet competitive way that games with my imaginary, silicon-based friends induces.

They say that everything on earth is a carbon-based lifeform, but I don't think it's true anymore. The characters on my computer screen are as real to me as the child in the kitchen, at the moment. And they're winning. Again.

Pieces of conversation drift in from the hallway.

"No, it's okay. She's not really working. She's just playing this weird game on her computer."

Damn. I turn off the sound — blips and beeps and occasional bursts of canned applause — so that I can listen better.

Tiny Reebok-clad footsteps approach my door. A pause. A tentative knock. I hit PAUSE and the screen freezes as the child opens the door.

I turn around. "What's up?"

"Will you teach Lonny how to bet?"

Wow. That was nowhere on my list of expected questions. The child and I have been playing poker for about six months now, not for money, just beans and M&Ms. But other people may not think this is such a hot idea.

I look at Lonny-with-a-Y, who is standing a step behind, waiting for the verdict. She doesn't look like she's from a fundamentalist family. She's wearing an Earth Day t-shirt, and has two earrings in one ear. Which doesn't mean liberal in San Francisco, but doesn't shout conservative, Bible-thumping, games-are-the-devil, either.

I hit QUIT — the pixel people had me soundly beaten — and turn my chair so I'm facing Lonny. "How come?"

She shuffles from one foot to the other. "I've got two brothers — Danny and David. And they won't let me play poker 'cause they say girls don't know how. But I do, sort of. I mean, I know what cards are good, and what beats what. But *she* said you could..."

"...Teach her the rest," the child finishes, fiddling with the bowl of paper clips on my file cabinet. "You know, betting and bluffing and all that."

I consider it further. Do her parents care that their sons are playing? Is that different than if I taught their little *girl* to play? I start to get caught up in a burst of righteous feminist indignation, based on nothing but my own fantasy, then catch myself.

"Okay, sure. Let's see what you know." The three of us troop into the kitchen. I pull the shuffling practice deck out of a drawer and toss it to Lonny-with-a-Y. We all sit down at the kitchen table.

"Shuffle up and deal out three hands of whatever game you know how to play. Only deal them face-up."

"Wait — that's not how my brothers…"

The child interrupts. "It's like training wheels."

I nod. "Right now, we're just watching the luck happen."

Lonny shrugs and starts to shuffle. I get out the jar of dried poker beans and issue us each about fifty.

"Five-card draw?" she asks. I nod and she deals.

It only takes a few hands for me to realize Lonny doesn't really *get* betting. She's stuck on the idea that you only bet if you've got good cards. I replenish her supply of beans and we keep playing.

About midway through her second pile of beans, I can almost see the light bulb go on in her brain. Sometimes you bet on what you've got; other times you bet for intimidation, or to make someone *think* she knows what you have. The only sure thing is when you have the nuts — when no one else's cards can possibly beat you. The rest is where skill and cunning come in.

I like Lonny-with-a-Y. She has spunk, she's intelligent and isn't overtly bossy or whiny. I approve; when she goes off to the bathroom, I ask the child if she wants to invite her friend to stay for dinner, since it's Friday, and not a school night. She does.

I call Lonny's mother, whose name is Marjorie. It's fine with her, but both her boys have scouts tonight, and could I bring Lonny home? Around nine? Done.

I make fish sticks and salad for dinner. I start to sprinkle bacon bits on the salad, but Lonny asks, quietly but firmly, if I'll leave them off hers. Her family's Jewish, she explains, and they don't really keep kosher, but they don't eat pork, and is that okay?

If it's okay with God, it's fine with me.

There's one last Corona in the fridge and, miraculously, a lime as well. The kids want to split another can of Dr. Pepper, but it's too late in the day for more sugar. I pour two glasses of milk. When I put hers down, Lonny informs me, a bit apologetically – and a little late – that she is also lactose-intolerant. The milk goes back into the carton. I give them orange juice with a few drops of raspberry Italian syrup and a splash of club soda for fizz.

Lonny has a second helping of salad, and asks if we can play some more poker after the dishes are done.

I check the clock. It's a little after 8:00, and her house is about ten minutes away. "Sure. But don't worry about the dishes. You're a guest. Just stack them in the sink. I'll take care of them later. We can play for another 45 minutes."

Lonny gets a look on her face like someone's just made her queen, and I realize that with two brothers she probably pulls more than her share of KP.

"Can we play the real way now?" she asks. "Face-down?"

Fine by me. They clear the table. I deal three hands. The child bets five beans before the draw. I see Lonny hesitate, fingering her pile of beans.

I want to tell her, honey, they're only beans, and there are plenty more where those came from. But that's not the point, and it's not a lesson I want either of them to learn. The danger is that later on, getting one more twenty from an ATM machine will seem just about as easy as getting another handful of beans. I stay quiet, let Lonny make her own decision.

She bites her lower lip and pushes five beans into the pot. Me too. The child takes one card. Lonny draws three; so do I, hoping to improve a pair of eights. I don't. The child, the opener, bets fifteen beans.

The kitchen is completely silent. Lonny looks at her cards, at her beans, at the child. And then she surprises me. She raises another fifteen beans, counting them out one by one, thirty beans. That leaves only four beans in front of her, but the pile in the center of the table is impressive.

I fold. The child sits with her arms crossed over her chest, staring at Lonny. Then she smiles, a wicked smile, one I'm not sure I like, and says, very quietly, "I'll raise your last four."

Showdown at the fourth-grade corral.

Lonny pushes her last beans in. "What've you got?"

The child looks pretty damn smug as she turns over her cards. "Two big pair. Kings and tens."

There is a pause. I have one hand on the jar of beans, expecting to see Lonny's face crumple in disappointment, but it doesn't. Instead she grins, a huge, ear-to-ear grin.

"Too bad," says Lonny-with-a-Y. She turns over her three 3s and scoops up the whole pile of beans.

Her brothers may be in for a surprise.

8 *Seven-Card Stud*

The child took a deck of cards to school and taught the class how to play seven-card stud for Talent Day. She didn't tell me about this plan beforehand. I probably would have talked her out of it, although part of me wants very much to have been there to watch.

She walked in the door a few minutes ago, bearing a note from her teacher. Poker is gambling. "Stud" is not an appropriate vocabulary word in the fourth grade. These are not family values.

The child is confused. She was showing off a skill that she's been patiently learning for several months. Up until now, this has always been a good thing.

It's my fault, I tell her. I have neglected to mention that poker is not at the top of the list of Essential Things Every Nine-Year-Old Girl Should Know. I get her an unleaded Dr. Pepper and settle in for what may be a lengthy chat.

She asks about "stud" first. "How come Ms. Whiteman says it's a bad word? Isn't that the name of the game?"

"It is. But it means other things, too."

"Like what?"

"Lots. But the one I think your teacher doesn't like is…" I parse my sentence carefully. "A kind of horse. A stud horse is a stallion who's rented out to farmers who want their mares to have babies. So a guy who looks like he's only interested in sex is sometimes called a stud."

The child absorbs this information. I wonder if it's too early for a glass of wine.

We haven't had THE major sex talk yet, just touched on random bits and pieces as they've come up: how she was conceived; me having my period; a flasher in the park one day; yes, a penis is different from what you have. But we haven't gotten to SEX yet, certainly not seamy, x-rated stud-like sex.

And now we do, a little. She's not interested in any details at the moment, just the basic concept of what's "dirty" and what's not. And why a card game would be named after a horse that does…that sort of thing.

I decide that it is not too early for a little Cabernet after all. I've already lost my shot at Role Model of the Year.

I go get the dictionary, and we learn just how versatile a word *stud* is – horse, virile guy, upright board in a wall, nail or rivet in blue jeans, small pierced-ear earring, metal protrusion in a snow tire. Not, alas, an explanation of why the poker game is called that.

It becomes a research project, a quest. I drag out many reference books: a slang dictionary, Hoyle's *Rules of Games*, two poker books, and the P volume of the encyclopedia. We learn that stud poker is the opposite of draw poker, and that the term originated in 1864. An hour later, we still don't know *why*.

"I got in trouble for saying stud once." I tell her, as I refill my wine glass.

"How come?"

"You know how if something's really great you'd say it was cool. Or neat. Or groovy?"

She giggles at *groovy*.

"Well, when I was in sixth grade, the word was 'stud.' Like: *Wow, your new shirt's really stud!* All my friends said it. I said it. Then one day I said it at home, and my mom hit the roof."

"The horse thing, right?"

"Maybe. I was just as baffled as you were. I didn't know it was a dirty word. I just wanted to sound cool."

"Stud," the child corrects me.

"Yeah. I wanted to sound stud. Anyway, my mom got mad and swatted me and told me to never, ever, *ever* use that word again, and sent me to my room."

The child looks at me for a minute and then says, very quietly, "I'm glad you didn't hit me or yell at me on account of I took the cards to school."

"Oh, hon." I get up and hug her. I would never, in a billion thoughts, punish her for being innocent and confused. She reaches up and pats my arm. I stroke her hair, then begin to cry into it.

"Are you *cry*ing?"

"A little."

"How come?"

"Bunch of stuff. The grown-up part of me is crying at the idea that anyone would yell at you or hurt you. And I'm also remembering the 'stud' day, and how it felt to get punished when I hadn't done anything wrong."

"But you didn't *know* it was a bad word and say it on purpose, did you?"

"Not the first time." I disengage and sit back in my chair so I can look at her. "But after that, I did, sometimes, just to piss off my mom. She was going to yell at me anyway. Hand me a Kleenex?"

She does, and then is silent for a while. I start to worry that I've just dumped too big a load of old angst on her tiny shoulders. She finally reaches over and pats my hand. "I'm glad she's not in charge of *me*," she says. "You're lots better. Can I have some Triscuits?"

I nod. I'm glad I'm not passing on the legacy of intolerance – or whatever it was – that made life a minefield between my mother and me.

She comes back with the yellow box of Triscuits. "So what are you going to do about my teacher?"

Damn. I pull myself back to the present. "How does this sound? I'll write her a letter, and tell her about all the other things that *stud* means. I'll tell her that she's going to have a hard time stopping the whole fourth grade from talking about building a house or getting pierced ears. Or that when she reads a story that talks about the star-studded sky, she *really* doesn't really want thirty kids giggling and thinking that it's dirty."

The child nods solemnly. "That is very true."

"But I'll also promise her that you won't give the other kids any more gambling lessons, and that you'll leave the deck of cards at home. What do you think?"

She makes a face. "It sounds like you're telling her she's right and that it really is bad to play poker."

"Some people think any kind of gambling is wrong. I'm just not one of them. We can play poker at home all you want, but it's not a school game – okay? I'm letting Ms. Whiteman have that one. She's probably terrified that next week you'll be running a little casino out on the playground and cheating first-grade kids out of their lunch money."

"I never *cheat*!" the child says indignantly.

I burst out laughing. True, and so irrelevant. "I know. I was kidding. So, do you want to play a little seven-card – STUD –" I give it a real leering emphasis, "after dinner?"

She smiles. "I think there might be a deck of cards in my knapsack."

9 *Gargling*

The child has a cold. Not a miserable, stay in bed, too sick to move cold, just the sniffles. But her throat is scratchy, one ear is stopped up, and her head is filling with Jell-O; she's rapidly losing the ability to breathe through her left nostril and is wheezing softly.

I give her the Tylenol cold stuff for kids – two spoonfuls because she's an older kid – and a handful of chewable vitamin C. All that helps. But her throat is still sore, so I take her into the bathroom to gargle with salt water.

Gargling isn't something I think a lot about. It's not an activity I do on a regular basis. I gargle when my throat's sore. It certainly never occurred to me, until this very minute, that it would be yet another skill I would have to teach someone.

But how hard can it be?

She sits on the toilet while I stand over the bathroom sink. "I'm going to take a mouthful of salt water," I tell her before I actually do. "Maybe two-thirds of a mouthful. I'll just hold it in my mouth, NOT swallowing. Then I'll tip my head back, so my mouth is pointing up towards the ceiling, and sort of gurgle it in my throat, like this."

I try to make the gargle noise, but it's not a sound you can make dry. The muscles in my throat contract; nothing either visual or vocal happens. I have to demonstrate, fully loaded. Three times. My powers of description are severely limited once my mouth is full of salt water, and the child is full of questions.

"Why do I have to do this?" She gives me the kind of look usually reserved for someone who is teaching you the penguin mating dance on the hope that you will join their cult.

"Because there are germs in your throat. Salt water kills them."

"They're not germs. A cold is a virus. We learned that in Health."

Point for the small one. "You're right. But viruses don't like salt water either. Look, it works. Trust me."

She is skeptical, but agrees to try. I put some salt in her Harry Potter cup, fill it midway with warm tap water, stir it, and hand it to her.

Now she looks at me like I'm Lucretia Borgia, and she knows what comes next, but takes the glass, gets a mouthful, tilts her head back and makes a sound like a broken garbage disposal.

Water comes gushing out of her mouth and down the front of her sweatshirt, soaking a good five inches of it. She glares at me. "Yuck. It tastes really bad!"

I remove the sweatshirt and wrap a towel around her shoulders. "I know. Will you try again? It's really pretty easy, once you get the hang of it. It's a useful thing to be able to do."

Such a look. I can tell that, in her book, this making a rude noise with your mouth stuff cannot possibly be useful. I am the only grown-up in the world who does this, and I'm just trying to make her as weird as I am.

"Please," I say. "Give it another shot?"

She rolls her eyes, but complies. More water down the front of her. Most of it misses the towel completely and runs down into the elastic of her sweatpants.

"One more time?" I ask faintly. I don't remember it being this difficult.

She shakes her head and folds her arms across her chest.

"Just once more? I'll call Tien Fu and we can have hot-and-sour soup for dinner. I'll even rent a movie." Ordinarily, I try not to stoop to bribes. But I was thinking of renting a movie anyway, figuring that an afternoon of lying on the couch under the big comforter will give the Tylenol a fighting chance. And hot-and-sour soup, as far as I'm concerned, is the second most powerful remedy for blasting a sore throat out of existence.

Unless this gargling bout improves in the next few minutes, the soup will take sole possession of first place.

The child eyes the glass of salt water warily. "Okay. But this is the last time." She scrunches her eyes tightly shut, takes a mouthful of water and tilts back her head. The horrible noise starts, then turns into a gargle. A real gargle!

"That's it!" I am, perhaps, a bit too enthusiastic.

She is startled, makes an *uh* of surprise — and inhales.

Damn.

The salt water goes "down the wrong pipe" as my mother used to say. The child gags and coughs. Water spews everywhere. It's hard to imagine an entire bathroom being hosed by one child-sized mouthful of water, but it can be done.

She is gasping and snorting, trying to expel all the fluids from her breathing parts, which were wheezy to begin with. I pat her on the back, which is entirely ineffectual, but makes me feel marginally better.

After a minute, the chaos subsides. The child, who started out with the sniffles, is now red-faced, teary-eyed, and soaking wet. She stares at me for a few seconds and then says, with wounded dignity, "If you don't mind, I'd like to change my clothes now."

I can only nod. I'll clean up the bathroom, which looks like a steerage cabin on the Titanic half an hour after the iceberg. We've taken on water. I get a sponge and a roll of paper towels and begin to mop. I'm glad she was using a plastic cup. This could have been worse. Really.

I am almost done mopping when she appears in the doorway, wearing my sweatpants (rolled up a bit) and a clean, dry sweatshirt. "I want to rent *Pirates of the Caribbean*," she says quietly. "And while you're out getting soup, would you mind buying some plain old cough drops?"

10 *Dancing at Dusk*

I marvel at the way the child moves, unconscious of her body, or maybe so conscious that it's all in synch. She is limber, flexible, runs like the wind and sleeps in any position she wants, reads lying flat on her belly with her head propped up in her hands, and she's not stiff when she gets up.

My neck has been sore for a week, from typing and bending over piles of papers. Even with a good desk chair and an ergonomic keyboard rest and all the other pseudo-orthopedic office furniture, my neck is constantly stiff.

I'm sitting at the kitchen table, sipping at a glass of wine, waiting for the Advil to kick in, watching the child not know that she's being watched. It is seven in the evening, late spring, and the light in the back yard is soft, golden, deepening into shadows where the houses block the setting sun. Twilight always seems thicker and richer than ordinary light, magic somehow.

And the child is dancing in it.

I envy her fluidity and her confidence. Not in the present – I'm relatively confident of the things I do well. But the nine-year old I once was is a shy child who spent most of her childhood reading, because books were safer than other people. And that shy child envies the confidence of this beaming one. Envies the ease in which she inhabits her body, the ease with which she accepts praise as an ordinary gift.

The radio is on, tuned to the light classical station – wind-down, end of the day music. The sliding door from the kitchen to the back yard is open, and the music wafts gently out into that soft light. It is an ethereal setting, and the child is dancing.

Her eyes are closed and she floats and spins and dips across the grass. She is not a willowy child. She is as short and sturdy as everyone else in my family. But she is so graceful it makes my heart ache, makes my eyes sting with not-quite-shed tears.

Am I crying because she is beautiful? Or because in my own childhood I was told that I was not? I don't want her to turn from this fairy child dancing at dusk to the stiff adolescent I'm afraid she will become, as if my past is a legacy, genetic and inevitable.

She is dancing with the cat in her arms now, not as if the cat were a partner – the cat would never tolerate that for a moment – but as if it were a baby, a treasure. Cradling it as she continues to pirouette across our tiny patch of lawn.

If time could compress like an accordion, would the bookish nine-year-old I once was play with my own child? Would they like each other? Would the then-me come over and dance in the setting sun, or would she linger at the edge of the yard, all bound feet and bound soul?

Baggage left unattended will be confiscated. Oh, if only that were true.

A tear runs down my cheek and I wipe it away. I don't want the child to think I'm sad, that anything's wrong. I couldn't explain to her that she's so beautiful it makes me cry without eliciting an embarrassed, slightly grimacing, "Ah, jeez..."

The light is fading now, and the child is hugging her arms to herself. Getting chilly. She will come inside soon, into the warmth and smell of spaghetti cooking on the stove.

After dinner, I will read to her. I'll sit next to her in the big over-stuffed chair in the sunroom, feel the weight of her body against mine, her head resting on my shoulder as the chapter goes on and the lithe dancer turns into a sleepy little girl. I will put my arm around her, my face in her hair, breathe in the aroma of girl child and sunlight and spring breezes.

And just for a moment, by magic or osmosis, I will dance inside myself, unfettered.

In the House of the Seven Librarians

ONCE UPON A TIME, the Carnegie Library sat on a wooded bluff on the east side of town: red brick and fieldstone, with turrets and broad windows facing the trees. Inside, green glass-shaded lamps cast warm yellow light onto oak tables ringed with spindle-backed chairs.

Books filled the dark shelves that stretched high up toward the pressed-tin ceiling. The floors were wood, except in the foyer, where they were pale beige marble. The loudest sounds were the ticking of the clock and the quiet, rhythmic *thwack* of a rubber stamp on a pasteboard card.

It was a cozy, orderly place.

Through twelve presidents and two world wars, the elms and maples grew tall outside the deep bay windows. Children leaped from *Peter Pan* to *Oliver Twist* and off to college, replaced at Story Hour by their younger brothers, cousins, daughters.

Then the library board – men in suits, serious men, men of money – met and cast their votes for progress. A new library, with fluorescent lights, much better for the children's eyes. Picture windows, automated systems, ergonomic plastic chairs. The town approved the levy, and the new library was built across town, convenient to the community center and the mall.

Some books were boxed and trundled down Broad Street, many others stamped DISCARD and left where they were, for a book sale in the fall. Interns from the university used the latest technology to transfer the cumbersome old card file and all the records onto floppy disks and microfiche. Progress, progress, progress.

The Ralph P. Mossberger Library (named after the local philanthropist and car dealer who had written the largest check) opened on a drizzly morning in late April. Everyone attended the ribbon-cutting ceremony and stayed for the speeches, because there would be cake after.

Everyone except the seven librarians from the Carnegie Library on the bluff across town.

Quietly, without a fuss (they were librarians, after all), while the town looked toward the future, they bought supplies: loose tea and English biscuits, packets of Bird's pudding and cans of beef barley soup. They rearranged some of the shelves, brought in a few comfortable armchairs, nice china and teapots, a couch, towels for the shower, and some small braided rugs.

Then they locked the door behind them.

Each morning they woke and went about their chores. They shelved and stamped and cataloged, and in the evenings, every night, they read by lamplight.

Perhaps, for a while, some citizens remembered the old library, with the warm nostalgia of a favorite childhood toy that had disappeared one summer, never seen again. Others assumed it had been torn down long ago.

And so a year went by, then two, or perhaps a great many more. Inside, time had ceased to matter. Grass and brambles grew thick and tall around the fieldstone steps, and trees arched overhead as the forest folded itself around them like a cloak.

Inside, the seven librarians lived, quiet and content.

Until the day they found the baby.

Librarians are guardians of books. They guide others along their paths, offering keys to help unlock the doors of knowledge. But these seven had become a closed circle, no one to guide, no new minds to open onto worlds of possibility. They kept themselves busy, tidying orderly shelves and mending barely frayed bindings with stiff netting and glue, and began to bicker.

Ruth and Edith had been up half the night, arguing about whether or not subway tokens (of which there were half a dozen in the Lost and Found box) could be used to cast the *I Ching*. And so Blythe was on the stepstool in the 299s, reshelving the volume of hexagrams, when she heard the knock.

Odd, she thought. It's been some time since we've had visitors.

She tugged futilely at her shapeless cardigan as she clambered off the stool and trotted to the front door, where she stopped abruptly, her hand to her mouth in surprise.

A wicker basket, its contents covered with a red-checked cloth, as if for a picnic, lay in the wooden box beneath the Book Return chute. A small, cream-colored envelope poked out from one side.

"How nice!" Blythe said aloud, clapping her hands. She thought of fried chicken and potato salad — of which she was awfully fond — a Mason jar of lemonade, perhaps even a cherry pie? She lifted the basket by its round-arched handle. Heavy, for a picnic. But then, there *were* seven of them. Although Olive just ate like a bird, these days.

She turned and set it on top of the Circulation Desk, pulling the envelope free.

"What's *that?*" Marian asked, her lips in their accustomed moue of displeasure, as if the basket were an agent of chaos, existing solely to disrupt the tidy array of rubber stamps and file boxes that were her domain.

"A present," said Blythe. "I think it might be lunch."

Marian frowned. "For you?"

"I don't know yet. There's a note..." Blythe held up the envelope and peered at it. "No," she said. "It's addressed to 'The Librarians. Overdue Books Department.'"

"Well, that would be me," Marian said curtly. She was the youngest, and wore trouser suits with silk t-shirts. She had once been blond. She reached across the counter, plucked the envelope from Blythe's plump fingers, and sliced it open it with a filigreed brass stiletto.

"Hmph," she said after she'd scanned the contents.

"It *is* lunch, isn't it?" asked Blythe.

"Hardly." Marian began to read aloud:

This is overdue. Quite a bit, I'm afraid. I apologize. We moved to Topeka when I was very small, and Mother accidentally packed it up with the linens. I have traveled a long way to return it, and I know the fine must be large, but I have no money. As it is a book of fairy tales, I thought payment of a first-born child would be acceptable. I always loved the library. I'm sure she'll be happy there.

Blythe lifted the edge of the cloth. "Oh, my stars!"

A baby girl with a shock of wire-stiff black hair stared up at her, green eyes wide and curious. She was contentedly chewing on the corner of a blue book, half as big as she was. *Fairy Tales of the Brothers Grimm*.

"The Rackham illustrations," Blythe said as she eased the book away from the baby. "That's a lovely edition."

"But when was it checked out?" Marian demanded.

Blythe opened the cover and pulled the ruled card from the inside pocket. "October 17th, 1938," she said, shaking her head. "Goodness, at two cents a day, that's…" She shook her head again. Blythe had never been good with figures.

They made a crib for her in the bottom drawer of a file cabinet, displacing acquisition orders, zoning permits, and the instructions for the mimeograph, which they rarely used.

Ruth consulted Dr. Spock. Edith read Piaget. The two of them peered from text to infant and back again for a good long while before deciding that she was probably about nine months old. They sighed. Too young to read.

So they fed her cream and let her gum on biscuits, and each of the seven cooed and clucked and tickled her pink toes when they thought the others weren't looking. Harriet had been the oldest of nine girls, and knew more about babies than she really cared to. She washed and changed the diapers that had been tucked into the basket, and read *Goodnight Moon* and *Pat the Bunny* to the little girl, whom she called Polly – short for Polyhymnia, the muse of oratory and sacred song.

Blythe called her Bitsy, and Li'l Precious.

Marian called her "the foundling," or "That Child You Took In," but did her share of cooing and clucking, just the same.

When the child began to walk, Dorothy blocked the staircase with stacks of Comptons, which she felt was an inferior encyclopedia, and let her pull herself up on the bottom drawers of the card catalog. Anyone looking up Zithers or Zippers (*see "Slide Fasteners"*) soon found many of the cards fused together with grape jam. When she began to talk, they

made a little bed nook next to the fireplace in the Children's Room.
It was high time for Olive to begin the child's education.

Olive had been the children's librarian since before recorded time, or so
it seemed. No one knew how old she was, but she vaguely remembered
waving to President Coolidge. She still had all of her marbles, though
every one of them was a bit odd and rolled asymmetrically.

She slept on a daybed behind a reference shelf that held *My First
Encyclopedia* and *The Wonder Book of Trees*, among others. Across the
room, the child's first "big-girl bed" was yellow, with decals of a fairy
and a horse on the headboard, and a rocket ship at the foot, because
they weren't sure about her preferences.

At the beginning of her career, Olive had been an ordinary-sized
librarian, but by the time she began the child's lessons, she was not
much taller than her toddling charge. Not from osteoporosis or dow-
ager's hump or other old-lady maladies, but because she had tired of
stooping over tiny chairs and bending to knee-high shelves. She had
been a grown-*up* for so long that when the library closed, she had
decided it was time to grow *down* again, and was finding that much
more comfortable.

She had a remarkably cozy lap for a woman her size.

The child quickly learned her alphabet, all the shapes and colors, the
names of zoo animals, and fourteen different kinds of dinosaurs, all of
whom were dead.

By the time she was four, or thereabouts, she could sound out the
letters for simple words – *cup* and *lamp* and *stairs*. And that's how she
came to name herself.

Olive had fallen asleep over *Make Way for Ducklings*, and all the
other librarians were busy somewhere else. The child was bored.
She tiptoed out of the Children's Room, hugging the shadows of the
walls and shelves, crawling by the base of the Circulation Desk so that
Marian wouldn't see her, and made her way to the alcove that held the
Card Catalog. The heart of the library. Her favorite, most forbidden
place to play.

Usually she crawled underneath and tucked herself into the corner formed of oak cabinet, marble floor, and plaster walls. It was a fine place to play Hide-and-Seek, even if it was mostly just Hide. The corner was a cave, a bunk on a pirate ship, a cupboard in a magic wardrobe.

But that afternoon she looked at the white cards on the fronts of the drawers, and her eyes widened in recognition. Letters! In her very own alphabet. Did they spell words? Maybe the drawers were all *full* of words, a huge wooden box of words. The idea almost made her dizzy.

She walked to the other end of the cabinet and looked up, tilting her neck back until it crackled. Four drawers from top to bottom. Five drawers across. She sighed. She was only tall enough to reach the bottom row of drawers. She traced a gentle finger around the little brass frames, then very carefully pulled out the white cards inside and laid them on the floor in a neat row:

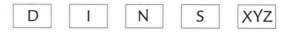

She squatted over them, her tongue sticking out of the corner of her mouth in concentration, and tried to read.

"Sound it out." She could almost hear Olive's voice, soft and patient. She took a deep breath.

"Duh-in-s — " and then she stopped, because the last card had too many letters, and she didn't know any words that had *X*s in them. Well, xylophone. But the *X* was in the front, and that wasn't the same. She tried anyway. "Duh-ins-zzzigh," and frowned.

She squatted lower, so low she could feel cold marble under her cotton pants, and put her hand on top of the last card. One finger covered the *X* and her pinkie covered the *Z* (another letter that was useless for spelling ordinary things). That left *Y*. *Y* at the end was good. funn*Y*. happ*Y*.

"Duh-ins-see," she said slowly. "Dinsy."

That felt very good to say, hard and soft sounds and hissing *S*s mixing in her mouth, so she said it again, louder, which made her laugh, so she said it again, very loud: "DINSY!"

There is nothing quite like a loud voice in a library to get a lot of attention very fast. Within a minute, all seven of the librarians stood in the doorway of the alcove.

"What on earth?" said Harriet.

"*Now* what have you..." said Marian.

"What have you spelled, dear?" asked Olive in her soft little voice.

"I made it myself," the girl replied.

"Just gibberish," murmured Edith, though not unkindly. "It doesn't mean a thing."

The child shook her head. "Does so. Olive," she said, pointing to Olive. "Do'thy, Edith, Harwiet, Bithe, Ruth." She paused and rolled her eyes. "Mawian," she added, a little less cheerfully. Then she pointed to herself. "And Dinsy."

"Oh, now, Polly," said Harriet.

"Dinsy," said Dinsy.

"Bitsy?" Blythe tried hopefully.

"*Dinsy,*" said Dinsy.

And that was that.

———

At three every afternoon, Dinsy and Olive made a two-person circle on the braided rug in front of the bay window, and had Story Time. Sometimes Olive read aloud from *Beezus and Ramona* and *Half Magic*, and sometimes Dinsy read to Olive, *The King's Stilts*, and *In the Night Kitchen*, and *Winnie-the-Pooh*. Dinsy liked that one especially, and took it to bed with her so many times that Edith had to repair the binding. Twice.

That was when Dinsy first wished upon the Library.

———

A NOTE ABOUT THE LIBRARY:

Knowledge is not static; information must flow in order to live. Every so often one of the librarians would discover a new addition. *Harry Potter and the Sorcerer's Stone* appeared one rainy afternoon, Rowling shelved neatly between Rodgers and Saint-Exupéry, as if it had always been there. Blythe found a book of Thich Nhat Hanh's writings in the 294s one day while she was dusting, and Feynman's lectures on physics showed up on Dorothy's shelving cart after she'd gone to make a cup of tea.

It didn't happen often; the Library was selective about what it chose to

190 | *Ellen Klages*

add, rejecting flash-in-the-pan best-sellers, sifting for the long haul, looking for those voices that would stand the test of time next to Dickens and Tolkien, Woolf and Gould.

The librarians took care of the books, and the Library watched over them in return. It occasionally left treats: a bowl of ripe tangerines on the Formica counter of the Common Room; a gold foil box of chocolate creams; seven small, stemmed glasses of sherry on the table one teatime. Their biscuit tin remained full, the cream in the Wedgwood jug stayed fresh, and the ink pad didn't dry out. Even the little pencils stayed needle sharp, never whittling down to finger-cramping nubs.

Some days the Library even hid Dinsy, when she had made a mess and didn't want to be found, or when one of the librarians was in a dark mood. It rearranged itself, just a bit, so that in her wanderings she would find a new alcove or cubbyhole, and once a secret passage that led to a previously unknown balcony overlooking the Reading Room. When she went back a week later, she found only blank wall.

And so it was, one night when she was sixish, that Dinsy first asked the Library for a boon. Lying in her tiny yellow bed, the fraying *Pooh* under her pillow, she wished for a bear to cuddle. Books were small comfort once the lights were out, and their hard, sharp corners made them awkward companions under the covers. She lay with one arm crooked around a soft, imaginary bear, and wished and wished until her eyelids fluttered into sleep.

The next morning, while they were all having tea and toast with jam, Blythe came into the Common Room with a quizzical look on her face and her hands behind her back.

"The strangest thing," she said. "On my way up here I glanced over at the Lost and Found. Couldn't tell you why. Nothing lost in ages. But this must have caught my eye."

She held out a small brown bear, one shoebutton eye missing, bits of fur gone from its belly, as if it had been loved almost to pieces.

"It seems to be yours," she said with a smile, turning up one padded foot, where DINSY was written in faded laundry-marker black.

Dinsy wrapped her whole self around the cotton-stuffed body and skipped for the rest of the morning. Later, after Olive gave her a snack – cocoa and a Lorna Doone – Dinsy cupped her hand and blew a kiss to the oak woodwork.

"Thank you," she whispered, and put half her cookie in a crack between two tiles on the Children's Room fireplace when Olive wasn't looking.

Dinsy and Olive had a lovely time. One week they were pirates, raiding the Common Room for booty (and raisins). The next they were princesses, trapped in the turret with *At the Back of the North Wind*, and the week after that they were knights in shining armor, rescuing damsels in distress, a game Dinsy especially savored because it annoyed Marian to be rescued.

But the year she turned seven-and-a-half, Dinsy stopped reading stories. Quite abruptly, on an afternoon that Olive said later had really *felt* like a Thursday.

"Stories are for babies," Dinsy said. "I want to read about *real* people." Olive smiled a sad smile and pointed toward the far wall, because Dinsy was not the first child to make that same pronouncement, and she had known this phase would come.

After that, Dinsy devoured biographies, starting with the orange ones, the Childhoods of Famous Americans: *Thomas Edison, Young Inventor*. She worked her way from Abigail Adams to John Peter Zenger, all along the west side of the Children's Room, until one day she went around the corner, where Science and History began.

She stood in the doorway, looking at the rows of grown-up books, when she felt Olive's hand on her shoulder.

"Do you think maybe it's time you moved across the hall?" Olive asked softly.

Dinsy bit her lip, then nodded. "I can come back to visit, can't I? When I want to read stories again?"

"For as long as you like, dear. Anytime at all."

So Dorothy came and gathered up the bear and the pillow and the yellow toothbrush. Dinsy kissed Olive on her papery cheek and, holding Blythe's hand, moved across the hall, to the room where all the books had numbers.

Blythe was plump and freckled and frizzled. She always looked a little flushed, as if she had just that moment dropped what she was doing to rush over and greet you. She wore rumpled tweed skirts and a shapeless cardigan whose original color was impossible to guess. She had bright, dark eyes like a spaniel's, which Dinsy thought was appropriate, because Blythe *lived* to fetch books. She wore a locket with a small rotogravure picture of Melvil Dewey and kept a variety of sweets — sour balls and mints and Necco wafers — in her desk drawer.

Dinsy had always liked her.

She was not as sure about Dorothy.

Over *her* desk, Dorothy had a small framed medal on a royal-blue ribbon, won for "Excellence in Classification Studies." She could operate the ancient black Remington typewriter with brisk efficiency, and even, on occasion, coax chalky gray prints out of the wheezing old copy machine.

She was a tall, rawboned woman with steely blue eyes, good posture, and even better penmanship. Dinsy was a little frightened of her, at first, because she seemed so stern, and because she looked like magazine pictures of the Wicked Witch of the West, or at least Margaret Hamilton.

But that didn't last long.

"You should be very careful not to slip on the floor in here," Dorothy said on their first morning. "Do you know why?"

Dinsy shook her head.

"Because now you're in the non*friction* room!" Dorothy's angular face cracked into a wide grin.

Dinsy groaned. "Okay," she said after a minute. "How do you file marshmallows?"

Dorothy cocked her head. "Shoot."

"By the *Gooey* Decimal System!"

Dinsy heard Blythe tsk-tsk, but Dorothy laughed out loud, and from then on they were fast friends.

The three of them used the large, sunny room as an arena for endless games of I Spy and Twenty Questions as Dinsy learned her way around the shelves. In the evenings, after supper, they played Authors and Scrabble, and (once) tried to keep a running rummy score in Base Eight.

Dinsy sat at the court of Napoleon, roamed the jungles near Timbuktu, and was a frequent guest at the Round Table. She knew all the kings of England and the difference between a pergola and a folly. She knew the names of 112 breeds of sheep, and loved to say "Barbados Blackbelly" over and over, although it was difficult to work into conversations. When she affectionately, if misguidedly, referred to Blythe as a "Persian Fat-Rumped," she was sent to bed without supper.

A NOTE ABOUT TIME:

Time had become quite flexible inside the library. (This is true of most places with interesting books. Sit down to read for twenty minutes, and suddenly it's dark, with no clue as to where the hours have gone.)

As a consequence, no one was really sure about the day of the week, and there was frequent disagreement about the month and year. As the keeper of the date stamp at the front desk, Marian was the arbiter of such things. But she often had a cocktail after dinner, and many mornings she couldn't recall if she'd already turned the little wheel, or how often it had slipped her mind, so she frequently set it a day or two ahead — or back three — just to make up.

One afternoon, on a visit to Olive and the Children's Room, Dinsy looked up from *Little Town on the Prairie* and said, "When's my birthday?"

Olive thought for a moment. Because of the irregularities of time, holidays were celebrated a bit haphazardly. "I'm not sure, dear. Why do you ask?"

"Laura's going to a birthday party, in this book," she said, holding it up. "And it's fun. So I thought maybe I could have one."

"I think that would be lovely," Olive agreed. "We'll talk to the others at supper."

"Your birthday?" said Harriet as she set the table a few hours later.

"Let me see." She began to count on her fingers. "You arrived in April, according to Marian's stamp, and you were about nine months old, so —" She pursed her lips as she ticked off the months. "You must have been born in July!"

"But when's my birth*day?*" Dinsy asked impatiently.

"Not sure," said Edith as she ladled out the soup. "No way to tell," Olive agreed.

"How does July fifth sound?" offered Blythe, as if it were a point of order to be voted on. Blythe counted best by fives.

"Fourth," said Dorothy. "Independence Day. Easy to remember?"

Dinsy shrugged. "Okay." It hadn't seemed so complicated in the Little House book. "When is that? Is it soon?"

"Probably." Ruth nodded.

A few weeks later, the librarians threw her a birthday party.

Harriet baked a spice cake with pink frosting, and wrote DINSY on top in red licorice laces, dotting the *I* with a lemon drop (which was rather stale). The others gave her gifts that were thoughtful and mostly handmade:

A set of Dewey Decimal flash cards from Blythe.

A book of logic puzzles (stamped discard more than a dozen times, so Dinsy could write in it) from Dorothy.

A lumpy orange-and-green cardigan Ruth knitted for her.

A snow globe from the 1939 World's Fair from Olive.

A flashlight from Edith, so that Dinsy could find her way around at night and not knock over the wastebasket again.

A set of paper finger puppets, made from blank card pockets, hand-painted by Marian. (They were literary figures, of course, all of them necessarily stout and squarish — Nero Wolfe and Friar Tuck, Santa Claus, and Gertrude Stein.)

But her favorite gift was the second boon she'd wished upon the Library: a box of crayons. (She had grown very tired of drawing gray pictures with the little pencils.) It had produced Crayola crayons, in the familiar yellow-and-green box, labeled LIBRARY PACK. Inside were the colors of Dinsy's world: Reference Maroon, Brown Leather, Peplum

Beige, Reader's Guide Green, World Book Red, Card Catalog Cream, Date Stamp Purple, and Palatino Black.

It was a very special birthday, that fourth of July. Although Dinsy wondered about Marian's calculations. As Harriet cut the first piece of cake that evening, she remarked that it was snowing rather heavily outside, which everyone agreed was lovely, but quite unusual for that time of year.

⁓

Dinsy soon learned all the planets, and many of their moons. (She referred to herself as Umbriel for an entire month.) She puffed up her cheeks and blew onto stacks of scrap paper. "Sirocco," she'd whisper. "Chinook. Mistral. Willy-Willy," and rated her attempts on the Beaufort scale. Dorothy put a halt to it after Hurricane Dinsy reshuffled a rather elaborate game of Patience.

She dipped into fractals here, double dactyls there. When she tired of a subject — or found it just didn't suit her — Blythe or Dorothy would smile and proffer the hat. It was a deep green felt that held one thousand slips of paper, numbered 001 to 999. Dinsy'd scrunch her eyes closed, pick one, and, like a scavenger hunt, spend the morning (or the next three weeks) at the shelves indicated.

Pangolins lived at 599 (point 31), and Pancakes at 641. Pencils were at 674 but Pens were a shelf away at 681, and Ink was across the aisle at 667. (Dinsy thought that was stupid, because you had to *use* them together.) Pluto the planet was at 523, but Pluto the Disney dog was at 791 (point 453), near Rock and Roll and Kazoos.

It was all very useful information. But in Dinsy's opinion, things could be a little *too* organized.

The first time she straightened up the Common Room without anyone asking, she was very pleased with herself. She had lined up everyone's teacup in a neat row on the shelf, with all the handles curving the same way, and arranged the spices in the little wooden rack: ANISE, BAY LEAVES, CHIVES, DILL WEED, PEPPERCORNS, SALT, SESAME SEEDS, SUGAR.

"Look," she said when Blythe came in to refresh her tea, "Order out of chaos." It was one of Blythe's favorite mottoes.

Blythe smiled and looked over at the spice rack. Then her smile faded and she shook her head.

"Is something wrong?" Dinsy asked. She had hoped for a compliment.

"Well, you used the alphabet," said Blythe, sighing. "I suppose it's not your fault. You were with Olive for a good many years. But you're a big girl now. You should learn the *proper* order." She picked up the salt container. "We'll start with Salt." She wrote the word on the little chalkboard hanging by the icebox, followed by the number 553.632. "Five-five-three-point-six-three-two. Because – ?"

Dinsy thought for a moment. "Earth Sciences."

"Ex-actly." Blythe beamed. "Because salt is a mineral. But, now, chives. Chives are a garden crop, so they're..."

Dinsy bit her lip in concentration. "Six-thirty-something."

"Very good." Blythe smiled again and chalked CHIVES 635.26 on the board. "So you see, Chives should always be shelved *after* Salt, dear."

Blythe turned and began to rearrange the eight ceramic jars. Behind her back, Dinsy silently rolled her eyes.

Edith appeared in the doorway.

"Oh, not again," she said. "No wonder I can't find a thing in this kitchen. Blythe, I've *told* you. Bay Leaf comes first. QK-four-nine – " She had worked at the university when she was younger.

"Library of Congress, my fanny," said Blythe, not quite under her breath. "We're not *that* kind of library."

"It's no excuse for imprecision," Edith replied. They each grabbed a jar and stared at each other.

Dinsy tiptoed away and hid in the 814s, where she read "Jabberwocky" until the coast was clear.

But the kitchen remained a taxonomic battleground. At least once a week, Dinsy was amused by the indignant sputtering of someone who had just spooned dill weed, not sugar, into a cup of Earl Grey tea.

⌣

Once she knew her way around, Dinsy was free to roam the library as she chose.

"Anywhere?" she asked Blythe.

"Anywhere you like, my sweet. Except the Stacks. You're not quite old enough for the Stacks."

Dinsy frowned. "I am *so*," she muttered. But the Stacks were locked, and there wasn't much she could do.

Some days she sat with Olive in the Children's Room, revisiting old friends, or explored the maze of the Main Room. Other days she spent in the Reference Room, where Ruth and Harriet guarded the big important books that no one could ever, ever check out — not even when the library had been open.

Ruth and Harriet were like a set of salt-and-pepper shakers from two different yard sales. Harriet had faded orange hair and a sharp, kind face. Small and pinched and pointed, a decade or two away from wizened. She had violet eyes and a mischievous, conspiratorial smile and wore rimless octagonal glasses, like stop signs. Dinsy had never seen an actual stop sign, but she'd looked at pictures.

Ruth was Chinese. She wore wool jumpers in neon plaids and had cat's-eye glasses on a beaded chain around her neck. She never put them all the way on, just lifted them to her eyes and peered through them without opening the bows.

"Life is a treasure hunt," said Harriet.

"Knowledge is power," said Ruth. "Knowing where to look is half the battle."

"Half the fun," added Harriet. Ruth almost never got the last word.

They introduced Dinsy to dictionaries and almanacs, encyclopedias and compendiums. They had been native guides through the country of the Dry Tomes for many years, but they agreed that Dinsy delved unusually deep.

"Would you like to take a break, love?" Ruth asked one afternoon. "It's nearly time for tea."

"I *am* fatigued," Dinsy replied, looking up from *Roget*. "Fagged out, weary, a bit spent. Tea would be pleasant, agreeable — "

"I'll put the kettle on," sighed Ruth.

Dinsy read *Bartlett's* as if it were a catalog of conversations, spouting lines from Tennyson, Mark Twain, and Dale Carnegie until even Harriet put her hands over her ears and began to hum "Stairway to Heaven."

One or two evenings a month, usually after Blythe had remarked "Well, she's a spirited girl," for the third time, they all took the night off, "For Library business." Olive or Dorothy would tuck Dinsy in early and read from one of her favorites while Ruth made her a bedtime treat — a cup of spiced tea that tasted a little like cherries and a little like varnish, and which Dinsy somehow never remembered finishing.

A LIST (WRITTEN IN DIVERS HANDS), TACKED TO THE WALL OF THE COMMON ROOM.

10 Things to Remember When You Live in a Library
1. We do not play shuffleboard on the Reading Room table.
2. Books should not have "dog's ears." Bookmarks make lovely presents.
3. Do not write in books. Even in pencil. Puzzle collections and connect-the-dots are books.
4. The shelving cart is not a scooter.
5. Library paste is not food.
   [Marginal note in a child's hand:
   True. It tastes like Cream of Wrong Soup.]
6. Do not use the date stamp to mark your banana.
7. Shelves are not monkey bars.
8. Do not play 982-pickup with the P-Q drawer (or any other).
9. The dumbwaiter is only for books. It is not a carnival ride.
10. Do not drop volumes of the Britannica off the stairs to hear the echo.

They were an odd, but contented family. There were rules, to be sure, but Dinsy never lacked for attention. With seven mothers, there was always someone to talk with, a hankie for tears, a lap or a shoulder to share a story.

Most evenings, when Dorothy had made a fire in the Reading Room and the wooden shelves gleamed in the flickering light, they would all sit in companionable silence. Ruth knitted, Harriet muttered over an acrostic, Edith stirred the cocoa so it wouldn't get a skin. Dinsy sat on the rug, her back against the knees of whoever was her favorite that week, and felt safe and warm and loved. "God's in his heaven, all's right with the world," as Blythe would say.

But as she watched the moon peep in and out of the clouds through the leaded-glass panes of the tall windows, Dinsy often wondered what it would be like to see the whole sky, all around her.

First Olive and then Dorothy had been in charge of Dinsy's thick dark hair, trimming it with the mending shears every few weeks when it began to obscure her eyes. But a few years into her second decade at the library, Dinsy began cutting it herself, leaving it as wild and spiky as the brambles outside the front door.

That was not the only change.

"We haven't seen her at breakfast in weeks," Harriet said as she buttered a scone one morning.

"Months. And all she reads is Salinger. Or Sylvia Plath," complained Dorothy. "I wouldn't mind that so much, but she just leaves them on the table for *me* to reshelve."

"It's not as bad as what she did to Olive," Marian said. "*The Golden Compass* appeared last week, and she thought Dinsy would enjoy it. But not only did she turn up her nose, she had the gall to say to Olive, 'Leave me alone. I can find my own books.' Imagine. Poor Olive was beside herself."

"She used to be such a sweet child." Blythe sighed. "What are we going to do?"

"Now, now. She's just at that age," Edith said calmly. "She's not really a child anymore. She needs some privacy, and some responsibility. I have an idea."

And so it was that Dinsy got her own room — with a door that *shut* — in a corner of the second floor. It had been a tiny cubbyhole of an office, but it had a set of slender curved stairs, wrought iron worked with lilies and twigs, which led up to the turret between the red-tiled eaves.

The round tower was just wide enough for Dinsy's bed, with windows all around. There had once been a view of the town, but now trees and ivy allowed only jigsaw-puzzle-shaped puddles of light to dapple the wooden floor. At night the puddles were luminous blue splotches of moonlight that hinted of magic beyond her reach.

On the desk in the room below, centered in a pool of yellow lamp-light, Edith had left a note: "Come visit me. There's mending to be done," and a worn brass key on a wooden paddle, stenciled with the single word: STACKS.

The Stacks were in the basement, behind a locked gate at the foot of the metal spiral staircase that descended from the 600s. They had always reminded Dinsy of the steps down to the dungeon in *The King's Stilts*. Darkness below hinted at danger, but adventure. Terra Incognita.

Dinsy didn't use her key the first day, or the second. Mending? Boring. But the afternoon of the third day, she ventured down the spiral stairs. She had been as far as the gate before, many times, because it was forbidden, to peer through the metal mesh at the dimly lighted shelves and imagine what treasures might be hidden there.

She had thought that the Stacks would be damp and cold, strewn with odd bits of discarded library flotsam. Instead they were cool and dry, and smelled very different from upstairs. Dustier, with hints of mold and the tang of vintage leather, an undertone of vinegar stored in an old shoe.

Unlike the main floor, with its polished wood and airy high ceil-ings, the Stacks were a low, cramped warren of gunmetal gray shelves that ran floor to ceiling in narrow aisles. Seven levels twisted behind the west wall of the library like a secret labyrinth that stretched from below the ground to up under the eaves of the roof. Floor and steps were translucent glass brick, and the six-foot ceilings strung with pipes and ducts were lit by single caged bulbs, two to an aisle.

It was a windowless fortress of books. Upstairs the shelves were mosaics of all colors and sizes, but the Stacks were filled with geometric monochrome blocks of subdued colors: eight dozen forest-green bound volumes of *Ladies' Home Journal* filled five rows of shelves, followed by an equally large block of identical dark red *LIFE*s.

Dinsy felt like she was in another world. She was not lost, but for the first time in her life, she was not easily found, and that suited her. She could sit, invisible, and listen to the sounds of library life going on around her. From Level Three she could hear Ruth humming in the

Reference Room on the other side of the wall. Four feet away, and it felt like miles. She wandered and browsed for a month before she presented herself at Edith's office.

A frosted glass pane in the dark wood door said MENDING ROOM in chipping gold letters. The door was open a few inches, and Dinsy could see a long workbench strewn with sewn folios and bits of leather bindings, spools of thread and bottles of thick beige glue.

"I gather you're finding your way around," Edith said, without turning in her chair. "I haven't had to send out a search party."

"Pretty much," Dinsy replied. "I've been reading old magazines." She flopped into a chair to the left of the door.

"One of my favorite things," Edith agreed. "It's like time travel." Edith was a tall, solid woman with long graying hair that she wove into elaborate buns and twisted braids, secured with number-two pencils and a single tortoiseshell comb. She wore blue jeans and vests in brightly muted colors – pale teal and lavender and dusky rose – with a strand of lapis lazuli beads cut in rough ovals.

Edith repaired damaged books, a job that was less demanding now that nothing left the building. But some of the bound volumes of journals and abstracts and magazines went back as far as 1870, and their leather bindings were crumbling into dust. The first year, Dinsy's job was to go through the aisles, level by level, and find the volumes that needed the most help. Edith gave her a clipboard and told her to check in now and then.

Dinsy learned how to take old books apart and put them back together again. Her first mending project was the tattered 1877 volume of *American Naturalist*, with its articles on "Educated Fleas" and "Barnacles" and "The Cricket as Thermometer." She sewed pages into signatures, trimmed leather, and marbleized paper. Edith let her make whatever she wanted out of the scraps, and that year Dinsy gave everyone miniature replicas of their favorite volumes for Christmas.

She liked the craft, liked doing something with her hands. It took patience and concentration, and that was oddly soothing. After supper, she and Edith often sat and talked for hours, late into the night, mugs of cocoa on their workbenches, the rest of the library dark and silent above them.

"What's it like outside?" Dinsy asked one night while she was waiting for some glue to dry.

Edith was silent for a long time, long enough that Dinsy wondered if she'd spoken too softly, and was about to repeat the question, when Edith replied.

"Chaos."

That was not anything Dinsy had expected. "What do you mean?"

"It's noisy. It's crowded. Everything's always changing, and not in any way you can predict."

"That sounds kind of exciting," Dinsy said.

"Hmm." Edith thought for a moment. "Yes, I suppose it could be."

Dinsy mulled that over and fiddled with a scrap of leather, twisting it in her fingers before she spoke again. "Do you ever miss it?"

Edith turned on her stool and looked at Dinsy. "Not often," she said slowly. "Not as often as I'd thought. But then I'm awfully fond of order. Fonder than most, I suppose. This is a better fit."

Dinsy nodded and took a sip of her cocoa.

A few months later, she asked the Library for a third and final boon.

The evening that everything changed, Dinsy sat in the armchair in her room, reading Trollope's *Can You Forgive Her?* (for the third time), imagining what it would be like to talk to Glencora, when a tentative knock sounded at the door.

"Dinsy? Dinsy?" said a tiny familiar voice. "It's Olive, dear."

Dinsy slid her READ! bookmark into chapter 14 and closed the book. "It's open," she called.

Olive padded in wearing a red flannel robe, her feet in worn carpet slippers. Dinsy expected her to proffer a book, but instead Olive said, "I'd like you to come with me, dear." Her blue eyes shone with excitement.

"What for?" They had all done a nice reading of *As You Like It* a few days before, but Dinsy didn't remember any plans for that night. Maybe Olive just wanted company. Dinsy had been meaning to spend an evening in the Children's Room, but hadn't made it down there in months.

But Olive surprised her. "It's Library business," she said, waggling her finger and smiling.

Now, that was intriguing. For years, whenever the Librarians wanted an evening to themselves, they'd disappear down into the Stacks after supper, and would never tell her why. "It's Library business," was all they ever said. When she was younger, Dinsy had tried to follow them, but it's hard to sneak in a quiet place. She was always caught and given that awful cherry tea. The next thing she knew it was morning.

"Library business?" Dinsy said slowly. "And I'm invited?"

"Yes, dear. You're practically all grown up now. It's high time you joined us."

"Great." Dinsy shrugged, as if it were no big deal, trying to hide her excitement. And maybe it wasn't a big deal. Maybe it was a meeting of the rules committee, or plans for moving the 340s to the other side of the window again. But what if it *was* something special...? That was both exciting and a little scary.

She wiggled her feet into her own slippers and stood up. Olive barely came to her knees. Dinsy touched the old woman's white hair affectionately, remembering when she used to snuggle into that soft lap. Such a long time ago.

A library at night is a still but resonant place. The only lights were the sconces along the walls, and Dinsy could hear the faint echo of each footfall on the stairs down to the foyer. They walked through the shadows of the shelves in the Main Room, back to the 600s, and down the metal stairs to the Stacks, footsteps ringing hollowly.

The lower level was dark except for a single caged bulb above the rows of *National Geographics*, their yellow bindings pale against the gloom. Olive turned to the left.

"Where are we going?" Dinsy asked. It was so odd to be down there with Olive.

"You'll see," Olive said. Dinsy could practically feel her smiling in the dark. "You'll see."

She led Dinsy down an aisle of boring municipal reports and stopped at the far end, in front of the door to the janitorial closet set into the stone wall. She pulled a long, old-fashioned brass key from the pocket of her robe and handed it to Dinsy.

"You open it, dear. The keyhole's a bit high for me."

Dinsy stared at the key, at the door, back at the key. She'd been fantasizing about "Library Business" since she was little, imagining all sorts of scenarios, none of them involving cleaning supplies. A monthly poker game. A secret tunnel into town, where they all went dancing, like the twelve princesses. Or a book group, reading forbidden texts. And now they were inviting her in? What a letdown if it was just maintenance.

She put the key in the lock. "Funny," she said as she turned it. "I've always wondered what went on when you – " Her voice caught in her throat. The door opened, not onto the closet of mops and pails and bottles of Pine-Sol she expected, but onto a small room, paneled in wood the color of ancient honey. An Oriental rug in rich, deep reds lay on the parquet floor, and the room shone with the light of dozens of candles. There were no shelves, no books, just a small fireplace at one end where a log crackled in the hearth.

"Surprise," said Olive softly. She gently tugged Dinsy inside.

All the others were waiting, dressed in flowing robes of different colors. Each of them stood in front of a Craftsman rocker, dark wood covered in soft brown leather.

Edith stepped forward and took Dinsy's hand. She gave it a gentle squeeze and said, under her breath, "Don't worry." Then she winked and led Dinsy to an empty rocker. "Stand here," she said, and returned to her own seat.

Stunned, Dinsy stood, her mouth open, her feelings a kaleidoscope.

"Welcome, dear one," said Dorothy. "We'd like you to join us." Her face was serious, but her eyes were bright, as if she was about to tell a really awful riddle and couldn't wait for the reaction.

Dinsy started. That was almost word for word what Olive had said, and it made her nervous. She wasn't sure what was coming, and was even less sure that she was ready.

"Introductions first." Dorothy closed her eyes and intoned, "I am Lexica. I serve the Library." She bowed her head once and sat down.

Dinsy stared, her eyes wide and her mind reeling as each of the librarians repeated what was obviously a familiar rite.

"I am Juvenilia," said Olive with a twinkle. "I serve the Library."

"Incunabula," said Edith.

"Sapientia," said Harriet.

"Ephemera," said Marian.

"Marginalia," said Ruth.

"Melvilia," said Blythe, smiling at Dinsy. "And I, too, serve the Library."

And then they were all seated, and all looking up at Dinsy.

"How old are you now, my sweet?" asked Harriet.

Dinsy frowned. It wasn't as easy a question as it sounded. "Seventeen," she said after a few seconds. "Or close enough."

"No longer a child." Harriet nodded. There was a touch of sadness in her voice. "That is why we are here tonight. To ask you to join us."

There was something so solemn in Harriet's voice that it made Dinsy's stomach knot up. "I don't understand," she said slowly. "What do you mean? I've been here my whole life. Practically."

Dorothy shook her head. "You have been *in* the Library, but not *of* the Library. Think of it as an apprenticeship. We have nothing more to teach you. So we're asking if you'll take a Library name and truly become one of us. There have always been seven to serve the Library."

Dinsy looked around the room. "Won't I be the eighth?" she asked. She was curious, but she was also stalling for time.

"No, dear," said Olive. "You'll be taking my place. I'm retiring. I can barely reach the second shelves these days, and soon I'll be no bigger than the dictionary. I'm going to put my feet up and sit by the fire and take it easy. I've earned it," she said with a decisive nod.

"Here, here," said Blythe. "And well done, too."

There was a murmur of assent around the room.

Dinsy took a deep breath, and then another. She looked around the room at the eager faces of the seven librarians, the only mothers she had ever known. She loved them all, and was about to disappoint them, because she had a secret of her own. She closed her eyes so she wouldn't see their faces, not at first.

"I can't take your place, Olive," she said quietly, and heard the tremor in her own voice as she fought back tears.

All around her the librarians clucked in surprise. Ruth recovered first. "Well, of course not. No one's asking you to *replace* Olive, we're merely – "

"I can't join you," Dinsy repeated. Her voice was just as quiet, but it was stronger. "Not now."

"But why *not*, sweetie?" That was Blythe, who sounded as if she were about to cry herself.

"Fireworks," said Dinsy after a moment. She opened her eyes. "Six-sixty-two-point-one." She smiled at Blythe. "I know everything about them. But I've never *seen* any." She looked from face to face again.

"I've never petted a dog or ridden a bicycle or watched the sun rise over the ocean," she said, her voice gaining courage. "I want to feel the wind and eat an ice-cream cone at a carnival. I want to smell jasmine on a spring night and hear an orchestra. I want – " She faltered, and then continued, "I want the chance to dance with a boy."

She turned to Dorothy. "You said you have nothing left to teach me. Maybe that's true. I've learned from each of you that there's nothing in the world I can't discover and explore for myself in these books. Except the world," she added in a whisper. She felt her eyes fill with tears. "You chose the Library. I can't do that without knowing what else there might be."

"You're *leaving?*" Ruth asked in a choked voice.

Dinsy bit her lip and nodded. "I'm, well, I've – " She'd been practicing these words for days, but they were so much harder than she'd thought. She looked down at her hands.

And then Marian rescued her.

"Dinsy's going to college," she said. "Just like I did. And you, and you, and you." She pointed a finger at each of the women in the room. "We were girls before we were librarians, remember? It's her turn now."

"But how – ?" asked Edith.

"Where did – ?" stammered Harriet.

"I wished on the Library," said Dinsy. "And it left an application in the Unabridged. Marian helped me fill it out."

"I *am* in charge of circulation," said Marian. "What comes in, what goes out. We found her acceptance letter in the book return last week."

"But you had no transcripts," said Dorothy practically. "Where did you tell them you'd gone to school?"

Dinsy smiled. "That was Marian's idea. We told them I was home-schooled, raised by feral librarians."

And so it was that on a bright September morning, for the first time in ages, the heavy oak door of the Carnegie Library swung open. Everyone stood in the doorway, blinking in the sunlight.

"Promise you'll write," said Blythe, tucking a packet of sweets into the basket on Dinsy's arm.

The others nodded. "Yes, do."

"I'll try," she said. "But you never know how long *any*thing will take around here." She tried to make a joke of it, but she was holding back tears and her heart was hammering a mile a minute.

"You will come back, won't you? I can't put off my retirement forever." Olive was perched on top of the Circulation Desk.

"To visit, yes." Dinsy leaned over and kissed her cheek. "I promise. But to serve? I don't know. I have no idea what I'm going to find out there." She looked out into the forest that surrounded the library. "I don't even know if I'll be able to get back in, through all that."

"Take this. It's your library card. It will always get you in," said Marian. She handed Dinsy a small stiff pasteboard card with a metal plate in one corner, embossed with her name: DINSY CARNEGIE.

There were hugs all around, and tears and good-byes. But in the end, the seven librarians stood back and watched her go.

Dinsy stepped out into the world as she had come — with a wicker basket and a book of fairy tales, full of hopes and dreams.

Afterword

I DIDN'T BEGIN TO WRITE, or take my writing seriously, until I was almost forty. I began to scribble bedtime stories in the middle of the night, the year my mother was dying. They calmed the frightened child I woke up as.

After Mom died, my sister Mary and I went through a box of her letters, and found one she'd written to my grandmother the Christmas I was two-and-a-half: *Ellen wants a football helmet. Of course, we're not going to get her one, but....*

I read that and wanted to go back in time and give the kid a football helmet, just to see the delight on her face. Delight should be a daily occurrence – Cookie! Swingset! Green Socks! It became an even scarcer commodity the older and more responsible I got.

I'm still delighted now and then (frequently by things on eBay), but to tap into that (literally) unadulterated sense of delight and wonder, I write myself stories about being a kid.

They are not children's stories.

I go down my own personal rabbit hole to a time when I truly and deeply believed that if I looked in the right place at the right time, I'd find treasure. Something that, if not actually *magic*, was at least out of the ordinary, unanticipated. I needed to believe that there were hidden staircases and mysterious trunks in attics, a secret passage in the damp brick basement of the old drugstore on the corner.

Science fiction is, I've read, a literature of setting. For some, that means other planets, other worlds, other dimensions. For me, it's the past, but a slightly alternate past, a reality that existed – at least in my imagination – just below the surface of everyday life.

On weekends, my mom and dad would load me into the car and we'd go for a drive into the Ohio countryside, past farms and through little towns. At just about the moment when I was about to ask, "Are we there yet?", we'd round a curve and there would be a covered bridge.

They are splendid, anachronistic structures, out of place and time. They were my primal experience with the wonder of the unexpected; my first words were *cubba bee-gee!* I never knew which turn in the road would reveal one.

It's a feeling I haven't been able to shake.

My stories have been described as fantasy, dark fantasy, science fiction, *not* science fiction, children's, mainstream, and/or horror. (Often in different reviews of the same story.) I am a round peg in genre's polyhedral hole; I write about childhood, and it's an odd landscape, with contradictions around every corner.

It's a time of play and imagination, freedom from responsibility. But it's also a time of someone else's rules and supervision, both for safety and surveillance. Everything – and everyone – *might* be dangerous. Don't swallow your gum, cross Main Street, talk to strangers. Bad things could happen.

That's the flip side of the unexpected.

I was in first grade when my youngest sister, Sally, was born. She has Down Syndrome, was and is, mentally retarded. She's funny and affectionate and looks very much like me, except shorter and vaguely Oriental. But in black-and-white photos from 1961, I look frightened, holding this new baby. She is alien, irredeemably and profoundly "other." First contact.

Write what you know.

And so I write about fear and wonder, and discovering who you are and where you belong.

Many of my stories appear to have happy endings.

ELLEN KLAGES
San Francisco
December 2006